Vampire Diaries

Diaries

MOONSONG

Vampire Diaries

THE HUNTERS

~

MOONSONG

L. J. SMITH

Hodder
Children's
Books

a division of Hachette Children's Books

CHAPTER

1

Dear Diary,

I'm so scared.

My heart is pounding, my mouth is dry and my hands are shaking. I've faced so much and survived: vampires, werewolves, phantoms. Things I never imagined were real. And now I'm terrified. Why?

Simply because I'm leaving home.

And I know that it's completely, insanely ridiculous. I'm barely leaving home, really. I'm going to college, only a few hours' drive from this darling house where I've lived since I was a baby. No, I'm not going to start crying again. I'll be sharing a room with Bonnie and Meredith, my two best friends in the whole world. In the same dorm, only a couple of floors away will be my beloved

Stefan. My other best friend, Matt, will be just a short walk across campus. Even Damon will be in an apartment in the town nearby.

Honestly, I couldn't stick any closer to home unless I never moved out of this house at all. I'm being such a wimp. But it seems like I just got my home back – my family, my life – after being exiled for so long, and now I suddenly have to leave again.

I suppose I'm scared partly because these last few weeks of summer have been wonderful. We packed all the enjoyment we would have been having these past few months – if it hadn't been for fighting the kitsune, travelling to the Dark Dimension, battling the jealousy phantom, and all the other Extremely Not Fun things we've done – into three glorious weeks. We had picnics and sleepovers and went swimming and shopping. We took a trip to the county fair, where Matt won Bonnie a stuffed tiger and turned bright red when she squealed and leaped into his arms. Stefan even kissed me as we sat on the top of the Ferris wheel, just like any normal guy might kiss his girlfriend on a beautiful summer night.

We were so happy. So normal in a way I thought we could never be again.

That's what's frightening me, I guess. I'm scared that these few weeks have been a bright golden interlude and now that things are changing, we'll *be heading back into darkness and horror. It's like that poem we read in English class last autumn says: Nothing gold can stay. Not for me.*

Even Damon . . .

The clatter of feet in the hallway downstairs distracted her, and Elena Gilbert's pen slowed. She glanced up at the last couple of boxes scattered around her room. Stefan and Damon must be here to pick her up.

But she wanted to finish her thought, to express the last worry that had been nagging at her during these perfect weeks. She turned back to her diary, writing faster so that she could get her thoughts down before she had to leave.

Damon has changed. Ever since we defeated the jealousy phantom, he's been . . . kinder. Not just to me, not just to Bonnie, who he's always had a soft spot for, but even to Matt and Meredith. He can still be intensely irritating and unpredictable – he wouldn't be Damon without that – but he hasn't had that cruel edge to him. Not like he used to.

He and Stefan seem to have come to an understanding. They know I love them both, and yet they haven't let jealousy come between them. They're close, acting like true brothers in a way I haven't seen before. There's this delicate balance between the three of us that's lasted through the end of the summer. And I worry that any misstep on my part will bring it crashing down and that like their first love, Katherine, I'll tear the brothers apart. And then we'll lose Damon forever.

Aunt Judith called up, sounding impatient, 'Elena!'

'Coming!' Elena replied. She quickly scribbled a few more sentences in her diary.

Still, it's possible that this new life will be wonderful. Maybe I'll find everything I've been looking for. I can't hold on to high school, or to my life here at home, forever. And who knows? Maybe this time the gold will stay.

'*Elena!* Your ride is *waiting*!'

Aunt Judith was definitely getting stressed out now.

She'd wanted to drive Elena up to school herself. But Elena knew she wouldn't be able to say goodbye to her family without crying, so she'd asked Stefan and Damon to drive her instead. It would be less embarrassing to get emotional here at home than to weep all over Dalcrest's campus. Since Elena had decided to go with the Salvatore brothers, Aunt Judith had been working herself up about every little detail, anxious that Elena's college career wouldn't start off perfectly without her there to supervise. It was all because Aunt Judith loved her, Elena knew.

Elena slammed the blue-velvet-covered journal shut and dropped it into an open box. She climbed to her feet and headed for the door, but before she opened it, she turned to look at her room one last time.

It was so empty, with her favourite posters missing from the walls and half the books gone from her bookcase. Only a few clothes remained in her dresser and closet. The furniture was all still in place. But now that the room was stripped of most of her possessions, it felt more like an impersonal hotel room than the cosy haven of her childhood.

So much had happened here. Elena could remember cuddling up with her father on the window seat to read together when she was a little girl. She and Bonnie and Meredith – and Caroline, who had been her good friend, too, once – had spent at least a hundred nights here telling secrets, studying, dressing for dances and just hanging out. Stefan had kissed her here, early in the morning, and disappeared quickly when Aunt Judith came to wake her. Elena remembered Damon's cruel, triumphant smile as she invited him in that first time, what felt like a million years ago. And, not so long ago, her joy when he had appeared here one dark night, after they all thought he was dead.

There was a quiet knock at the door, and it swung open. Stefan stood in the doorway, watching her.

'About ready?' he said. 'Your aunt is a little worried. She thinks you're not going to have time to unpack before orientation if we don't get going.'

Elena stood and went over to wrap her arms around him. He smelled clean and woodsy, and she nestled her head against his shoulder. 'I'm coming,' she said. 'It's just hard to say goodbye, you know? Everything's changing.'

Stefan turned towards her and caught her mouth softly in a kiss. 'I know,' he said when the kiss ended, and ran his finger gently along the curve of her bottom lip. 'I'll take these boxes down and give you one more minute. Aunt Judith will feel better if she sees the truck getting packed up.'

'OK. I'll be right down.'

Stefan left the room with the boxes, and Elena sighed, looking around again. The blue flowered curtains her mother had made for her when Elena was nine still hung over the windows. She remembered her mother hugging her, her eyes a little teary, when her baby girl told her she was too big for Winnie the Pooh curtains.

Elena's own eyes filled with tears, and she tucked her hair behind her ears, mirroring the gesture her mother had used when she was thinking hard. Elena was so young when her parents died. Maybe if they'd lived, she and her mother would be friends now, would know each other as equals, not just as mother and daughter.

Her parents had gone to Dalcrest College, too. That's

where they'd met, in fact. Downstairs on top of the piano sat a picture of them in their graduation robes on the sun-filled lawn in front of the Dalcrest library, laughing, impossibly young.

Maybe going to Dalcrest would bring Elena closer to them. Maybe she'd learn more about the *people* they'd been, not just the mum and dad she'd known when she was little, and find her lost family among the neoclassical buildings and the sweeping green lawns of the college.

She wasn't leaving, not really. She was moving forward.

Elena set her jaw firmly and headed out of her room, clicking off the light as she went.

Downstairs, Aunt Judith, her husband, Robert, and Elena's five-year-old sister, Margaret, were gathered in the hall, waiting, watching Elena as she came down the stairs.

Aunt Judith was fussing, of course. She couldn't keep still; her hands were twisting together, smoothing her hair or fiddling with her earrings. 'Elena,' she said, 'are you sure you've packed everything you need? There's so much to remember.' She frowned.

Her aunt's obvious anxiety made it easier for Elena to smile reassuringly and hug her. Aunt Judith held her tight, relaxing for a moment, and sniffed. 'I'm going to miss you, sweetheart.'

'I'll miss you, too,' Elena said, and squeezed her

closer, feeling her own lips tremble. She gave a shaky laugh. 'But I'll be back. If I forgot anything, or if I get homesick, I'll run right back for a weekend. I don't have to wait for Thanksgiving.'

Next to them, Robert shifted from one foot to the other and cleared his throat. Elena let go of Aunt Judith and turned to him.

'Now, I know college students have a lot of expenses,' he said. 'And we don't want you to have to worry about money, so you've got an account at the student store, but . . .' He opened his wallet and handed Elena a fistful of bills. 'Just in case.'

'Oh,' said Elena, touched and a little flustered. 'Thank you so much, Robert, but you really don't have to.'

He patted her awkwardly on the shoulder. 'We want you to have everything you need,' he said firmly. Elena smiled at him gratefully, folded the money and put it in her pocket.

Next to Robert, Margaret glared down obstinately at her shoes. Elena knelt before her and took her little sister's hands. 'Margaret?' she prompted.

Large blue eyes stared into her own. Margaret frowned and shook her head, her mouth a tight line.

'I'm going to miss you so much, Meggie,' Elena said, pulling her close, her eyes filling with tears again. Her little sister's dandelion-soft hair brushed against Elena's cheek. 'But I'll be back for Thanksgiving, and maybe you can come and visit me on campus. I'd love to show off my little sister to all my new friends.'

Margaret swallowed. 'I don't want you to go,' she said in a small miserable voice. 'You're always *leaving*.'

'Oh, sweetie,' Elena said helplessly, cuddling her closer. 'I always come back, don't I?'

Elena shivered. Once again, she wondered how much Margaret remembered of what had *really* happened in Fell's Church during the last year. The Guardians had promised to change everyone's memories of those dark months when vampires, werewolves and kitsune had nearly destroyed the town – and when Elena herself had died and risen again – but there seemed to be exceptions. Caleb Smallwood remembered, and sometimes Margaret's innocent face looked strangely knowing.

'Elena,' Aunt Judith said again, her voice thick and weepy, 'you'd better get going.'

Elena hugged her sister one more time before letting her go. 'OK,' she said, standing and picking up her bag. 'I'll call you tonight and let you know how I'm settling in.'

Aunt Judith nodded, and Elena gave her another quick kiss before wiping her eyes and opening the front door.

Outside, the sunlight was so bright she had to blink. Damon and Stefan were leaning against the truck Stefan had rented, her stuff packed into the back. As she stepped forward, they both glanced up and, at the same time, smiled at her.

Oh. They were so beautiful, the two of them, that seeing them could still leave her shaken after all this time. Stefan, her love Stefan, his leaf-green eyes shining at the sight of her, was gorgeous with his classical profile and that sweet little kissable curve to his bottom lip.

And Damon – all luminescent pale skin, black velvety eyes and silken hair – was graceful and deadly all at once. His brilliant smile made something inside her stretch and purr like a panther recognising its mate.

Both pairs of eyes watched her lovingly, possessively.

The Salvatore brothers were hers now. What was she going to do about it? The thought made her frown and made her shoulders hunch nervously. Then she consciously smoothed the wrinkles in her forehead away, relaxed and smiled back at them. What would come, would come.

'Time to go,' she said, and tilted her face up towards the sun.

CHAPTER

2

Meredith held the tyre gauge firmly against the valve of her left rear tyre while she checked it. The pressure was fine.

The pressure on all four tyres was fine. The antifreeze, oil and transmission fluids were all topped up, the car battery was new and the jack and spare tyre were in perfect shape. She should have known. Her parents weren't the kind to stay home from work to see her off to college. They knew she didn't need coddling, but they'd show their love by making sure all the preparations were made, that she was safe and perfectly ready for anything that might happen. Of course, they wouldn't *tell* her that they had checked everything, either; they'd want her to continue protecting herself.

There wasn't anything she had to do now except leave. Which was the one thing she didn't want to do.

'Come with me,' she said without looking up, despising the faint quiver she heard in her own voice. 'Just for a couple of weeks.'

'You know I can't,' Alaric said as he brushed his hand lightly over her back. 'I wouldn't want to leave if I came with you. It'll be better this way. You'll get to enjoy the first weeks of college like all the other new students, without anyone holding you back. Then I'll come up and visit soon.'

Meredith turned to face him and found Alaric gazing back at her. His mouth tensed, just the tiniest tightening, and she could see that parting again, after only a few weeks together, was just as hard for him as it was for her. She leaned in and kissed him softly.

'Better than if I'd gone to Harvard,' she murmured. 'Much closer.'

As the summer had ended, she and Matt had realised they couldn't leave their friends and head off to out-of-state colleges as they'd planned. They'd all been through so much together, and they wanted to *stay* together, to protect one another, more than they wanted to go anywhere else.

Their home had been nearly destroyed more than once, and only Elena's blackmail of the Celestial Court had restored it and saved their families. They *couldn't* leave.

Not while they were the only ones standing against the darkness out there, the darkness that would be drawn forever to the Power of the magical ley lines that crossed the area around Fell's Church. Dalcrest was close enough that they'd be able to come back if danger threatened again.

They needed to protect their home.

So Stefan had gone down to the administrative offices at Dalcrest and used his vampire mojo. Suddenly Matt had the football scholarship to Dalcrest he'd turned down in favour of Kent State back in the spring, and Meredith was not only expected as an incoming freshman but was housed in a triple room in the best dorm on campus with Bonnie and Elena. The supernatural had worked *for* them, for a change.

Still, she'd had to give up a couple of dreams to get here. Harvard. Alaric by her side.

Meredith shook her head. *Those* dreams were incompatible, anyway. Alaric couldn't have come to Harvard with her. He was staying here in Fell's Church to research the origins of all the supernatural things that had happened during the town's history. Luckily, Duke University was letting him count this towards his dissertation on the paranormal. And he'd be able to monitor the town for danger at the same time. They'd have to be apart for now, no matter where Meredith chose to go, but at least Dalcrest was a manageable drive away.

Alaric's skin had a soft tan and a scattering of golden freckles across his cheekbones. Their faces were so close she could feel the warmth of his breath.

'What're you thinking?' His voice was a low murmur.

'Your freckles,' she said. 'They're gorgeous.' Then she took a breath and pulled away. 'I love you,' Meredith said, and then rushed on before a wave of longing could overwhelm her, 'I have to go.' She picked up one of the suitcases sitting by the car and swung it into the boot.

'I love you, too,' Alaric said, and caught her hand and held it tightly for a moment, looking into her eyes. Then he let go and put the last suitcase into the boot and slammed the lid.

She kissed him, quick and hard, and hurried herself into the driver's seat. Once she was safely seated, belted in, the engine running, she let herself look at him again.

'Bye,' she said through the open window. 'I'll call you tonight. Every night.'

Alaric nodded. His eyes were sad, but he smiled and held up a hand in farewell.

Meredith backed out of the driveway carefully. Her hands were at ten and two, and she kept her eyes on the road and her breathing steady. Without even looking, she knew Alaric was standing in the driveway, watching her car drive out of sight. She pressed her lips together firmly. She was a Sulez. She was a vampire hunter, a star student and completely level-headed in all situations.

She didn't need to cry; after all, she would see Alaric again. Soon. In the meantime, she would be a true Sulez: ready for anything.

Dalcrest was *beautiful*, Elena thought. She'd been here before, of course. She, Bonnie and Meredith had driven all the way up for a frat party during junior year, when Meredith had been dating a college boy. And she dimly remembered her parents bringing her for an alumni family event when she was little.

But now that she was part of the college, now that it would be her home for the next four years, everything looked different.

'Pretty swanky,' Damon commented as the car swept between the great gilded gates at the college's entrance and drove on past buildings of faux Georgian brick and neoclassical marble. 'For America, that is.'

'Well, we can't all grow up in Italian palaces,' Elena answered absently, very conscious of the light pressure of his thigh alongside hers. She was sitting in the front of the truck between Stefan and Damon, and there wasn't a lot of room. Having both of them so close was awfully distracting.

Damon rolled his eyes and drawled to Stefan, 'Well, if you have to play human and attend college *again*, little brother, at least you didn't choose too hideous a spot. And, of course, the company will make up for every inconvenience,' he added gallantly with a glance at Elena. 'But I still think that it's a waste of time.'

'And yet, here you are,' Elena said.

'*I'm* only here to keep you out of trouble,' he retorted.

'You'll have to excuse Damon,' Stefan said to Elena lightly. 'He doesn't understand. He was thrown out of university back in the old days.'

Damon laughed. 'But I had great fun while I was there,' he said. 'There were all kinds of pleasures a man of means could have at university. I imagine things have changed a bit though.'

They were needling each other, Elena knew, but there wasn't that hard, bitter edge to their sparring that used to be there. Damon was smiling over her head at Stefan with a wry affection, and Stefan's fingers were loose and relaxed on the steering wheel.

She put a hand on Stefan's knee and squeezed. Damon tensed next to her, but when she glanced over at him, he was gazing ahead through the windscreen, his face neutral. Elena took her hand off Stefan's knee. The last thing she wanted to do was disturb the delicate balance between the three of them.

'Here we are,' Stefan said, pulling up to an ivy-covered building. 'Pruitt House.'

The dorm loomed above them, a tall brick building

with a turret on one side, windows glittering in the afternoon sun.

'It's supposed to be the nicest dorm on campus,' Elena said.

Damon opened his door and hopped out, then turned to give Stefan a long look. 'The best dorm on campus, is it? Have you been using your powers of persuasion for *personal gain*, young Stefan?' He shook his head. 'Your morals are disintegrating.'

Stefan got out on his own side and turned to give Elena a courteous hand down. 'It's possible you're finally rubbing off on me,' he said to Damon, his lips twitching slightly with amusement. 'I'm in the turret in a single. There's a balcony.'

'How nice for you,' Damon said, his eyes moving quickly between them. 'This is a dormitory for both boys and girls, then? The sins of the modern world.' His face was thoughtful for a moment; then he gave a brilliant smile and began to pull luggage out of the back.

He had seemed almost lonely to Elena for that second – which was ridiculous, Damon was never *lonely* – but that fleeting impression was enough to make her say impetuously, 'You could come to college with us, Damon. It's not too late, not if you used your Power to enroll. You could live on campus with us.'

She felt Stefan freeze. Then he took a slow breath and slid up next to Damon, reaching for a stack of boxes. 'You could,' he said casually. 'It might be more fun than you think to try college again.'

Damon shook his head, scoffing, 'No, thank you. I parted ways with academia several centuries ago. I'll be much happier in my new apartment in town, where I can keep an eye on you without having to slum with students.'

He and Stefan smiled at each other with what looked like perfect understanding.

Right, Elena thought, with a curious mixture of relief and disappointment. She hadn't seen the new apartment yet, but Stefan had assured her that Damon would be, as usual, living in the lap of luxury, at least so far as the closest town could offer.

'Come along, kiddies,' Damon said, picking up several suitcases effortlessly and heading into the dorm. Stefan hoisted his tower of boxes and followed him.

Elena grabbed a box of her own and came after them, admiring their natural grace, their elegant strength. As they passed a few open doors, she heard a girl mock wolf-whistle, then giggle breathlessly with her roommate.

A box tipped from Stefan's enormous pile as he started up the staircase, and Damon caught it easily despite the suitcases. Stefan gave him a casual nod of thanks.

They'd spent centuries as enemies. They'd *killed* each other, once. Hundreds of years of hating each other, bound together by misery, jealousy and sorrow. Katherine had done that to them, trying to have them both when they each wanted only her.

Everything was different now. They'd come so far. Since Damon had died and come back, since they had battled and defeated the jealousy phantom, they'd come to be partners. There was an unspoken acknowledgment that they would work together to protect a little group of humans. More than that, there was a cautious, but very real, affection between them. They relied on each other; they'd be sorry to lose each other again. They didn't talk about it, but she knew it was true.

Elena squeezed her eyes shut for just a second. She knew they both loved her. They both knew that she loved them. *Even though*, her mind corrected conscientiously, *Stefan is my true love*. But something else in her, that imaginary panther, stretched and smiled. *But Damon, my Damon . . .*

She shook her head. She couldn't break them apart, couldn't let them fight over her. She wouldn't do what Katherine had done. If the time came for her to choose, she would choose Stefan. Of course.

Would you? the panther purred lazily, and Elena tried to push the thought away.

Everything could fall apart so easily. And it was up to her to make sure that never happened again.

CHAPTER

3

Bonnie fluffed her red curls as she hurried across Dalcrest's great lawn. It was so pretty here. Little flagstone paths bordered the lawn, leading off to the various dorms and classroom buildings. Brightly coloured flowers – petunias, impatiens, daisies – were growing everywhere, by the sides of the path and in front of the buildings.

The human scenery was pretty awesome, too, Bonnie thought, surreptitiously eyeing a bronzed guy lying on a towel near the edge of the lawn. Not surreptitiously enough, though – the guy lifted his shaggy dark head and winked at her. Bonnie giggled and walked faster, her cheeks warm. Honestly, shouldn't he be *unpacking* or setting up his room or something? Not just lying around half naked and winking at passing girls like a big . . . *flirt*.

The bag of stuff Bonnie had bought in the campus bookstore clunked gently in her hand. Of course, she hadn't been able to buy books yet, as they wouldn't sign up for classes until the next day, but it turned out the bookstore sold *everything*. She'd got some great stuff: a Dalcrest mug, a teddy bear wearing its own cute little Dalcrest T-shirt and a few things that would come in handy, like an efficiently organised shower caddy and a collection of pens in every colour of the rainbow. She had to admit she was pretty excited about starting college.

Bonnie shifted the bag to her left hand and flexed the cramping fingers of her right. Excited or not, all this stuff she'd bought was *heavy*.

But she needed it. This was her plan: she was going to become a new person at college. Not *entirely* new; she liked herself fine, for the most part. But she was going to become more of a leader, more mature, the kind of person about whom people said, 'Ask Bonnie,' or, 'Trust Bonnie,' rather than, 'Oh, *Bonnie*,' which was completely different.

She was determined to step out of the shadows of Meredith and Elena. They were both *terrific*, of course, her absolute best friends, but they didn't even realise how terrifyingly in charge they were all the time. Bonnie wanted to become a terrific, fully in-charge person in her own right.

Plus maybe she'd meet a really special guy. That would be nice. Bonnie couldn't actually *blame* Meredith or Elena for the fact that all the way through high school, she'd had plenty of dates but no serious boyfriends. But the simple fact was that, even if everyone thought you were cute, if your two closest friends were gorgeous and smart and powerful, the kind of guy who was looking to fall in love might find you a little bit . . . fluffy . . . in comparison.

She had to admit, though, that she was relieved that she and Meredith and Elena were all living together. She might not want to be stuck in their shadows, but they were still her best friends. And, after all . . .

Thud. Someone crashed into Bonnie's side and she lost her train of thought completely. She staggered backwards. A large male body lurched into her again, briefly crushing her face against his chest, and she tripped, falling against someone else's side. There were guys all around her, shoving one another back and forth, joking around and arguing, paying no attention to her as she was jostled among them, until a strong hand suddenly steadied her in the midst of the turmoil.

By the time she found her feet, they were moving off again, five or six male bodies swiping and shoving at one another, not stopping to apologise, as if they hadn't even noticed her as anything more than an inanimate obstacle in their path.

Except for one of them. Bonnie found herself staring

at a worn blue T-shirt and a slim torso with well-muscled arms. She straightened up and smoothed her hair, and the hand gripping her arm let go.

'Are you all right?' a low voice asked.

I'd be better if you hadn't almost knocked me down, Bonnie was about to say snippily. She was out of breath, and her bag was heavy, and this guy and his friends seriously needed to watch where they were going. Then she looked up, and her eyes met his.

Wow. The guy was *gorgeous*. His eyes were a clear, true blue, the blue of the sky at dawn on a summer morning. His features were sharply cut, the eyebrows arched, the cheekbones high, but his mouth was soft and sensual. And she'd never seen hair quite that colour before, except on the youngest kids, that pure white-blond that made her think of tropical beaches under a summer sky . . .

'Are you OK?' he repeated more loudly, a frown of concern crinkling his perfect forehead.

God. Bonnie could feel herself blushing right up to the roots of her hair. She had just been staring at him with her mouth open.

'I'm fine,' she said, trying to pull herself together. 'I guess I wasn't watching where I was going.'

He grinned, and a tiny *zing!* shot right through Bonnie. His smile was gorgeous, too, and it lit up his whole face. 'That's nice of you to say,' he said, 'but I think maybe *we* should have been watching where we were going instead of shoving each other all over the path. My friends sometimes get a little . . . rowdy.'

He glanced past her, and Bonnie looked back over her shoulder. His friends had stopped and were waiting for him further down the path. As Bonnie watched, one of them, a tall dark guy, smacked another on the back of the head, and a moment later they were scuffling and shoving again.

'Yeah, I can see that,' said Bonnie, and the gorgeous white-blond guy laughed. His rich laugh made Bonnie smile, too, and pulled her attention back to those *eyes*.

'Anyway, please accept my apology,' he said. 'I'm really sorry.' He held out his hand. 'My name's Zander.'

His grip was nice and firm, his hand large and warm around hers. Bonnie felt herself blushing again, and she tossed her red curls back and stuck her chin bravely in the air. She wasn't going to act all flustered. So what if he was gorgeous? She was friends – sort of, anyway – with *Damon*. She ought to be immune to gorgeous guys by now. 'I'm Bonnie,' she said, smiling up at him. 'This is my first day here. Are you a freshman, too?'

'Bonnie,' he said thoughtfully, drawing her name out a little like he was tasting it. 'No, I've been here for a while.'

'Zander . . . Zander,' the guys down the path began chanting, their voices getting faster and louder as they repeated it. '*Zander . . . Zander . . . Zander*.'

Zander winced, his attention slipping back towards

his friends. 'I'm sorry, Bonnie, I've got to run,' he said. 'We've got sort of a . . .' he paused, '. . . club thing going on. But, like I said, I'm really sorry we almost knocked you over. I hope I'll see you again soon, OK?'

He squeezed her hand once more, gave her a lingering smile, and walked away, picking up speed as he got closer to his friends. Bonnie watched him rejoin the group of guys. Just before they turned past a dorm, Zander looked back at her, flashed that gorgeous smile and waved.

Bonnie raised her hand to wave back, accidentally clunking the heavy bag against her side as he turned away.

Amazing, she thought, remembering the colour of his eyes. *I might be falling in love.*

Matt leaned against the wobbly pile of suitcases he'd stacked by the entrance to his dorm room. 'Darn it,' he said as he jiggled the key in the door's lock. Had they given him the right key?

'Hey,' a voice said behind him, and Matt jerked, tumbling a suitcase down onto the floor. 'Whoops, sorry about that. Are you Matt?'

'Yeah,' Matt said, giving the key one last twist and, just like that, the door finally opened. He turned, smiling. 'Are you Christopher?' The school had told him his roommate's name and that he was on the football team, too, but the two of them hadn't got in touch. Christopher looked OK. He was a big guy with a linebacker build, friendly smile and short sandy hair that he rubbed at with one hand as he stepped back to make way for the cheerful middle-aged couple following him.

'Hi there, you must be Matt,' said the woman, who was carrying a rolled-up rug and a Dalcrest pennant. 'I'm Jennifer, Christopher's mum, and this is Mark, his dad. It's so nice to meet you. Are your folks here?'

'Uh, no, I just drove up by myself,' Matt said. 'My hometown, Fell's Church, isn't too far from here.' He grabbed his suitcases and lugged them into the room, hurrying to get out of Christopher's family's way.

Their room was pretty small. There was a bunk bed along one wall, a narrow space in the middle of the room and two desks and dressers crammed side by side on the other wall.

The girls and Stefan were no doubt living in luxury, but it hadn't seemed quite right to let Stefan use his Power to get Matt a good housing assignment. It was bad enough that Matt took someone else's slot as a student and someone else's space on the football team.

Stefan had talked him into doing just that. 'Look, Matt,' he'd said, his green eyes serious. 'I understand how you feel. I don't like influencing people to get what I want either. But the fact is, we need to stay together. With the lines of Power that run through this whole part of the country, we have to be on our guard. We're the only ones who *know*.'

Matt had to agree, when Stefan put it like that. He'd turned down the plush dorm room Stefan had offered to arrange for him, though, and taken what the housing office assigned him. He had to hang on to at least a shred of his honour. Plus if he was in the same dorm as the others, it would have been hard to say no to rooming with Stefan. He liked Stefan fine, but the idea of living with him, of watching him with Elena, the girl Matt had lost and still loved despite all that had happened, was too much. And it would be fun to meet new people, to expand his horizons a bit after spending his whole life in Fell's Church.

But the room *was* awfully small.

And Christopher seemed to have a ton of stuff. He and his parents went up and down the stairs, hauling in a sound system, a little refrigerator, a TV, a Wii. Matt shoved his own three suitcases into the corner and helped them bring it all in.

'We'll share the fridge and the entertainment stuff, of course,' Christopher told him, glancing at Matt's bags, which clearly contained nothing but clothes and maybe some sheets and towels. 'If we can figure out where to put it all.' Christopher's mum was prowling around the room, directing his dad on where to move things.

'Great, thanks—' Matt started to say, but

Christopher's dad, having finally managed to wedge the TV on top of one of the dressers, turned to look at Matt.

'Hey,' he said. 'It just hit me – if you're from Fell's Church, you guys were the state champions last year. You must be some player. What position do you play?'

'Uh, thanks,' Matt said. 'I play quarterback.'

'First string?' Christopher's dad asked him.

Matt blushed. 'Yeah.'

Now they were all staring at him.

'Wow,' Christopher said. 'No offense, man, but why are you going to *Dalcrest*? I mean, I'm excited just to play college ball, but you could have gone, like, Division One.'

Matt shrugged uncomfortably. 'Um, I had to stay close to home.'

Christopher opened his mouth to say something else, but his mother gave a tiny shake of her head and he closed it again. *Great*, Matt thought. They probably thought he had family problems.

He had to admit it warmed him a little, though, to be with people who acknowledged what he'd given up. The girls and Stefan didn't really understand football. Even though Stefan had played on their high school team with him, his mindset was still very much that of the Renaissance European aristocrat: sports were enjoyable pastimes that kept the body fit. Stefan didn't really care.

But Christopher and his family – they *got* what it meant for Matt to pass up the chance of playing for a top-ranked college football team.

'So,' Christopher said, a little too suddenly, as if he'd been trying to think of a way to change the subject, 'which bed do you want? I don't care whether I take top or bottom.'

They all looked over at the bunk beds, and that's when Matt saw it for the first time. It must have arrived while he was downstairs helping with Christopher's luggage. A cream-coloured envelope sat on the bottom bunk, made of a fancy thick paper stock like a wedding invitation. On the front was written in calligraphy 'Matthew Honeycutt'.

'What's that, dear?' Christopher's mum asked curiously.

Matt shrugged, but he was beginning to feel a thrum of excitement in his chest. He'd heard something about invitations certain people at Dalcrest received, ones that just mysteriously appeared, but he'd always thought they were a myth.

Flipping the envelope over, he saw a blue wax seal bearing the impression of an ornate letter V.

Huh. After gazing at the envelope for a second, he folded it and slipped it into his back pocket. If it was what he thought it was, he was supposed to open it alone.

'I guess that's fate telling us the bottom bunk's yours,' Christopher said amiably.

'Yeah,' Matt said distractedly, his heart pounding hard. 'Excuse me for a minute, OK?'

He ducked out into the hall, took a deep breath and opened the envelope. Inside was more thick fancy paper with calligraphy on it and a narrow piece of black fabric. He read:

Fortis Aeturnus

For generations, the best and brightest of Dalcrest College have been chosen to join the Vitale Society. This year, you have been selected.

Should you wish to accept this honour and become one of us, come tomorrow night at eight o'clock to the main campus gate. You must be blindfolded and dressed as befits a serious occasion.

Tell no one.

The little pulse of excitement in Matt's chest increased until he could hear his heart pounding in his ears. He sank down along the wall and took a deep breath.

He'd heard stories about the Vitale Society. The handful of well-known actors, famous writers and great Civil War generals that Dalcrest counted among its alumni were all rumoured to have been members. To belong to the legendary society was supposed to ensure your success, to link you to an incredible secret network that would help you throughout your life.

More than that, there was talk of mysterious deeds,

of secrets revealed only to members. And they were supposed to have amazing parties.

But they were just gossip, the stories of the Vitale Society, and no one ever straight-out admitted to belonging to it. Matt always figured the secret society was a myth. The college itself so vehemently denied any knowledge of the Vitale Society that Matt suspected the admissions people might have made the whole thing up, trying to make the college seem a little more exclusive and mysterious than it really was.

But here – he looked down at the creamy paper clutched in his hands – was evidence that all the stories might be true. It could be a joke, he supposed, a trick someone was playing on a few of the freshmen. It didn't *feel* like a joke, though. The seal, the wax, the expensive paper; it seemed like a lot of effort to go to if the invitation wasn't genuine.

The most exclusive, most secret society at Dalcrest was real. And they wanted *him*.

CHAPTER

4

'Trust Bonnie to meet a cute guy on her first day at college,' Elena said. She carefully drew the nail polish brush over Meredith's toenail, painting it a tannish pink. They'd spent the evening at freshman orientation with the rest of their dormmates, and now all they wanted to do was relax. 'Are you sure this is the colour it's supposed to be?' Elena asked Meredith. 'It doesn't look like a summer sunset to me.'

'I like it,' Meredith said, wiggling her toes.

'Careful! I don't want polish on my new bedspread,' Elena warned.

'Zander is just *gorgeous*,' Bonnie said, stretching out luxuriously on her own bed on the other side of the room. 'Wait till you meet him.'

Meredith smiled at Bonnie. 'Isn't it an amazing

feeling? When you've just met somebody and you feel like there's something between you, but you're not quite sure what's going to happen?' She gave an exaggerated sigh, rolling her eyes up in a mock swoon. 'It's all about the anticipation, and you get a thrill just seeing him. I love that first part.' Her tone was light, but there was something lonely in her face. Elena was sure that, as composed and calm as Meredith was, she was already missing Alaric.

'Sure,' Bonnie said amiably. 'It's awesome, but I'd like to get to the *next* stage for once. I want to have a relationship where we know each other really well, a serious boyfriend instead of just a crush. Like you guys have. That's even better, isn't it?'

'I think so,' said Meredith. 'But you shouldn't try to hurry through the we-just-met stuff, because you've only got a limited time to enjoy it. Right, Elena?'

Elena dabbed a cotton bud around the edges of Meredith's polished toenails and thought about when she had first met Stefan. With all that had happened since then, it was hard to believe it was only a year ago.

What she remembered most was her own determination to have Stefan. No matter what had got in her way, she had known with a clear, firm purpose that he would be *hers*. And then, in those early days, once he *was* hers, it was glorious. It felt as if the missing piece of herself had slotted into place.

'Right,' she said finally, answering Meredith. 'Afterwards, things get more complicated.'

At first, Stefan had been a prize that Elena wanted to win: sophisticated and mysterious. He was a prize Caroline wanted, too, and Elena would never let Caroline beat her. But then Stefan had let Elena see the pain and passion, the integrity and nobility he held inside him, and she had forgotten the competition and loved Stefan with her whole heart.

And now? She still loved Stefan with everything she had, and he loved her. But she loved Damon, too, and sometimes she understood him – plotting, manipulative, dangerous Damon – better than she did Stefan. Damon was like her in some ways: he, too, would be relentless in pursuing what he wanted. She and Damon connected, she thought, on some deep, core, instinctive level that Stefan was too good, too honourable to understand. How could you love two people at the same time?

'Complicated,' Bonnie scoffed. 'More complicated than never being sure if somebody likes you or not? More complicated than having to wait by the phone to see if you have a date for Saturday night or not? I'm ready for complicated. Did you know that forty-nine per cent of college-educated women meet their future husbands on campus?'

'You made that statistic up,' Meredith said, rising and picking her way towards her own bed, careful not to smudge her polish.

Bonnie shrugged. 'OK, maybe I did. But I bet it's a really high percentage, anyway. Didn't your parents meet right here, Elena?'

'They did,' Elena said. 'I think they had a class together sophomore year.'

'How romantic,' Bonnie said happily.

'Well, if you get married, you have to meet your future spouse somewhere,' Meredith said. 'And there are a lot of possible future spouses at college.' She frowned at the silky cover on her bed. 'Do you think I can dry my nails faster if I use the hairdryer, or will it mess up the polish? I want to go to sleep.'

She examined the hairdryer as if it were the focal point of some science experiment, her face intent. Bonnie was watching her upside down, her head tipped back off the end of the bed and her red curls brushing the floor, tapping her feet energetically against the wall. Elena felt a great swell of love for both of them. She remembered the countless sleepovers they'd had all through school, back before their lives had become . . . complicated.

'I love having the three of us together,' she said. 'I hope the whole year is going to be just like this.' That was when they first heard the sirens.

Meredith peered through the blinds, collecting facts, trying to analyse what was going on outside Pruitt

House. An ambulance and several police cars were parked across the street, their lights silently blinking red and blue. Floodlights lit the quad a ghastly white, and it was crawling with police officers.

'I think we should go out there,' she said.

'Are you kidding me?' Bonnie asked from behind her. 'Why would we want to do that? I'm in my *pyjamas*.' Meredith glanced back. Bonnie was standing, hands on hips, brown eyes indignant. She was indeed wearing cute ice-cream-cone-printed pyjamas.

'Well, quick, put on some jeans,' Meredith said.

'But *why*?' asked Bonnie plaintively.

Meredith's eyes met Elena's across the room, and they nodded briskly to each other.

'Bonnie,' Elena said patiently, 'we have a responsibility to check out everything that's going on around here. We might just want to be normal college students, but we *know* the truth about the world – the truth other people don't realise, about vampires and werewolves and monsters – and we need to make sure that what's going on out there isn't part of that truth. If it's a *human* problem, the police will deal with it. But if it's something else, it's *our* responsibility.'

'Honestly,' grumbled Bonnie, already reaching for her clothes, 'you two have a – a saving-people complex or something. After I take psychology, I'm going to *diagnose* you.'

'And then we'll be sorry,' Meredith said agreeably.

On their way out of the door, Meredith grabbed the long velvet case that held her fighting stave. The stave was special, designed to fight both human and supernatural adversaries, and was made to specifications handed down through her family for generations. Only a Sulez could have a staff like this. She caressed it through the case, feeling the sharp spikes of different materials that dotted its ends: silver for werewolves, wood for vampires, white ash for Old Ones, iron for all eldritch creatures, tiny hypodermics to fill with poisons. She knew she couldn't take the stave out of its case on the quad, not surrounded by police officers and innocent bystanders, but she felt stronger when she could feel the weight of it in her hand.

Outside, the mugginess of the Virginia September day had given way to a chilly night, and the girls walked quickly towards the crowd around the quad.

'Don't look like we're heading straight over there,' Meredith whispered. 'Pretend we're going to one of the buildings. Like the student centre.' She angled off slightly, as if she was heading past the quad, and then led them closer, glancing over at the police tape surrounding the grass, pretending to be surprised by the activity next to them. Elena and Bonnie followed her lead, looking around wide-eyed.

'Can I help you ladies?' one of the campus security men asked, stepping forward to block their progress.

Elena smiled at him appealingly. 'We were just on our way to the student centre, and we saw everyone out here. What's going on?'

Meredith craned her head to look past him. All she could see were groups of police officers talking to one another and more campus security. Some officers were on their hands and knees, searching carefully through the grass. *Crime scene analysts*, she thought vaguely, wishing she knew more about police procedure than what she'd seen on TV.

The security officer stepped sideways to block her view. 'Nothing serious, just a girl who ran into a bit of trouble walking out here alone.' He smiled reassuringly.

'What kind of trouble?' Meredith asked, trying to see for herself.

He shifted, blocking her line of sight again. 'Nothing to worry about. Everyone's going to be OK this time.'

'This time?' Bonnie asked, frowning.

He cleared his throat. 'You girls just stick together at night, OK? Make sure to walk in pairs or groups when you're out around campus, and you'll be fine. Basic safety stuff, right?'

'But what happened to the girl? Where is she?' Meredith asked.

'Nothing to worry about,' he said, more firmly this time. His eyes were on the black velvet case in Meredith's hand. 'What have you got in there?'

'Pool cue,' she lied. 'We're going to play pool in the student centre.'

'Have a good time,' he said, in a tone of voice that was clearly a dismissal.

'We will,' Elena said sweetly, her hand on Meredith's arm. Meredith opened her mouth to ask another question, but Elena was pulling her away from the officer and towards the student centre.

'Hey,' Meredith objected quietly, when they were out of earshot. 'I wasn't done asking questions.'

'He wasn't going to tell us anything,' Elena said. Her mouth was a grim straight line. 'I bet a lot more happened than someone getting into a little trouble. Did you see the ambulances?'

'We're not really going to the student centre, are we?' Bonnie asked plaintively. 'I'm too tired.'

Meredith shook her head. 'We'd better loop back behind the buildings to our dorm, though. It'll look suspicious if we head straight back where we came from.'

'That was creepy, right?' Bonnie said. 'Do you think –' she paused, and Meredith could see her swallow – 'do you think something really bad happened?'

'I don't know,' Meredith said. 'He said a girl ran into a little bit of trouble. That could mean anything.'

'Do you think someone attacked her?' Elena asked.

Meredith shot her a significant look. 'Maybe,' she said. 'Or maybe some*thing* did.'

'I hope not,' Bonnie said, shivering. 'I've had enough somethings to last me forever.' They'd crossed behind the science building, down a darker, lonelier path, and circled back towards their dorm, its brightly lit entryway like a beacon before them. All three sped up, heading for the light.

'I've got my key,' Bonnie said, feeling in her jeans pocket. She opened the door, and she and Elena hurried into the dorm.

Meredith paused and glanced back towards the busy quad, then, past it, at the dark sky above campus. Whatever 'trouble' had happened, and whether the cause was human or something else, she knew she needed to be in top condition, ready to fight.

She could almost hear her father's voice saying, '*Fun time is over, Meredith*.' It was time to focus on her training again, time to work towards her destiny as a protector, as a Sulez, to keep innocent people safe from the darkness.

CHAPTER
5

The sun was way too bright. Bonnie shielded her eyes with one hand and glanced anxiously around as she walked across the quad towards the bookstore. It had taken her a long time to fall asleep after getting back to their room the night before. What if some crazy person was stalking the campus?

It's broad daylight, she told herself. *There are people everywhere. I have nothing to be afraid of.* But bad things could happen during the day, too. Girls got lured into cars by horrible men, or hit over the head and taken to dark places. Monsters didn't just lurk in the night. After all, she knew several *vampires* who strolled around during the day all the time. Damon and Stefan didn't scare her, not anymore, but there were other daytime monsters. *I just want to feel safe for once*, she thought wistfully.

She was coming up to the area the police had been searching the night before, still blocked off with yellow tape. Students were standing nearby in groups of two or three, talking in low voices. Across the path, Bonnie spied a reddish-brown stain that she thought might be blood, and she walked faster as she passed it.

There was a rustling in the bushes. She sped up even more, picturing a wild-eyed attacker hiding in the undergrowth, and glanced around nervously. No one was looking in her direction. Would they help her if she screamed?

She risked another look back at the bush – should she just take off running? – and stopped, embarrassed by the furious thumping of her heart. A cute little squirrel hopped hesitantly from under the branches. It sniffed the air, then dashed across the path and up a tree behind the police tape.

'Honestly, Bonnie McCullough, you're a moron,' she muttered to herself. A guy passing her in the other direction overheard her and snickered, making her blush furiously.

By the time she got to the bookstore, her blushing was under control. Having the typical redhead's complexion was a pain – everything she felt was broadcast by the flush or paleness of her skin. With any luck, though, she'd be able to handle a simple trip to buy books without humiliating herself.

Bonnie had started getting acquainted with the

bookstore during her shopping spree yesterday, but she hadn't really investigated the *book* side of the store. Today, though, she had the book list for the classes she'd registered for, and she needed to stock up for some serious studying. She'd never been a huge fan of school, but maybe college would be different. With a resolute squaring of her shoulders, she turned determinedly away from the shiny stuff and towards the textbooks.

The book lists were awfully *long*, though. She found the fat *Introduction to Psychology* textbook with a sense of satisfaction: this would definitely give her the terminology to diagnose her friends. The freshman English seminar she was assigned to covered a slew of novels, so she wandered through the fiction section, pulling *The Red and the Black*, *Oliver Twist* and *The Age of Innocence* off the shelves as she passed.

She rounded a corner in search of the rest of the *W*s, intent on adding *To the Lighthouse* to her growing stack of books, and froze.

Zander. Beautiful, beautiful Zander was draped gracefully next to a bookshelf, his white-blond head bent over a book. He hadn't seen her yet, so Bonnie immediately ducked back into the previous aisle.

She leaned against the wall, breathing hard. She could feel her cheeks heating up again, that awful telltale blush.

Carefully, she peeked back around the corner. He

hadn't noticed her; he was still reading intently. He was wearing a grey T-shirt today, and his soft-looking hair curled a bit at the nape of his neck. His face looked sort of sad with those gorgeous blue eyes hidden beneath his long lashes and no sign of that fabulous smile. There were dark shadows under his eyes.

Bonnie's first instinct was to sneak away. She could wait and find the Virginia Woolf book tomorrow; it wasn't as if she was going to read it today. She really didn't want Zander to think she was stalking him. It would be better if *he* saw *her* somewhere, when she wasn't paying attention. If he approached her, she'd know he was interested.

After all, maybe he *wasn't* interested in Bonnie. He'd been kind of flirtatious when he'd run into her, but he'd nearly knocked her down. What if he was just being friendly? What if he didn't even remember her?

Nope, better to take off this time and wait till she was better prepared. She wasn't even wearing eyeliner, for heaven's sake. Making up her mind, Bonnie turned firmly away.

But, on the other hand . . .

She hesitated. There'd been a connection between them, hadn't there? She'd felt something when her eyes met his. And he'd smiled at her like he was really seeing her, past the fluff and fluster.

And what about the resolution she'd made the day

before, walking to her dorm from this very same bookstore? If she was going to become a terrific, confident, stepping-out-of-the-shadows kind of person, she couldn't run away every time she saw a boy she liked.

Bonnie had always admired the way that Elena managed to get what she wanted. Elena just went after it and *nothing* got in her way. When Stefan had first come to Fell's Church, he hadn't wanted anything to do with Elena, certainly not to fall into her arms and start some kind of amazing eternal romance. But Elena hadn't cared. She was going to have Stefan, even if it killed her.

And, well, it *had* killed her, hadn't it? Bonnie shivered.

She shook her head a little. The point was, if you wanted to find love, you couldn't be afraid of trying, could you?

She stuck her chin determinedly into the air. At least she wasn't blushing anymore. Her cheeks were so cold, she was probably as white as a snowwoman, but she definitely wasn't blushing. So that was something.

Before she could change her mind again, she walked quickly around the corner back into the aisle where Zander stood reading.

'Hi!' she said, her voice squeaking a tiny bit. 'Zander!'

He looked up, and that amazing, beautiful smile spread across his face.

'Bonnie!' he said enthusiastically. 'Hey, I'm really glad to see you. I was thinking about you earlier.'

'You *were*?' she asked, and immediately wanted to kick herself at how overly enthusiastic she sounded.

'Yeah,' he said softly. 'I was.' His sky-blue eyes held hers. 'I was wishing I'd got your phone number.'

'You were?' Bonnie asked again, and this time didn't even worry about how she sounded.

'Sure,' he said. He scuffed his feet against the carpet, as though he was a little nervous, and a warmth blossomed inside her. He was nervous talking to *her*! 'I was thinking,' Zander went on, 'maybe we could do something sometime. I mean, if you wanted to.'

'Oh,' Bonnie said. 'I mean, yes! I would want to. If you did.'

Zander smiled again, and it was as if their little corner of the fiction section was lit up with a glowing light. She had to keep herself from staggering backwards, he was so gorgeous.

'How about this weekend?' he asked, and Bonnie, feeling suddenly as light and buoyant as though she might float up into the air, smiled back.

Meredith stepped her left foot behind her and raised her right heel, moving into a back stance as she brought her hands up sharply, fists together, in a blocking move. Then she slid her foot sideways into a front stance and punched forward with the fist of her left hand. She loved running through a taekwondo form. Each movement was choreographed, and the only thing to do was to practise over and over until the whole form flowed in a model of precision, grace and control. Taekwondo forms were perfectible, and Meredith enjoyed perfection.

The most glorious thing about them was that once she knew her forms so well that they were as natural as breathing, she would be ready for anything. In a fight, she would be able to sense what her opponent's next move would be and counter with a block or a kick or a punch without even thinking.

She turned swiftly, blocked high with her right hand and low with her left. It was the preparation, Meredith knew. If she was so prepared that her body could sense what move she needed to make without her brain having to get involved, then she would be able to truly protect herself and everyone else around her.

A few weeks ago, when she and her friends had been under attack from the phantom and she'd sprained her ankle, only Stefan had been left with Power enough to defend Fell's Church.

Stefan, a *vampire*.

Meredith's lips tightened as she automatically kicked forward with her right foot, slid into a tiger stance and blocked with her left hand.

She liked Stefan, and she trusted him, she really did, but still . . . She could picture generation upon generation of Sulezes rolling over in their graves, cursing her, if they knew that she had left herself and her friends so vulnerable, with only a vampire between themselves and danger. Vampires were the enemy.

Not *Stefan*, of course. She knew, despite all her training, that she could put her faith in Stefan. Damon, on the other hand . . . However useful Damon had been in a couple of battles, however reasonably pleasant and, frankly, out-of-character he had behaved for the last few weeks, Meredith couldn't bring herself to trust him.

But if she trained hard, if she perfected herself as a warrior, she wouldn't have to. She moved into a right front stance and, sharp and clean, punched forward with her right hand.

'Nice punch,' said a voice behind her.

She turned to see a short-haired African American girl leaning against the door of the practice room, watching her.

'Thanks,' Meredith said, surprised.

The girl strolled into the room. 'What are you,' she asked, 'a black belt?'

'Yes,' Meredith said, and couldn't help adding proudly, 'in taekwondo *and* karate.'

'Hmm,' the girl said, her eyes sparkling. 'I do taekwondo and aikido myself. My name's Samantha. I've been looking for a sparring partner. Interested?'

Despite the casualness of her tone, Samantha was

bouncing eagerly on the balls of her feet, a mischievous smile flickering at the corners of her mouth. Meredith's eyes narrowed.

'Sure,' she said, her attitude light. 'Show me what you've got.'

Samantha's smile broadened. She kicked off her shoes and stepped onto the practice mat next to Meredith. They faced off, assessing each other. She was a head shorter than Meredith, thin, but wiry and sleekly muscled, and she moved as gracefully as a cat.

The anticipation in the girl's eyes betrayed Samantha's belief that Meredith would be easy to beat. She was thinking that Meredith was one of those trainees who was all form and technique with no real fighting instinct. Meredith knew that kind of fighter well, had met them often enough in competitions. If that was what Samantha thought of her, she was in for a surprise.

'Ready?' Samantha asked. At Meredith's nod, she immediately launched a punch while bringing the opposite-side foot around in an attempt to sweep Meredith off her feet. Meredith reacted instinctively, blocking the blow, dodging the foot, then sweeping a kick of her own, which Samantha avoided, grinning with simple pleasure.

They exchanged a few more blows and kicks, and, against her will, Meredith was impressed. This girl was fast, faster than most of the fighters she had faced before, even at black-belt level, and much stronger than she looked.

She was too cocky, though, an aggressive fighter instead of a defensive one; the way she'd hurried to strike the first blow showed that. Meredith could use that cockiness against her.

Samantha shifted her weight, and Meredith slid in below her defenses, giving a fast spin heel kick that hit Samantha firmly on the upper thigh. She staggered a bit, and Meredith moved out of range quickly.

Samantha's face changed immediately. She was getting angry now, Meredith could tell, and that, too, was a weakness. She was frowning, her lips tight, while Meredith kept her own face purposefully blank. Samantha's fists and feet were moving quickly, but she lost some accuracy as she sped up.

Meredith pretended to fall back under the assault, feinting to keep her opponent off-balance, allowing herself to be backed towards a corner while still blocking Samantha's blows. When she was almost cornered, she jammed her arm against Samantha's fist, stopping her before she could fully extend her blow, and swept a foot under hers.

Samantha tripped, caught by Meredith's low kick, and fell heavily to the mat. She lay there and just stared up at her for a moment, face stunned, while Meredith hovered over her, suddenly uncertain. Had she hurt Samantha? Was the girl going to be angry and storm off?

Then Samantha's face blossomed into a wide, glowing smile. 'That was awesome!' she said. 'Can you show me that move?'

CHAPTER

6

Cautiously, Matt felt along the path with his foot until he found grass, then inched his way onto it, holding his hands out in front of him until he was touching the rough bark of a tree. There probably weren't too many people hanging around outside the main campus gate, but he'd just as soon have no one see him, blindfolded, dressed in his weddings-and-funerals suit and tie, and looking, he was sure, like an idiot.

On the other hand, he did want whoever was coming to get him to be able to spot him. It would be better to look like an idiot out in the open now and become part of the Vitale Society than to hide and spend the rest of the night blindfolded in the bushes. Matt inched his way back towards where he thought the gate must be and stumbled. Waving his hands, he managed to catch his balance again.

He suddenly wished he had told someone where he was going. What if somebody other than the Vitale Society had left him the invitation? What if this was a plan to get him on his own, some kind of trap? Matt ran his finger beneath his sweaty too-tight collar. After all the weird things that had happened to him in the last year, he couldn't help being paranoid.

If he vanished now, his friends would never know what had happened to him. He thought of Elena's laughing blue eyes, her clear, searching gaze. She would miss him if he disappeared, he knew, even if she had never loved him the way he wanted her to. Bonnie's laugh would lose its carefree note if Matt were gone, and Meredith would become more tense and fierce, push herself harder. He mattered to them.

The Vitale Society's invitation was clear, though: tell no one. If he wanted to get in the game, he had to play by their rules. Matt understood rules.

Without warning, someone – two someones – grabbed his arms, one on each side. Instinctively, Matt struggled, and he heard a grunt of exasperation from the person on his right.

'*Fortis aeturnus.*' The person on his left hissed it like a password, his breath warm on Matt's ear.

He stopped fighting. That was the heading on the letter from the Vitale Society, wasn't it? It was Latin, he was pretty sure. He wished he'd taken the time to find out what it meant. He let the people holding his arms guide him across the grass and onto the road.

'Step up,' the one on his left whispered, and Matt moved forward carefully, climbing into what seemed to be the back of a van. Firm hands pushed his head down to keep him from banging it on the van's roof, and Matt was reminded of that terrible time this past summer when he'd been arrested, accused of attacking Caroline. The cops had pushed his head down just like that when they put him handcuffed into the back of the squad car. His stomach sank with remembered dread, but he shook it off. The Guardians had erased everyone's memories of Caroline's false accusations, just as they'd changed everything else.

The hands guided him to a seat and strapped a seat belt around him. There seemed to be people sitting on each side of him, and Matt opened his mouth to speak – to say what, he didn't know.

'Be still,' the mysterious voice whispered, and he closed his mouth obediently. He strained his eyes to see something past the blindfold, even a hint of light and shadow, but everything was dark. Footsteps clattered across the floor of the van; then the doors slammed and the engine started up.

Matt sat back. He tried to keep track of the turns the van took but lost count of the rights and lefts after a few minutes and instead just sat quietly, waiting to see what would happen next.

After about fifteen minutes, the van came to a halt. The people on either side of him sat up straighter, and he tensed, too. He heard the front doors open and close and then footsteps come around the van before the back doors opened.

'Remain silent,' the voice that spoke to him earlier ordered. 'You will be guided towards the next stage of your journey.'

The person next to Matt brushed against him as he rose, and Matt heard him stumble on what sounded like gravel underfoot as he was led away. He listened alertly, but, once that person had left, he heard only the nervous shifting of the other people seated in the van. He jumped when hands took his arms once more. Somehow they'd snuck up on him again; he hadn't heard a thing.

The hands helped him out of the van, then guided him across what felt like a sidewalk or courtyard, where his shoes thudded against gravel and then pavement. His guides continued to lead him up a series of stairs, through some kind of hallway, then back down again. He counted three flights down before he was stopped again.

'Wait here,' the voice said, and then his guides stepped away.

Matt tried to figure out where he was. He could hear people, probably his companions from the van, shifting quietly, but no one spoke. Judging by the echoes their movements produced, they were in a large space: a gym? A basement? Probably a basement, after all those stairs down.

From behind him came the quiet click of a door closing.

'You may now remove your blindfolds,' a new voice said, deep and confident.

Matt untied his blindfold and looked around, blinking as his eyes adjusted to the light. It was a faint, indirect light, which supported his basement theory, but if this was a basement, it was the fanciest one he'd ever seen.

The room was huge, stretching into dimness at its other end, and the floor and walls were panelled in a dark, heavy wood. Arches and pillars supported the ceiling at intervals, and there were various carvings on them: the clever, twisted face of what might be a sprite leered at him from a pillar; the figure of a running deer spanned one archway. Red velvet chairs and heavy wooden tables lined the walls. Matt and the others were facing a great central archway, topped by a large ornate letter V made of different kinds of glittering, highly polished metals elaborately welded together. Below the V ran the same motto that had appeared on the invitation: *fortis aeturnus*.

Glancing at the people near him, Matt saw that he wasn't the only one feeling confused and apprehensive. There were maybe fifteen other people standing there, and they seemed like they came from different years: there was no way that tall, stooping guy with the full beard was a freshman.

A small, round-faced girl with short ringlets of brown hair caught Matt's eye. She raised her eyebrows at him, widening her mouth in an exaggerated expression of bewilderment. He grinned back at her, his spirits lightening. He shifted closer to her and had just opened his mouth to whisper an introduction when he was interrupted.

'Welcome,' said the deep, authoritative voice that had instructed them to take off their blindfolds, and a young man stepped up to the central archway, directly below the huge *V*. Behind him came a circle of others, seemingly a mix of guys and girls, all clothed in black and wearing masks. The effect ought to have been over the top, Matt thought, but instead the masked figures seemed mysterious and aloof, and he suppressed a shiver.

The guy beneath the arch was the only one not wearing a mask. He had curly dark hair and was a bit shorter than the silent figures around him. He smiled warmly as he stretched out his hands towards Matt and the others.

'Welcome,' he said again, 'to a secret. You may have heard rumours of the Vitale Society, the oldest and most illustrious organisation of Dalcrest. This is a society often spoken of in whispers, but about which no one knows the truth. No one except its members. I am Ethan Crane, the current president of the Vitale Society, and I'm delighted that you have accepted our invitation.'

He paused and looked around. 'You have been invited to pledge because you are the best of the best. Each of you has different strengths.' He gestured to the tall, bearded guy Matt had noticed. 'Stuart Covington here is the most brilliant scientific mind of the senior class, perhaps one of the most promising scientists in the country. His articles on biogenetics have already been published in numerous journals.'

Ethan walked into the crowd and stopped next to Matt. This close up, Matt could see that Ethan's eyes were an almost golden hazel, full of warmth. 'Matt Honeycutt enters Dalcrest as a starting player on the football team after leading his high school to the state championship last year. He could have had his choice of college football programmes, and he chose to come to Dalcrest.' Matt ducked his head modestly, and Ethan squeezed his shoulder before walking on to stop next to the cute round-faced girl.

'Junior Chloe Pascal is, as those of you who attended last year's campus art show know, the most talented artist on campus. Her dynamic, exciting sculptures have won her the Gershner Award for two years running.' He patted Chloe on the arm as she blushed.

Ethan went on, passing from one member of their

little group to another, listing accomplishments. Matt was only half listening as he looked around at the rapt expressions on the faces of the other candidates, but he got the impression of a wide range of talents, and that this was indeed a gathering of the best of the best, an assembly of campus achievers. He seemed to be the only freshman.

He felt like Ethan had lit a glowing candle inside him: he, Matt, who had been the least special of his group of friends, was being singled out.

'As you can see,' Ethan said, circling back to the front of the group, 'each of you has different skills. Brains, creativity, athleticism, the ability to lead others. These qualities, when brought together, can make you the most elite and powerful group, not only on campus, but throughout life. The Vitale Society is an organisation with a long history, and once you are a member of the society, you are one for life. Forever.' He held up one finger in caution, his face serious. 'However, this meeting is but the first step on the road to becoming a Vitale. And it is a difficult road.' He smiled at them again. 'I believe – *we* believe – that all of you have what it takes to become a Vitale. You would not have been invited to pledge if we didn't think you were worthy.'

Matt straightened his shoulders and held his head high. Least remarkable member of his group of friends or not, he'd *saved the world* – or at least his hometown

– more than once. Even if he'd just been one of a team then, he was pretty sure he could handle whatever the Vitale Society could throw at him.

Ethan smiled directly at him. 'If you are prepared to pledge the Vitale Society, to keep our secrets and earn our trust, step forward now.'

Without hesitating, Matt stepped forward. Chloe and the bearded guy – Stuart – stepped with him and, looking around, Matt saw that every one of the pledges had moved forward together.

Ethan came towards Matt and took hold of the lapel of his suit. 'There,' he said, quickly pinning something on it and letting Matt go. 'Wear this at all times, but discreetly. You must keep your involvement with the society secret. You will be contacted. Congratulations.' He gave Matt a brief, genuine smile, and moved on to Chloe, saying the same thing to her.

Matt turned his lapel up and looked at the tiny dark blue *V* that Ethan had pinned to it. He'd never thought much before about fraternities, or secret societies, or any kind of organisation that wasn't a sports team. But this, being the only freshman the legendary Vitale Society wanted, was different. They saw something in him, something *special*.

CHAPTER 7

'It would have been difficult to find a group of settlers less suited to building a brand-new colony than the one hundred and five men who sailed up the river from the Chesapeake Bay in 1607 and founded Jamestown,' Professor Campbell lectured from the front of Elena's class. 'While there were a couple of carpenters, a mason, a blacksmith and maybe a dozen labourers among them, they were far outnumbered by the self-proclaimed gentlemen who made up almost half the party.'

He paused and smiled sardonically. '"Gentlemen" in this case signifies men without a profession or trade. Many of them were lazy, idle men who had joined the London Company's expedition in the hope of making a profit without realising how much work founding a colony in the New World was really going to entail. The settlers landed in the spring, and by the end of September, half of them were dead. By January, when Captain Newport returned with supplies and more colonists, only thirty-eight of the original settlers remained.'

Lazy and clueless, Elena wrote neatly in her notebook. *Dead in less than a year*.

History of the South was her very first class, and college was already proving to be an eye-opening experience. Her high school teachers had always stressed courage and enterprise when they talked about Virginia's early settlers, not haplessness.

'On Thursday, we'll talk about the legend of John Smith and Pocahontas. We're going to discuss the facts and how they differ from Smith's own account, as he had a tendency towards self-promotion,' Professor Campbell announced. 'The reading assignment is in the syllabus, so please come prepared for a lively discussion next time.' He was a plump, energetic little man, whose small black eyes swept the class and landed unerringly on Elena as he added, 'Elena Gilbert? Please stay after class for a moment. I'd like to speak with you.'

She had time to wonder, nervously, how he knew which of his students she was while the rest of the class straggled out of the room, a few stopping to ask him questions. She hadn't spoken up during his lecture, and there were about fifty students in the class.

As the last of her classmates disappeared through the door, she approached his desk.

'Elena *Gilbert*,' he said avuncularly, his bright eyes searching hers. 'I do apologise for taking up your time. But when I heard your name, I had to ask.'

He paused, and Elena dutifully replied, 'Had to ask what, Professor?'

'I know the name Gilbert, you see,' he said, 'and the more I look at you, the more you remind me of someone – two someones – who were once very dear friends of mine. Could you possibly be the daughter of Elizabeth Morrow and Thomas Gilbert?'

'Yes, I am,' said Elena slowly. She ought to have expected that she might meet someone who knew her parents here at Dalcrest, but all the same it felt weird to hear their names.

'Ah!' He laced his fingers across his stomach and gave her a satisfied smile. 'You look so much like Elizabeth. It startled me when you came into the room. But there's a touch of Thomas in you, too, make no mistake about that. Something about your expression, I think. Seeing you takes me right back to my own days as an undergraduate. She was a lovely girl, your mother, just lovely.'

'You went to school here with my parents?' Elena asked.

'I certainly did.' Professor Campbell's small black eyes widened. 'They were two of my best friends here.

Two of the best friends I ever had. We lost track of each other over the years, I'm afraid, but I heard about the accident.' He unlaced his fingers and hesitantly touched her arm. 'I'm so sorry.'

'Thank you.' Elena bit her lip. 'They never talked much about their college years. Maybe as I got older, they would have . . .' Her voice trailed off, and she realised with dismay that her eyes had filled with tears.

'Oh, my dear, I didn't mean to upset you.' Professor Campbell patted his jacket pockets. 'And I've never got a tissue when I need one. Oh, please don't cry.'

His comical expression of distress made her give him a watery-eyed smile, and he relaxed and smiled in return. 'There, that's better,' he said. 'You know, if you'd like to hear more about your parents and what they were like back then, I'd be happy to tell you about them. I've got all kinds of stories.'

'Really?' she said hopefully. She felt a flicker of excitement. Aunt Judith talked with Elena about her mother sometimes, but the memories she shared were mostly from their childhood. And Elena really didn't know much about her father's past at all: he'd been an only child and his parents were dead.

'Certainly, certainly,' Professor Campbell said cheerfully. 'Come to my office hours, and I'll tell you all about our hijinks back in the old days. I'm there every Monday and Friday from three to five, and I'll put out a welcome mat for you. Metaphorically speaking, of course. Serve you some of the horrible department coffee.'

'Thank you, Professor Campbell,' Elena said. 'I'd love that.'

'Call me James,' he said. 'It's nothing at all. Anything I can do to make you feel at home here at Dalcrest.' He cocked his head to one side and looked at her quizzically, his eyes as bright and curious as a small animal's. 'After all, as the daughter of Elizabeth and Thomas, you must be a very special girl.'

The big black crow outside the open lecture room window paced back and forth, clenching and unclenching its powerful talons around the branch on which it was perched. Damon wanted to transform back into his vampire self, climb through the window and have a quick but *effective* interrogation session with that professor.

But Elena wouldn't like that.

She was so *naive*, dammit.

Yes, yes, she was his lovely, brilliant, clever princess, but she was ridiculously naive, too; they all were. Damon irritably preened his ruffled feathers back into iridescent sleekness. They were just so *young*. At this point, Damon was able to look back and say that no one learned anything in life, not for her first hundred years or so. You had to be immortal, really, to have the time to learn to look out for yourself properly.

Take Elena, gazing so trustfully at her professor. After all she'd been through, all she'd seen, she was so easy to lull into complacency – all the man had to do was dangle the promise of information about her parents in front of her and she'd happily trot off to meet him in his office whenever he suggested. Sentimental ninny. What could the man possibly tell her that would be of any real importance? Nothing could bring her parents back.

The professor wasn't a danger, most likely. Damon had probed him with his Power, felt nothing but the flickering of a human mind, no dark surge of answering Power coming from the little man, no swell of disturbing or violent emotion. But he couldn't be *sure*, could he? Damon's Power couldn't detect every monster, couldn't predict every twist of the human heart.

But the real problem here was Elena. She'd forgotten, clearly, that she'd lost all her Power, that the Guardians had stripped her back to being just a vulnerable, fragile mortal girl again. She thought, wrongly, that she could protect herself.

They were all like that. Damon had been infuriated at first to slowly realise that he was starting to feel as though all of them were *his* humans. Not just his lovely Elena and the little redbird, but *all* of them, the witch Mrs Flowers and the hunter and that meathead of a boy as well. Those last two didn't even like him, but he felt compelled to keep an eye on them, to prevent them from damaging themselves through their innate stupidity.

Damon wasn't the one who wanted to be here. No, the 'let's all join hands and dance off to further our educations together' idea wasn't his, and he'd treated it with the proper scorn. He wasn't Stefan. He wasn't going to waste his time pretending to be one of the mortal children.

But he had found, to his dismay, that he didn't want to lose them, either.

It was embarrassing. Vampires were not pack animals, not like humans. He wasn't supposed to care what happened to them. These children should be *prey*, and nothing more.

But being dead and coming back, fighting the jealousy phantom and letting go of the sick envy and misery that had held him captive ever since he was a human had changed Damon. With that hard ball of hate gone from the middle of his chest, where it had lived for so long, he found himself feeling lighter. Almost as if he . . . *cared*.

Embarrassing or not, it felt surprisingly comfortable, having this connection to the little group of humans. He'd have died – again – rather than admit it aloud, though.

He clacked his beak a few times as Elena said goodbye to her professor and left the classroom. Then

Damon spread his wings and flapped down to a tree next to the building's entrance.

Nearby, a thin young man was posting on another tree a flyer with a girl's picture and Damon flew over to get a closer look. *Missing Student*, the top of the flyer said, and below the picture were details of a night-time disappearance: no clues, no leads, no evidence, no idea where nineteen-year-old Taylor Harrison might be. Suspicion of foul play. The promise of a reward from her anxious family for information leading to her safe return.

Damon let out a rough caw. There was something *wrong* here. He'd known it already – had felt something a little off about this campus as soon as he'd arrived two days ago, although he hadn't quite been able to put his finger on it. Why else would he have been so worried about his princess?

Elena came out of the building and started across the quad, tucking her long golden hair behind her ears, oblivious to the black crow that swooped from tree to tree above her. Damon was going to find out what was going on here, and he was going to do it before whatever it was touched *any* of his humans.

Especially Elena.

CHAPTER

8

'Ugh, I don't think there's a single thing on the hot lunch bar I'd ever consider eating,' Elena said to Stefan. 'Half the stuff I can't even identify.' He watched patiently as she passed on to the salad bar.

'This isn't much better,' she said, lifting a watery spoonful of cottage cheese and letting it slop back into the container for emphasis. 'I thought the food at college would be more edible than in our high school cafeteria, but apparently I was wrong.'

Stefan made a vague sound of agreement and looked around for a place for them to sit. He wasn't eating. Human food didn't have much taste for him now, and he'd used his Power to call down a dove to his balcony that morning. That had provided enough blood to hold him until the evening, when he would need to hunt again.

Once Elena finally made herself a salad, he led her to the empty table he'd spotted.

She kissed him before she sat down and a shiver of delight ran through him as their minds touched. The familiar link between them slid into place, and he felt Elena's joy, her contentment at being with him and at their new, nearly normal, lives. Below this, a touch of excitement fizzed through her, and Stefan sent a questioning thought between them, wondering what had happened since they'd seen each other that morning.

Elena broke the kiss and answered his unspoken question.

'Professor Campbell, my history professor, knew my parents when they were in college,' she said. Her voice was calm, but her eyes were bright, and Stefan could sense how big this was for her. 'He was a really good friend of theirs. He can tell me stories about them, parts of their lives I never knew before.'

'That's great,' he said, pleased for her. 'How was the class?'

'It was all right,' she said, beginning to eat her salad. 'We're talking about the colonial days for the first couple of weeks.' She looked up, her fork poised in mid-air. 'How about you? What was your philosophy class like?'

'Fine.' Stefan paused. *Fine* wasn't really what he

meant. It had been strange to be sitting in a college classroom again. He'd attended college a few times during his long history, seen the changing fads in education. At first, his classmates had been a select number of wealthy young men, and now there was a more diverse mix of boys and girls. But there was an essential sameness to all those experiences. The professor lecturing, the students either bored or eager. A certain shallowness of thought, a shy ducking away from exposing deeper feelings.

Damon was right. Stefan didn't belong here; he was just playing a role, again. Killing some of his limitless time. But Elena – he looked at her, her shining blue eyes fixed on him – she *did* belong here. She deserved the chance at a normal life, and he knew she wouldn't have come to college without him.

Could he say any of this to her? He didn't want to dim the excitement in those lapis lazuli eyes, but he had sworn to himself that he would always be honest with her, would treat her as an equal. He opened his mouth, hoping to explain some of what he felt.

'Did you hear about Daniel Greenwater?' a girl asked nearby, her voice high with curiosity as she and her friends slid into the empty chairs at the other end of the table. Stefan closed his mouth and turned his head to listen.

'Who's Daniel Greenwater?' someone else asked.

'Look,' the first girl said, unfolding a newspaper she

held. Glancing over, Stefan saw it was the campus paper. 'He's a freshman, and he just vanished. He left the student centre when it closed last night, and his roommate says he never came back to the room. It's really creepy.'

Stefan's eyes met Elena's across the table, and she raised an eyebrow thoughtfully. Could this be something they should look into?

Another girl at the other end of the table shrugged. 'He probably just got stressed out and went home. Or maybe his roommate killed him. You know you get automatic As if your roommate dies.'

'That's a myth,' Stefan said absently, and the girls looked up at him in surprise. 'Could I see the paper for a moment, please?'

They passed it over, and he studied the picture on the front. A high school yearbook photo smiled up at him, a skinny floppy-haired guy with a slight overbite and friendly eyes. A face he recognised. He had thought the name sounded familiar.

'He lives in our dorm,' he said softly to Elena. 'Remember him from orientation? He seemed happy to be here. I don't think he would have left, not of his own free will.'

Elena stared at him, her wide eyes apprehensive now. 'Do you think something bad happened to him? There was something weird going on in the quad the first night we were here.' She swallowed. 'They said a girl had got into some trouble, but the cops wouldn't really tell us anything. Do you think it might be related to Daniel Greenwater's disappearance?'

'I don't know,' Stefan said tightly, 'but I'm worried. I don't like anything out of the ordinary.' He stood up. 'Are you ready to go?' Elena nodded, although half her lunch was still on her tray. He handed the paper politely back to the girls and followed Elena outside.

'Maybe we're paranoid because we're used to terrible things happening,' she said, once they were on the path heading back up the hill towards their dorm. 'But people disappear all the time. Girls get harassed or attacked sometimes. It's unfortunate, but it doesn't mean there's a sinister plot behind it all.'

Stefan paused, staring at a flyer stuck to a tree by the cafeteria. *Missing Student*, the heading said, with a picture of a girl beneath it. 'Promise me you'll be careful, Elena,' he said. 'Tell Meredith and Bonnie, too. And Matt. None of you should be wandering around campus by yourselves. Not at night, anyway.'

Elena nodded, her face pale, staring at the picture on the flyer. Stefan felt a sharp pang of regret even through his anxiety. She had been so excited when they met for lunch, and now that enthusiasm had drained away.

He wrapped his arm around her waist, wanting to hold her, to keep her safe. 'Why don't we go out tonight?' he said. 'I've got a study group to go to, but it shouldn't last too long. We could go off campus for dinner. Maybe you could stay over tonight? I'd feel better if I knew you were safe.'

She looked at him, her eyes suddenly sparkling with laughter. 'Oh, as long as that's the only reason you'd want me in your room,' she said, smiling. 'I'd hate to think you had designs on my virtue.'

Stefan thought of Elena's creamy skin and silky golden hair, of her warmth, the rich wine of her blood. The idea of her in his arms again, without her aunt Judith or his landlady, Mrs Flowers, down the hall, was intoxicating.

'Of course not,' he murmured, bowing his head towards hers. 'I have no designs. I live only to serve you.' He kissed her again, sending all his love and longing to her.

Above their heads, Stefan heard a strident cawing and the flapping of wings, and, his lips still against Elena's, he frowned. She seemed to sense his sudden tension and pulled away from him, following his gaze towards the black crow wheeling above them.

Damon. Watching them, watching Elena, as always.

'Excellence.' Ethan's voice rang out across the outdoor basketball court where the pledges were gathered. Dawn was breaking, and there was no one around except for Ethan and the sleepy-faced pledges. 'As you know from our first meeting, each of you here exemplifies the peak of one or more types of achievement. But that's not enough.' He paused, looking from face to face. 'It's not enough for each of you to have a piece of the best. You *can* encompass all these attributes in yourself. Over the course of the pledge period, you will discover worlds inside yourselves that you've never imagined.'

Matt shuffled his sneakers against the asphalt and tried to keep the skeptical expression off his face. Expecting him to achieve the heights of academic or artistic success, he knew, was a long shot.

He wasn't particularly modest, but he was realistic, and he could list his best qualities: athlete, good friend, honourable guy. He wasn't stupid, either, but if excelling in intellect and creativity were prerequisites for being part of the Vitale Society, he might as well give up now.

Rubbing the back of his neck, he glanced around at his fellow pledges. It was reassuring to see that most of them were wearing expressions of barely restrained panic: apparently 'encompassing all these attributes' wasn't something they'd reckoned on either. Chloe, the cute round-faced girl he'd noticed at the first gathering, caught his eye and winked, just a quick brush of her lashes, and he smiled back, feeling oddly happy.

'Today,' Ethan announced, 'we will work on athleticism.' Matt sighed with relief. Athleticism he could do.

All around him, he saw faces fall. The intellectuals, the leaders, the budding creative geniuses – they weren't looking forward to testing their athletic prowess. A low rebellious murmur swelled among them.

'Don't sulk,' said Ethan, laughing. 'I promise you, by the time you become full members of the society, each of you will have reached your peak of physical perfection. For the first time, you will feel what it is to be truly *alive*.' His eyes glittered with possibility.

He went on to outline the pledges' task. They were about to embark on a twenty-five kilometre run, with several obstacles along the way. 'Be prepared to get dirty,' he said cheerfully. 'But it will be wonderful. When you finish, you'll have achieved something new. You are welcome to assist one another. But be aware: if you do not complete the run in three hours, you will not be invited to continue to the next step in the pledging process.' He smiled. 'Only the best can become members of the Vitale Society.'

Matt looked around and saw that the pledges, even those who looked like they had never left the science lab or the library, were retying their sneakers and stretching, wearing determined expressions.

'Holy cow,' a voice beside him said. It was a nice voice, with a real twang to it, a voice that came from somewhere deeper in the South than Virginia, and Matt was smiling even before he looked around and saw that it was Chloe. 'I figure you're about the only person here who isn't going to have a *lot* of trouble with this,' she said.

She was so cute. Little dimples showed in her cheeks when she smiled, and her short dark hair fell in curls behind her ears. 'Hey, I'm Matt,' he said, grinning back at her.

'I knew that,' she said cheerfully. 'You're our football star.'

'And you're Chloe, the amazing artist,' he said.

'Oh.' She blushed. 'I don't know about that.'

'I'd love to see your work sometime,' he told her, and her smile widened.

'Any tips for today?' she asked. 'I never run unless I'm about to miss the bus, and I think I'm about to regret that.'

Her face was so appealing that Matt momentarily felt like hugging her. Instead, he frowned thoughtfully up at the sky. 'Under these kinds of conditions,' he said, 'the best thing to do is incline your arms at a fifty-degree angle to the ground and run with a light bounding step.'

Chloe stared at him for a minute and then giggled. 'You're teasing me,' she said. 'That's not fair. I have no idea about this stuff.'

'I'll help you,' he said, feeling good. 'We can do it together.'

CHAPTER

9

Where r u? Elena texted impatiently. Stefan was supposed to meet her at her dorm room more than twenty minutes ago. Surely his study group was over by now? She was *starving*.

She paced around the room, occasionally glancing at the dark tree branches beyond the windows. It wasn't like Stefan to be late.

She checked her phone. It was too soon to try to reach him again. Outside, something dark moved and she gasped. Then she shook her head. It was just the branches of the trees out there, waving in the breeze. She moved closer, trying to see past the reflections on the glass. Their room was on the third floor; there wouldn't be anyone sitting that high up. At least not anyone human. Elena shuddered.

'Elena,' said a cool, clear voice from outside.

With a squeak that sounded like a frightened rabbit, she jerked backwards, pressing one hand to her pounding heart. After a moment, she stepped up to the window and threw it open.

'Damon,' she said. 'You scared me to death. What are you doing out there?'

There was a flash of white teeth in the shadows. A mocking tone rang through his answer. 'Waiting for you to invite me into your room, of course.'

'You don't need an invitation,' she said. 'You helped me move in.'

'I know,' Damon said, smiling. 'I'm being a gentleman.'

She hesitated. She trusted him, of course she did, but this seemed so intimate. Damon outside in the dark, Elena alone in her bedroom, neither of her roommates around. He'd been in her room at home, but Aunt Judith and Robert had been just down the hall. She wondered if Stefan would mind her being alone here with Damon, but she shook off the thought. He trusted Elena, that was what mattered.

'*Elena*,' Damon's voice was soft but insistent. 'Let me in before I fall.'

Rolling her eyes, she said, 'You'd never fall. And if you did, you'd fly. But you can come in anyway.'

With a soft *whoosh*, faster than her eye could follow, Damon was suddenly beside her. She had to step back a pace. Eyes and hair as dark as night, pale luminous skin, perfectly cut features. He even smelled good. His lips looked so soft . . .

Elena caught herself leaning towards him, her own lips parting, and pulled away. 'Stop it,' she said.

'I'm not doing anything,' he said innocently. When Elena arched a skeptical eyebrow at him, he shrugged and shot her a brief, brilliant smile. *There*, she thought. *That's why Stefan might mind Damon being here.* 'Oh, all right. I'm only teasing you.'

He looked around the room and quirked an eyebrow of his own. 'Why, Elena,' he said, 'I'm almost disappointed. You and your friends are running so true to type here.'

She followed his eyes. Bonnie's side of the room was a mess, a tumble of stuffed animals, rejected outfits and Dalcrest paraphernalia. In contrast, Meredith's area was rigidly tidy, books lined up alphabetically, a single silver pen on the desk next to her slim silver laptop, her bed neatly draped in a silk duvet in subtly patterned grey and white. Her dresser and closet were closed, but inside, Elena knew, Meredith's clothes would be organised by type, colour and season. Damon was right: just by looking at their parts of the room, you could tell that Meredith was rational, sophisticated, carefully controlled and private, while Bonnie was fluffy, fun-loving and disorganised.

What about Elena's own things? What did they say

about her? She looked over her part of the room with a critical eye. Framed art prints from her favourite exhibits, her silver brush and comb lined up on her dresser, deep-blue sheets that she knew set off her eyes and hair. Someone who held on to what she liked and didn't change easily? Someone who was very aware of what suited her? She wasn't sure.

Damon smiled at her again, without the mocking edge this time. 'Don't give it a second's thought, princess,' he said affectionately. 'You're more than your possessions.'

'Thanks,' Elena said shortly. 'So, did you just drop in my window to say hello?'

He reached out and tucked a stray lock of hair behind her ear. They were standing very close together, and she backed away a little. 'I thought maybe, now that you're a college girl, we could go out tonight and have some fun.'

'Fun?' Elena said, still distracted by his mouth. 'What kind of fun?'

'Oh, you know,' he said, 'just a little dinner, a few drinks. Friend stuff. Nothing too daring.'

'Right,' she said firmly. 'It sounds nice. But I can't tonight. Stefan and I are going out to dinner.'

'Of course,' Damon said. He gave her a firm little nod and what was so obviously supposed to be a supportive smile that she had to stifle a giggle. Supportive, friendly and unassuming were not natural looks on Damon's face.

He was trying so very hard to be her *friend* even though they all knew there was more than that between them. Since he had died and come back, she knew he had been trying to change his relationships with Stefan and with her, to be with them in a way he never had before. It couldn't be easy on poor Damon, trying to be good. He was out of practice.

Elena's phone chimed. She read the text from Stefan:

I'm sorry. The study group's running late. I think it'll be at least another hour. Meet later?

'Problem?' Damon was watching her, the same innocent, friendly smile on his face, and affection for him washed over her. Damon was her friend. Why shouldn't she go out with him?

'Change of plans,' she said briskly. 'We'll go out, but just for a little while. I need to be back here to meet Stefan in an hour.' She texted Stefan quickly to let him know she was going to grab some food and looked up to see a triumphant smile on Damon's face as he reached to take her arm.

Bonnie walked across campus, practically skipping in time to the happy tune in her head. A *date* with *Zan*der, la *la* la *la la*. It was about time, too. She'd been eagerly anticipating seeing him again all week, and although they'd talked on the phone, she hadn't laid eyes on him around campus at all, even though of course she'd been looking.

At last she was about to see him. La *la* la *la la*. Lovely, gorgeous Zander.

She had on jeans and a sort of silvery, draping top that at least made it *look* like she might have some cleavage. It was a good outfit, she thought, understated enough for just hanging out but also a little bit special. Just in case they decided to go out clubbing or something at the last minute. Zander hadn't told her what he'd planned, just asked her to meet him outside the science building. La *la* la *la la*, she hummed.

Bonnie's footsteps slowed, and the tune in her head died off as she saw flickering lights illuminating a group of people up ahead. They were gathered in the courtyard in front of one of the dorms.

Approaching, she realised it was a group of girls holding candles. The wavering light from the candles sent shadows across their serious faces. Propped against the wall of the dorm were three blown-up photos, two girls and a guy. All across the grass in front of them were heaped flowers, letters and teddy bears.

Hesitant to break the silence, Bonnie touched the arm of one of the girls. 'What's going on?' she whispered.

'It's a candlelight vigil for the missing people,' the girl whispered back.

Missing people? Bonnie scanned the faces in the photographs. Young, smiling, about her age. 'Are they all students here?' she asked, horrified. 'What happened to them?'

'Nobody knows,' the girl said, her gaze serious. 'They just vanished. You didn't hear about this?'

Bonnie's stomach dropped. She knew that a girl was attacked – or something – on the quad the first night, but she hadn't known about any disappearances. No wonder her gut instinct had warned her to be scared walking across campus the other day. She could have been in danger. 'No,' she said slowly. 'I didn't hear anything.' She dropped her eyes and bowed her head, silent as she sent out a fervent hope that these three happy-looking people would be found, safe and sound.

In the distance, a siren began to wail.

'Something's happened.'

'Do you think someone was attacked?'

A babble of frightened voices rose as the sirens got closer. A girl near Bonnie began to sob, a hurt, scared sound.

'All right, what's the trouble here?' said a new, authoritative voice, and Bonnie looked up to see two campus police officers shouldering their way through the crowd.

'We . . . uh . . .' The girl who had spoken to Bonnie gestured at the photos and flowers against the wall. 'We were having a vigil. For the missing people.'

'What are those sirens for?' another girl asked, her voice rising.

'Nothing to worry about,' said the officer, but his face softened as he looked at the sobbing girl. Bonnie realised with a slight shock that he wasn't much older than she was. 'Miss?' he said to the crying girl. 'We'll help you get home.'

His partner looked around at the crowd. 'It's time to break things up and head inside,' he said sternly. 'Stick together and be careful.'

'I thought you said there was nothing to worry about,' said another girl angrily. 'What aren't you telling us?'

'There's nothing you don't know already,' the man said patiently. 'People are missing. You can never be too careful.'

If there's nothing to worry about, why do we have to be careful? Bonnie wondered, but she bit back the words and hurried away down the path, towards the science building where Zander had suggested they meet.

The idea of trying to have a vision, to see if she could learn anything about the missing people, nudged at her mind, but she pushed it away. She hated that. She hated the loss of control when she slid into one of her visions.

It was unlikely to work, anyway. Her visions had always been about people she knew, about immediate problems facing them. She didn't know any of the missing people. She bit her lip and walked faster. The excitement about her date had fizzled out, and she didn't feel safe now. But at least if she got to Zander, she wouldn't be alone.

When she arrived at the science building, though, Zander wasn't there. Bonnie hesitated and looked around nervously. This corner of campus seemed to be deserted.

She tried the door of the science building, but it was locked. Well *of course* it was – there weren't any classes this late. She shook the handle of the front door in frustration. She reached into her bag, then groaned as she realised she'd left her phone back in her room.

Suddenly, she felt very exposed. The campus police had said to stick together, not to wander around alone at night, but here she was, all by herself. A cool breeze ruffled her hair and she shivered. It was getting awfully dark.

'Bonnie. *Psst*, Bonnie!'

Zander's voice. But where was he?

She saw nothing but the dark quad, streetlights throwing little circles of light on the paths. Above her, leaves rustled in the wind.

'Bonnie! Up here.'

Looking up, she finally spotted Zander on the roof, peering down over the side at her, his pale hair almost glowing in the moonlight.

'What're you doing up there?' she called to him, confused.

'Come on up,' he invited, pointing to the fire escape ladder on the side of the building. It was lowered to just a couple of feet above the ground.

'Really?' Bonnie said dubiously. She walked over to the fire escape. She could make it onto the ladder, she was pretty sure, but she was going to look clumsy and awkward scrambling up on it. And what if she got caught? She hadn't actually read the campus regulations thoroughly, but wouldn't climbing the fire escape up to the roof of a closed building be against the rules?

'Come on, Bonnie,' Zander called. His feet clanging loudly against the iron steps, he ran down the fire escape, shimmied down the ladder and leaped to the ground, landing catlike on his feet beside her. He went down on one knee and held his hands out together. 'I'll boost you up so you'll be able to reach.'

Bonnie swallowed, then stepped up onto Zander's hands and stretched for the ladder. Once she swung her leg up onto the bottom rung, it was a piece of cake, although the slightly rusty metal was rough against her hands. She spared a moment to thank all the powers of the universe that she had decided to wear jeans rather than a skirt tonight.

Zander trailed behind her up the fire escape from one landing to another until finally they arrived on the roof.

'Are we allowed to be up here?' Bonnie asked nervously.

'Well,' Zander said slowly, 'probably not. But I come up here all the time, and no one's ever told me not to.' He smiled that warm, wonderful smile at her and added, 'This is one of my favourite places.'

It was a nice view, she had to admit that. Below them, the campus stretched, leafy and green and mysterious.

If anyone else had brought her up here, though, she would have complained about the rusty fire escape and the concrete roof, suggested that maybe a date should involve *going somewhere*. This was a date, wasn't it? She froze momentarily in a panic, trying to recall exactly what Zander had said when he suggested meeting here. She didn't remember the words themselves, but they definitely had a date-y feel to them: she wasn't a kid anymore, she knew when she was being asked out.

And Zander was so cute, it was worth making an effort.

'It's pretty up here,' she said lamely and then, looking around at the flat dirty concrete, 'I mean being so high up.'

'We're closer to the stars,' he said, and took her hand. 'Come on over here.' His hand was warm and strong, and Bonnie held on to it tightly. He was right, the stars were beautiful. It was cool to be able to see them more clearly, here above the trees.

He led her over to the corner of the roof, where a ratty old army blanket was spread out with a pizza box and some cans of soda. 'All the comforts of home,' he said. Then, quietly, 'I know this isn't a very fancy date, Bonnie, but I wanted to share this with you. I thought you would appreciate what's special about being up here.'

'I absolutely do,' she said, flattered. A secret little cheer went up inside her: *Hurray! Zander definitely knows we're on a date!*

Pretty soon she found herself tucked up against his side, his arm around her shoulders, eating hot, greasily delicious pizza and looking at the stars.

'I come up here alone a lot,' he told her. 'One time last year I just lay here and watched a big fat full moon get swallowed up by the earth's shadow in an eclipse. It was nearly pitch black without the light of the full moon, but I could still see its dark red shape in the sky.'

'The Vikings thought eclipses were caused by two wolves, one who wanted to eat the sun, and one who wanted to eat the moon,' she said idly. 'I forget which one wanted to eat the moon, but whenever either a solar or a lunar eclipse happened, people were supposed to make a lot of noise to scare the wolf away.'

Zander looked down at her. 'That's a random piece of information to know.' But he smiled as he said it.

Bonnie wriggled with delight under the sheer force of his smile. 'I'm interested in mythology,' she said. 'Druid and Celtic, mostly, but myths and stories in general. The Druids were into the moon, too: they had a whole astrology based on the lunar calendar.' She sat up straighter, enjoying the admiring look on Zander's face. 'Like, right now, from late August to late September, we're in the month of the Artist Moon. But in a couple of weeks, we'll be in the month of the Dying Moon.'

'What does that mean?' he asked. He was very close to her, gazing straight into her eyes.

'Well, it means it's a time of endings,' she said. 'It's all about dying and sleep. The Druid year begins again after Halloween.'

'Hmm.' Zander was still watching her intently. 'How do you know so much, Bonnie McCullough?' A little smile played around his mouth.

'Um, my ancestors were Druids and Celtics,' she said, feeling stupid. 'My grandmother told me we were descended from Druid priestesses, and that's why I see things sometimes. My grandmother does, too.'

'Interesting,' he said softly. His tone grew lighter. 'So you see things, do you?'

'I really do,' she said, seriously, staring back at him. She hadn't meant to tell him that. She didn't want to weird him out, not on their first date, but she also didn't want to lie to him.

So blue. Zander's eyes were as deep as the sea, and she was falling further and further into them. There was nothing above her, nothing below, she was ceaselessly, gently falling.

With a wrench, Bonnie pulled her eyes away from Zander's. 'Sorry,' she said, shaking her head. 'That was weird. I think I almost fell asleep for a minute.'

'Don't worry about it,' he said, but his face looked stiff and strange. Then he flashed that warm, enchanting smile again and got to his feet. 'Come on, I want to show you something.'

Bonnie stood slowly. She felt a little strange still, and she pressed her hand briefly against her forehead.

'Over here,' he said, tugging her by the other hand. He led her to the corner of the roof and stepped up onto the narrow ledge running around it.

'*Zander*,' Bonnie said, horrified. 'Come down! You might fall!'

'We won't fall,' he said, smiling down at her. 'Climb on up.'

'Are you *crazy*?' she said. She'd never liked heights much. She remembered crossing a very high bridge once with Damon and Elena. They'd had to cross it to save Stefan, but she would never have been able to do it if Damon hadn't used his Power and convinced her she was an acrobat, a tightrope walker to whom heights were nothing. When he'd released her from his Power, after they crossed the bridge, her retroactive fear had been nauseating.

Still, she'd made it across that bridge, hadn't she? And she had promised herself she would be more confident, stronger, now that she was in college. She looked up at Zander, who was smiling at her, sweetly, eagerly, his hand extended. She took it and let him help her climb onto the ledge.

'Oh,' she said, once she was up there. The ground swam dizzyingly far below her, and she yanked her eyes away from it. '*Oh*. No, this is not a good idea.'

'Trust me,' he said, and took her other hand so that he was holding on to her securely. 'I won't let you fall.'

Bonnie looked into his blue, blue eyes again and felt comforted. There was something so candid and straightforward in his gaze. 'What should I do?' she asked, and was proud when her voice was steady.

'Close your eyes,' he said, and when she'd done that, 'and pick your right foot up off the ledge.'

'*What?*' she asked, and almost opened her eyes again.

'Trust me,' Zander said again, and this time there was a rich undercurrent of laughter in his voice. Hesitantly, Bonnie lifted her foot.

Just then, the wind picked up, and she felt like it was about to scoop her off the ledge and throw her into the sky like a kite whose string had snapped. She tightened her grip on Zander's hands.

'It's all right,' he said soothingly. 'It's amazing, Bonnie, I promise. Just let yourself be. Life isn't worth living if you don't take risks.'

Inhaling deeply and then letting the breath out, she forced herself to relax. The wind was blowing her curls everywhere, whistling in her ears, tugging at her clothes and her raised leg. As she relaxed into it, she felt almost as if she was being lifted, gently, into the sky, the air all around supporting her. It was like flying.

Bonnie realised she was laughing with sheer delight and opened her eyes, gazing straight into Zander's. He was laughing, too, and holding on to her tightly, anchoring her to the earth as she almost flew. She had never been so conscious of the blood thrumming through her veins, of each nerve catching the sensations of the air around her.

She had never felt so alive.

CHAPTER
10

The pub where Elena and Damon ended up was lively and full of people, but of course he made sure they didn't have to wait for a table. He lounged across one side of the booth, looking as arrogant and relaxed as a big gorgeous cat, and listened peaceably as Elena talked. She found herself gaily chatting away, filling him in on all the minutiae of her campus life so far, from finding out that Professor Campbell knew her parents to the personalities of the other students she'd met in her classes.

'The elevator was really crowded, and slow, and my lab partner's back was against the buttons. Somehow she accidentally pushed the alarm button, and the alarm started going off.' Elena took a sip of her soda. 'Suddenly, a voice came out of nowhere and asked, "Do you have an emergency?" And she said, "No, it was an accident," and the voice said, "What? I can't hear you." It went on like that, back and forth, until she started shouting "Accident! Accident!"'

Damon stopped tracing patterns in the condensation on his glass with one finger and glanced up at her through his lashes, his lips twitching into a smile.

'When the doors opened on the ground floor, there were four security men standing there with a medical kit,' Elena finished. 'We didn't know what to do, so we just walked past them. When we got out of the building, we started to run. It was so embarrassing, but we couldn't stop laughing.'

Damon let his slight smile expand into a grin – not his usual cool twist of the lips or his brief, brilliant and enigmatic there-then-gone smile, but an honest-to-God cheek-puffing, eye-squinching grin. 'I like you like this,' he said suddenly.

'Like what?' Elena asked.

'Relaxed, I suppose. Ever since we met, you've been in the middle of some crisis or another.' He raised his hand and brushed a curl away from her face, gently touching her cheek.

She was vaguely aware of the waiter standing by the booth, waiting for them to look up, as she answered with just a touch of flirtation, 'Oh, and I suppose you had nothing to do with that?'

'I wouldn't say I am the one who's most to blame,

no,' Damon said coolly, his grin fading. He looked up, his eyes sharp and knowing. 'Hello, Stefan.'

Elena froze in surprise. Not the waiter, then. Stefan. One look at him, and she winced, her stomach dropping. His face could have been carved from stone. He was looking at Damon's hand, still stretched across the table towards Elena.

'Hey,' she said tentatively. 'How was your study group?'

Stefan stared at her. 'Elena, I've been looking everywhere for you. Why didn't you answer your phone?'

Pulling out her phone, she saw that there were several messages and texts from Stefan. 'Oh, no, I'm so sorry,' she said. 'I didn't hear it ring.'

'We were supposed to meet,' he said stiffly. 'I came to your room and you were just *gone*. Elena, people have been disappearing all over campus.'

He had been scared, afraid that something terrible had happened to her. His eyes were still anxious. She started to reach out to comfort him. The fact that she'd lost the Power she'd had so briefly was hard for Stefan to accept, she knew. He thought her mortality made her fragile, and he was afraid he'd lose her. She should have thought it through, should have left him more of a message than a quick text saying she would return soon.

Before she could touch him, Stefan's gaze turned to

Damon. 'What's going on?' he asked his brother, his voice full of frustration. 'Is this why you followed us to college? To zero in on Elena?'

The look of hurt that crossed Damon's face was only a subtle shadow and was gone so quickly that Elena wasn't entirely sure she had actually seen it. His features settled into an expression of lazy disdain, and she tensed. The peace between the brothers was so fragile – she knew that – and yet she had let Damon flirt with her. She'd been so *stupid*.

'Someone should be keeping her safe, Stefan,' Damon drawled. 'You're too busy playing human again, aren't you? *Study groups.*' He lifted an eyebrow scornfully. 'I'm surprised you've even noticed that there's something going on around this campus. Would you rather have Elena alone and in danger than have her spending time with me?'

Tense lines were forming around Stefan's mouth. 'You're saying you don't have an ulterior motive here?' he asked.

Damon waved a hand disparagingly. 'You know what I feel for Elena. Elena knows what I feel for Elena. Even that sports-loving Mutt of yours knows how things are between us. But the problem isn't me, little brother – it's you and your jealousy. Your wanting to be an "ordinary human" –' Damon made quote marks with his fingers – 'and still carry on with Elena, who is hardly ordinary. You want to have your cake and eat it,

97

too. *I* haven't done anything wrong. Elena wouldn't have come with me if she didn't want to.'

Elena winced again. Was *this* the way it was always going to be? Was any minor misstep on her part going to set Damon and Stefan at each other's throats? 'Stefan . . . Damon,' she implored, but they ignored her.

They were glaring at each other. Stefan stepped closer, flexing his fists, and Damon clenched his jaw, silently daring Stefan to make a move. For the first time, Elena saw a resemblance between them.

'I can't do this,' she said. Her voice sounded small and soft to her own ears, but both Salvatore brothers heard her and whipped their heads towards her with inhuman speed.

'I can't do this,' she said again, louder and more firmly this time. 'I can't be Katherine.'

Damon scowled. '*Katherine?* Believe me, darling, nobody here wants you to be Katherine.'

Stefan, his face softening, said, 'Elena, sweetheart—'

She interrupted him. 'Listen to me.' She wiped her eyes. 'I've been walking on eggshells, trying to keep this – this *thing* between the three of us from tearing us apart. If anything good has come out of all the stuff that's happened, it's that you found each other, you started being brothers again. I can't—' She took a deep breath and tried to find a sensible matter-of-fact voice somewhere inside herself.

'I think we should take a break,' she said flatly. 'Stefan, I love you so much. You're my soulmate, you're *it* for me. You know that.' She looked up at him pleadingly, silently begging him to understand.

Then her eyes moved past him to Damon, who was staring at her with a furrowed brow. 'And Damon, you're part of me now. I . . . feel for you.' She looked back and forth between them, her hands clutching each other. 'I can't lose either of you. But I need to figure out who I am now, after everything that's happened, and I need to do it without worrying about destroying the relationship between you. And you need to figure out how you can be friends with each other, even if I'm in both your lives.'

Damon let out a skeptical noise, but Elena kept talking. 'I'll understand,' she gulped, 'if you can't wait for me. But I will always, always love you. Both of you. In different ways. But for now, I just can't be with you. *Either* of you.'

She was tearing up again, and her hands shook as she wiped her eyes.

Damon leaned across the table, a small twisted smile hovering on his lips. 'Elena, did you just break up with *both* of us?'

The tears dried up instantly. 'Damon, I *never* dated you,' she said angrily.

'I know,' he replied, and shrugged. 'But I've definitely just been dumped.' He glanced at Stefan, then quickly away, his expression closed off.

Stefan looked devastated. For a moment, his face was so bleak that it wasn't hard to believe he was more than five hundred years old. 'Whatever you want, Elena,' he said. He started to reach for her, then pulled his hand back to his side. 'No matter what, I will always love you. My feelings aren't going to change. Take whatever time you need.'

'OK,' she said. She stood up shakily. She felt as though she was going to be sick. Half of her wanted to pull Stefan to her, kiss him until that broken expression on his face went away. But Damon was watching her, his own face inscrutable, and touching either of them felt . . . wrong. 'I need to be by myself for a while,' she told them.

At any other time, she knew, both of them would have objected to the idea of her walking the campus alone. They would have argued, followed her if she wouldn't walk with them – anything to keep her safely under their protection.

Now, though, Stefan moved aside to let her out of the booth, his head bowed. Damon sat very still and watched her go, his eyes hooded.

Elena didn't look back at them as she crossed to the door of the pub. Her hands were shaking and her eyes were brimming with tears once more. But she also felt as if she'd carried something very heavy for a while and had finally been able to put it down.

This might be the best choice I've made in a long, long time, she thought.

Dear Diary,

Every time I remember the look on Stefan's face when I told him I needed space, my chest aches. It's like I can't breathe.

I never wanted to hurt Stefan. Never. How could I? We're so close, so wrapped up in each other that he's like a piece of my soul – without him, I'm not complete.

But . . .

I love Damon, too. He's my friend – my dark mirror image – the clever, plotting one who will do whatever it takes to get what he wants, but who has a kindness deep inside him that not everybody sees. I can't imagine living without Damon, either.

Stefan wants to hold on to me so tightly. He cares for his brother – he does – and Damon cares for him, too, and having me between them is messing that up.

All three of us have been held so closely together by the crises we've had to deal with recently – my death and rebirth, Klaus's attack, Damon's return from the edge of death, the phantom's attack – that every move we've made, every thought we've had, has been wrapped up with the other two. We can't go on like this.

I know I've done the right thing. Without me between them, they can become brothers again. And then I can sort out the tangled threads of my relationships with both of them without having to worry that any move I make will snap the tenuous bond between us.

It's the right decision. But still, I feel like I'm dying a slow death. How can I live for even a little while without Stefan?

All I can do is try to be strong. If I just keep going, I'll get through this time. And in the end, everything will be wonderful. It has to be.

CHAPTER

11

'Coffee, my dear?' Professor Campbell – *James*, Elena reminded herself – asked. At her nod, he bounced to his feet and bustled over to the tiny coffeemaker perched on top of a teetering stack of papers. He brought her a cup of coffee, creamed and sugared, and settled down happily in his chair, gazing across his crowded desk at her with an expression of innocent enjoyment. 'I think I have some cookies,' he offered. 'Not homemade, but they're reasonably tasty. No?'

Elena shook her head politely and sipped her coffee. 'It's very good,' she said, and smiled at him.

It had been a few days since she had told Stefan and Damon she needed to take a break from them. After a much-needed sob session with Bonnie and Meredith, she had done her best to be normal – going to class, having lunch with her friends, keeping up a brave mask. Part of this attempt at normality was coming to James's office hours, so that she could hear more about her parents. Even though they couldn't be there to comfort her, talking about them offered some solace.

'My God!' James cried out. 'You have Elizabeth's face, and then, when you smile, Thomas's dimple comes right out. Just the same as his – on only one side. It gave him a certain raffish charm.'

Elena wondered if she should thank James. He was complimenting her, in a way, but the compliments were really directed towards her parents, and it felt a little presumptuous to be grateful for them.

She settled for saying, 'I'm glad you think I look like my parents. I remember thinking when I was little that they were very elegant.' She shrugged. 'I guess all little kids think their parents are beautiful.'

'Well, your mother certainly was,' James said. 'But it's not just your looks. Your voice sounds like hers, and the comments you made in class this week reminded me of things your father would have said. He was very observant.' He delved into his desk drawers and, after a bit of rummaging, pulled out a tin of butter cookies. 'Sure you won't have one? Ah, well.' He chose one for himself and took a bite. 'Yes, as I was saying, Elizabeth was extremely lovely. I wouldn't have called Thomas lovely, but he had charm. Maybe that's how he managed to win Elizabeth's heart in the end.'

'Oh.' Elena stirred her coffee absently. 'She dated other guys, then?' It was ridiculous, but she had kind of imagined her parents as always being together.

James chuckled. 'She was quite the heartbreaker. I imagine you are, too, dear.'

Elena thought unhappily of Stefan's soft, dismayed green eyes. She had never wanted to hurt him. And Matt, who she had dated in high school and who had quietly gone on loving her. He hadn't fallen in love or even been really interested in anyone else since then. *Heartbreaker, yeah.*

James was watching her with bright, inquisitive eyes. 'Not a *happy* heartbreaker, then?' he said softly. Elena glanced at him in surprise, and he set his coffee cup down with a little *clink*. He straightened up. 'Elizabeth Morrow,' he said in a brisk businesslike voice, 'was a freshman when I met her. She was always making things, particularly amazing sets and costumes she designed for the theatre department. Your father and I were both sophomores at the time – we were in the same fraternity, and close friends – and he couldn't stop talking about this amazing girl. Once I got to know her, I was sucked into her orbit, too.'

He smiled. 'Thomas and I each had something special about us: I was academically gifted, and Thomas could talk anyone into anything. But we were both cultural barbarians. Elizabeth taught us about art, about theatre, about the world beyond the small

Southern towns where we'd grown up.' James ate another cookie, absentmindedly licking sugar off his fingers, then sighed deeply. 'I thought we'd be friends forever,' he said. 'But we went in different directions in the end.'

'Why?' Elena asked. 'Did something happen?'

His bright eyes shifted away from hers. 'Of course not,' he said dismissively. 'Just life, I suppose. But whenever I walk down the third-floor corridor, I can't help stopping to look at the photograph of us.' He gave a self-conscious laugh, patting his stomach. 'Mostly vanity, I suppose. I recognise my young self more easily than I do the fat old man I see in the mirror now.'

'What are you talking about?' Elena asked, confused. 'The third-floor corridor?'

James's mouth made a round O of surprise. 'Of course, you don't know all the college traditions yet. The long corridor on the third floor of this building has pictures from all the different periods of Dalcrest's history. Including a nice photo of your parents and yours truly.'

'I'll have to check it out,' Elena said, feeling a little excited. She hadn't seen many pictures of her parents from before they were married.

There was a tap on the door, and a small girl with glasses peeked in. 'Oh, I'm sorry,' she said, and started to withdraw.

'No, no, my dear,' James said jovially, getting to his

feet. 'Elena and I were just chatting about old friends. You and I need to have a serious talk about your senior thesis as soon as possible. Come in, come in.' He gave Elena an absurd little half bow. 'Elena, we'll have to continue this conversation later.'

'Of course,' she said, and rose, shaking James's offered hand.

'Speaking of old friends,' he said casually as she turned to go, 'I met a friend of yours, Dr Celia Connor, just before the semester started. She mentioned that you were coming here.'

Elena whipped back around, staring at him. He had met *Celia*? Images filled her mind: Celia held in Stefan's arms as he travelled faster than any human, desperate to save her life; Celia fending off the phantom in a room full of flames. How much did James know? What had Celia told him?

James smiled blandly back at her. 'But we'll talk later,' he said. After a moment, Elena nodded and stumbled out of his office, her mind racing. The girl who was waiting held the door open for her.

In the hall outside, Elena leaned against the wall and took stock for a moment. Would Celia have told James about Stefan and Damon being vampires, or anything about Elena herself? Probably not. Celia had become a friend by the end of their battle with the phantom. She would have kept their secrets. Plus, Celia was a very savvy academic. She wouldn't have told her colleagues anything that might make them think she was crazy, including that she had met actual vampires.

Elena shook off the unease she felt from the end of her conversation with James and thought instead of the picture he'd told her about. She climbed the stairs to the third floor to see if she could find it now.

It turned out that the 'third-floor corridor' was no problem to find. While the second floor was a maze of turning passageways and faculty offices subdivided from one another, when she stepped out of the stairwell on the third floor she discovered it was a long hall that ran from one end of the building to the other.

In contrast to the chatter of people at work on the second floor, the third floor seemed abandoned, silent and dim. Closed doors stood at regular intervals along the hall. Elena peered through the glass on one door, only to see an empty room.

All down the hall, between the doors, hung large photographs. Near the stairwell, where she began looking, they seemed as though they were from the turn of the century: young men in side-combed hair and suits, smiling stiffly; girls in high-necked white blouses and long skirts with their hair pulled up on top of their heads. In one, a row of girls carried garlands of flowers for some forgotten campus occasion.

There were photos of boat races and picnics, couples dressed up for dances, team pictures. In one photo, the cast of some student play – maybe from the 1920s or

30s, the girls with shingled flapper cuts, the guys with funny covers over their shoes – laughed hilariously on stage, their mouths frozen open, their hands in the air. A little further on, a group of young men in army uniforms gazed back at her seriously, jaws firmly set, eyes determined.

As she moved on down the hall, the photos changed from black-and-white to colour; the clothes became less formal; the hairstyles grew longer, then shorter; messier, then sleeker. Even though most of the people in the photographs looked happy, something about them made Elena feel sad. Maybe it was how fast time seemed to pass in them: all these people had been Elena's age, students like her, with their own fears and joys and heartbreaks, and now they were gone, grown old or even dead.

She thought briefly of a bottle tucked deep in her closet at home, containing the water of eternal life she'd accidentally stolen from the Guardians. Was that the answer? She pushed the thought away. It wasn't the answer *yet* – she knew that – and she'd made the very clear choice not to think about that bottle, not to decide anything, not now. She had time, she had more life to live naturally before she'd want to ask herself that question.

The picture James had talked about was close to the far end of the hall. In it, her father, her mother and James were sitting on the grass under a tree in the quad. Her parents were leaning forward in eager conversation, and James – a much thinner version, his face almost unrecognisable beneath a straggly beard – was sitting back and watching them, his expression sharp and amused.

Her mother looked amazingly young, her face soft, her eyes wide, her smile big and bright, but she was also somehow exactly the mother Elena remembered. Elena's heart gave a painful but happy throb at the sight of her. Her father was gawkier than the distinguished dad Elena had known – and his pastel-patterned shirt was a fashion disaster of epic proportions – but there was an essential *dadness* to him that made her smile.

She noticed the pin on his horrific pastel shirt first. She thought it was a smudge, but then, leaning forward, she made out the shape of a small, dark blue V. Looking at the other figures, she realised her mother and James were wearing the same pins, her mother's half-obscured by a long golden curl falling across it.

Weird. She tapped her finger slowly against the glass of the photograph, touching one V and then the others. She would ask James about the pins. Hadn't he mentioned that he and her dad had been in a fraternity? Maybe it had something to do with that. Didn't frat boys 'pin' their girlfriends?

Something nudged at the edges of her mind. She'd seen one of these pins somewhere. But she couldn't remember where, so she shrugged it off. Whatever it stood for, it was something she didn't know about her parents, another facet of their lives to be discovered here.

She couldn't wait to learn more.

CHAPTER
12

'**G**ood practice,' Christopher said, stopping next to Matt as he headed out of the locker room. 'You've got some great moves, man.'

'Thanks,' Matt said, glancing up from putting on his shoes. 'You were looking pretty good out there yourself.' He could tell Christopher was going to be a solid teammate, the kind of guy who did his job and focused on the big picture, working to help the rest of the team. He was a great roommate, too, generous and laid-back. He didn't even snore.

'Want to skip the dining hall and order a pizza?' Christopher asked. 'This is my night to beat you at *Guitar Hero* – I can feel it.'

Matt laughed. In the couple of weeks they'd been living together, he and Christopher had been working their way through all the Wii games Christopher had brought with him to college. 'All right, I'll see you back at the room.'

Christopher slapped him on the back, grinning widely. After he left, Matt took his time getting his things together, letting the other guys get out of the locker room ahead of him. He felt like walking back to the dorm alone tonight. They were a nice bunch of guys, but he was sore and tired. Between football practices and Vitale Society pledge activities, he'd never worked his body quite so hard. It felt good.

He felt good. Even the stupidest of the Vitale activities – and some of them were pretty stupid: they'd had to work in teams to build houses out of newspaper the other night – were kind of fun, because he was getting to know some amazing people. Ethan had been right. As a group, the pledges were smart, determined, talented, everything you'd expect. And *he* was one of them.

His classes were interesting, too. Back in high school he'd got OK grades but had mostly just done what he had to do to pass. The Civil War, geometry, chemistry, *To Kill a Mockingbird*: all his schoolwork had sort of blended into the background of his real life of friends and sports.

Some of what he was doing at Dalcrest was like that, too, but in most of his classes, he was starting to see connections between things. He was getting the idea that history, language, science and literature were all parts of the same thing – the way people thought and the stories they told – and it was really pretty interesting.

It was possible, Matt thought, with a self-mocking grin, that he was 'blossoming' in college, just like his high school guidance counsellor had predicted.

It wasn't fully dark yet, but it was getting late. He sped up, thinking about pizza.

There weren't a lot of people roaming the campus. He guessed they were either in the cafeteria or holed up in their rooms, afraid. He wasn't worried, though. He figured there were a lot more vulnerable targets than a football player.

A breeze started up, waving the branches of the trees in the quad and wafting the smell of grass towards Matt. It still felt like summer. In the bushes, a few early-evening fireflies blinked on and off. He rolled his shoulders, enjoying the stretch after a long practice.

Up ahead, someone screamed. A guy, Matt thought. The cry cut off suddenly.

Before he could even think, he was running towards the sound. His heart was pounding, and he tried to force his tired legs to move faster. That was a sound of pure panic, Matt thought. He strained his ears but didn't hear anything except his own ragged breaths.

As he came around the business building, a dark figure that had been bent over something in the grass took off, its long skinny legs flying. It was moving *fast*, and its face was completely concealed by a hoodie. Matt couldn't even see if it was a guy or a girl.

He angled his own stride to race after the figure in black but came to a sudden halt by the shape in the grass.

Not just a shape. For a moment, Matt's mind refused to process what he was seeing. The red and gold of a football jersey. Wet, thick liquid spreading across it. A familiar face.

Then everything snapped into focus. He dropped to his knees. 'Christopher, oh no, Christopher.'

There was blood everywhere. Matt frantically felt at Christopher's chest, trying to figure out where he could put pressure to try to stop the bleeding. *Everywhere, everywhere, it's coming from everywhere*. Christopher's whole body was shaking, and Matt pressed his hands against the soaking football jersey to try to hold him still. Fresh blood ran in thick crimson streams against the brighter red of the jersey's material.

'Christopher, man, hold on, it's going to be OK. You'll be OK,' Matt said, and pulled out his phone to dial 911. His hands were covered with blood now, and the phone was a slimy mess as he held it to his ear.

'Please,' he said, his voice shaking, 'I'm at Dalcrest College, near the business building. My roommate, someone attacked my roommate. He's bleeding a lot. He's not conscious.' The 911 operator started to ask him some questions and Matt tried to focus.

Suddenly Christopher opened his eyes, taking a deep gulp of air.

'Christopher,' Matt said, dropping his phone. 'Chris, they're sending an ambulance, hold on.'

The shaking got worse, his arms and legs vibrating in a rapid rhythm. His eyes settled on Matt's face, and his mouth opened.

'Chris,' Matt said, trying to hold him down, trying to be gentle, 'who did this? Who attacked you?'

Christopher gasped again, a hoarse gulping sound. Then the shaking stopped, and he was very still. His eyelids slid down over his eyes.

'Chris, please hold on,' Matt begged. 'They're coming. They'll help you.' He grabbed at Christopher, shook him a little, but he wasn't moving, wasn't breathing.

Sirens sounded in the distance, but Matt knew the ambulance was already too late.

CHAPTER

13

Bonnie clutched the banana-nut muffin to her chest as if it was some kind of sacred offering. She just couldn't bring herself to knock on Matt's door. Instead, she turned big pleading brown eyes on Meredith and Elena.

'Oh, *Bonnie*,' Meredith muttered, reaching past her, shifting the pile of bagels and the carton of orange juice she was carrying, and rapping loudly on the door.

'*I don't know what to say*,' Bonnie whispered back, agonised.

Then the door opened and Matt appeared, red-eyed and pale. He seemed somehow smaller and more hunched into himself than Bonnie had ever seen him. Overwhelmed with pity, she forgot all about being nervous and launched herself into his arms, dropping the muffin in the process.

'I'm so sorry,' she choked out, tears running down her face. Matt held on to her tightly, bending over and burying his head in her shoulder. 'It's OK,' she said finally, desperately, patting the back of his head. 'I mean, no, it's not . . . of course it's not . . . but we love you, we're here.'

'I couldn't help him,' Matt said dully, his face still pressed against Bonnie's neck. 'I tried my best, but he died anyway.'

Elena and Meredith joined them, wrapping their arms around Matt from either side.

'We know,' Elena said, rubbing his back. 'You did everything you could for him.'

Matt pulled out of their arms eventually and gestured around the room. 'All this stuff is his,' he said. 'His parents don't feel like they're ready to clear out his things yet, they told the police. It's killing me to see it all still here when he's not. I thought about packing it up for his parents, but there's a possibility that the police might want to look through his stuff.'

Bonnie shuddered at the thought of what Christopher's parents must be going through.

'Have something to eat,' Meredith said. 'I bet you haven't eaten for ages. Maybe it'll help you feel better.'

All three girls fussed around, fixing the breakfast they'd brought for Matt, then convincing him to taste something, anything. He drank some juice and picked at a bagel, his head lowered. 'I was at the police station all night,' he said. 'I had to keep going over and over what happened.'

'What *did* happen?' Bonnie asked tentatively.

Matt sighed. 'I really wish I knew. I just saw somebody dressed in black running away from Christopher. I wanted to chase him, but Chris needed my help. And then he died. I tried, but I couldn't do anything.' His forehead creased into a frown. 'The really weird thing, though,' he said slowly, 'is that, even though I saw a *person* running away, the police think Christopher was attacked by some kind of animal. He was . . . pretty ripped up.'

Elena and Meredith exchanged an alert glance. 'A vampire?' said Meredith. 'Or a werewolf, maybe?'

'I was wondering about that,' Matt admitted. 'It makes sense.' Without seeming to notice, he finished his bagel, and Elena took advantage of his distraction to slip some fruit onto his plate.

Bonnie wrapped her arms around herself. '*Why?*' she asked. 'Why is it that, wherever we go, weird, scary things happen around us? I thought that once we left Fell's Church things would be different.'

No one argued with her. For a little while, they all sat quietly, and Bonnie felt as if they were huddling together, trying to protect themselves from something cold and horrible.

Finally, Meredith reached out and took an orange slice off Matt's plate. 'The first thing we need to do, then, is to investigate and try to figure out if these attacks and disappearances are supernatural.' She chewed thoughtfully. 'As much as I hate to say it, we should probably get Damon on this. He's good at this kind of thing. And Stefan should know what's going on, too.' She looked at Elena, her voice gentle. 'I'll talk to them, OK, Elena?'

Elena shrugged. Bonnie could tell she was trying to keep her expression blank, but her lips were trembling. 'Of course,' she said after a minute. 'I'm sure they're both checking things out anyway. You know how paranoid they are.'

'Not without reason,' Meredith said dryly.

Matt's eyes were wet. 'Whatever happens, I need you to promise me something,' he said. 'Please, be careful. I can't – let's not lose anyone else, OK?'

Bonnie snuggled closer to him, putting her hand on his. Meredith reached over and placed her hand over both of theirs, and Elena added hers to the pile. 'We'll take care of one another,' Elena said.

'A vow,' said Bonnie, trying to smile. 'We'll always watch out for one another. We'll make sure everyone is safe.'

At that moment, as they murmured in agreement, she was sure they could do it.

* * *

Meredith pivoted and stepped forward, swinging her staff down to strike at Samantha's heavily padded knees. Samantha dodged the blow, then jabbed her own staff straight towards Meredith's head. Meredith blocked the blow, then thrust her staff at Samantha's chest.

Samantha staggered backwards and lost her footing.

'Wow,' she said, rubbing her collarbone and looking at Meredith with a mixture of resentment and appreciation. 'That *hurt*, even with the padding. I've never trained with anyone so strong before.'

'Oh, well,' Meredith said modestly, feeling absurdly pleased, 'I practise a lot.'

'Uh-huh,' Samantha said, eyeing her. 'Let's take a break.' She flopped down on the mat, and Meredith, her staff balanced lightly in one hand, sat beside her.

It wasn't *her* staff, of course, not her special hunting one. She couldn't bring her heirloom slayer staff to the gym – it was too clearly a customised deadly weapon. But she'd been delighted to learn that Samantha could fight with a four-foot-long *jo* staff and that she had an extra.

Samantha was quick and smart and fierce, one of the best sparring partners she'd ever had. Fighting, Meredith was able to block out the helpless feeling she'd had in Matt's room this morning. There was something so pathetic about seeing all Christopher's things sitting there ready for him, when he was never coming back. He had one of those weird little fake Zen gardens on his desk, the sand neatly groomed. Maybe only the day before, Christopher had picked up the tiny rake in his hand and smoothed the sand, and now he'd never touch anything again.

And it was her fault. Meredith squeezed her staff, her knuckles whitening. She had to accept that. If she had the power of being a potent force against darkness, a hunter and slayer of monsters, she had the responsibility, too. Anything that got through and killed someone in her territory was Meredith's failure and her shame.

She had to work harder. Practise more, go out patrolling the campus, keep people safe.

'Are you all right?' Samantha's voice broke through her thoughts. Startled, she saw Samantha staring at her with wide and solemn dark eyes, taking in her gritted teeth and clenched fists.

'Not entirely,' Meredith said dryly. 'Um.' She felt she had to explain her grimness. 'Did you hear about what happened last night, the guy who was killed?' Samantha nodded slowly, her expression unreadable. 'Well, he was the roommate of a really good friend of mine. And I was with my friend today, trying to help him. It was . . . upsetting.'

Samantha's face seemed to harden, and she scrambled up on her knees. 'Listen, Meredith,' she said, 'I promise you this isn't going to happen again. Not on my watch.'

'On your watch?' Meredith asked mildly. Suddenly, it felt hard to breathe.

'I have responsibilities,' Samantha said. She dropped her eyes to her hands. 'I'm going to catch this killer.'

'It's a big job,' Meredith said. It wasn't possible, was it? But Samantha was such a good fighter, and what she was saying . . . why would she think she was responsible for stopping the killer? 'What makes you think you can do it?' she asked.

'I know this is difficult to believe, and I shouldn't even be telling you, but I need your help.' Samantha was looking straight into her eyes, practically vibrating with earnestness. 'I'm a hunter. I was raised to . . . I have a sacred trust. All my family for generations, we've fought against evil. I'm the last of us. My parents were killed when I was thirteen.'

Meredith gasped, shocked, but Samantha shook her head fiercely, pushing Meredith's sympathy away. 'They hadn't finished training me,' she continued, 'and I need you to help me get better, get faster. I'm not strong enough yet.'

Meredith stared at her.

'Please, Meredith,' she said. 'I know it sounds crazy, but it's true. People are depending on me.'

Unable to stop herself, Meredith started to laugh.

'It's not a joke,' Samantha said, jumping to her feet, her fists clenched. 'This is . . . I shouldn't have said anything.' She stalked to the door, her back as straight as a soldier's.

'Samantha, wait,' Meredith called. She whirled round towards her with a face full of fury. Meredith took a quick breath and tried desperately to remember something she'd learned as a child but never had occasion to use. Crooking her pinkies together, she drew up her thumbs to make a triangle, the secret sign of greeting between two hunters.

Samantha just stared, her face perfectly blank. Meredith wondered if she'd remembered the sign correctly. Had Samantha's family even taught it to her? Meredith knew there were other families out there, but she had never met any of them before. Her parents had left the hunter community before she was born.

Then Samantha, moving as quickly as she ever had when they'd sparred, was in front of her, gripping her arms.

'For real?' she said. 'Are you serious?'

Meredith nodded, and Samantha threw her arms around her and clutched her tightly. Her heart was beating so hard that Meredith could feel it. Meredith stiffened at first – she wasn't the touchy-feely type, despite being best friends with wildly affectionate Bonnie for years – but then relaxed into the hug, feeling Samantha's slim, muscular body under her arms, so like her own.

She had the strangest feeling of familiarity, as if she

had been lost and had now found her true family at last. Meredith knew she could never say any of that, and part of her felt like she was betraying Elena and Bonnie just by thinking that way, but she couldn't help it. Samantha pulled away, smiling and weepy, wiping at her eyes and nose.

'I'm acting stupid,' she said. 'But this is the best thing that has ever happened to me. Together, we can fight this.' She gave a half-hysterical sniff and gazed at Meredith with huge shining eyes. 'I feel like I've made a new best friend,' she said.

'Yes,' Meredith said – not weeping, not laughing, cool as ever on the outside but, inside, feeling as though she was breaking into happy pieces – 'yes, I think you're right.'

CHAPTER 14

Matt hunched his shoulders miserably. He had come to the pledge meeting because he didn't want to stay in his room alone, but now he wished he hadn't. He'd been avoiding Elena, Meredith and Bonnie – it wasn't their fault, but so much violence had happened around all four of them in the past year, so much death. He'd thought it might be better being around other people – people who hadn't seen how much darkness there was in the world – but it wasn't.

He felt almost as if he was swathed in bubble wrap, thick and cloudy. As the other pledges moved and talked, he could watch them and hear them, but he felt separated from them; everything seemed muffled and dim. He felt fragile, too, as if removing the protective layer might make him fall apart.

As he stood in the crowd of pledges, Chloe came over and stood next to him, touching his arm reassuringly with her small, strong hand. A gap appeared in the bubble wrap, and he could really feel her with him. He put his hand over hers and squeezed it gratefully.

The pledge meeting was in the wood-panelled underground room where they'd first met. Ethan assured them this was just one of many secret hideouts – the others were open only to fully initiated members. Matt had discovered by now that even this pledge room had several entrances: one through an old house just outside campus, which must have been the one they brought them through that first time; one through a shed near the playing fields; and one through the basement of the library. The ground beneath the campus must be honeycombed with tunnels for so many entrances to end up in one place, he thought, and he had an unsettling picture of students walking on the sun-warmed grass while, a few metres below, endless dark tunnels opened underneath them.

Ethan was talking, and Matt knew that usually he would have been hanging on his every word. Today, Ethan's voice washed over him almost unheard, and Matt let his eyes follow the black-clad, masked figures of the Vitale members who paced the room behind Ethan. Dully, he wondered about them, about how the masks disguised them well enough that he was never sure if he recognised any of them around campus. Any of them except Ethan, that is. Matt wondered curiously what made the leader immune to such restrictions. Like the tunnels beneath the campus, the anonymity of the Vitales was slightly unsettling.

Eventually, the meeting ended and the pledges started to trickle out of the room. A few patted Matt on the back or murmured sympathetic words to him, and he warmed as he realised that they cared, that somehow they'd come to feel like friends through all the silly pledge bonding activities.

'Hold up a minute, Matt?' Ethan was next to him suddenly. At Ethan's glance, Chloe squeezed Matt's arm again and let go.

'I'll see you later,' she murmured. Matt watched as she crossed the room and went out of the door, her hair bouncing against the nape of her neck.

When he looked back at Ethan, Ethan's head was cocked to one side, his golden-brown eyes considering.

'It's good to see you and Chloe getting so close,' he declared, and Matt shrugged awkwardly.

'Yeah, well . . .' he said.

'You'll find that the other Vitales are the ones who can understand you best,' Ethan said. 'They'll be the ones who will stand by you all through college, and for the rest of your life.' He smiled. 'At least, that's what's happened to me. I've been watching you, Matt,' he went on.

Matt tensed. Something about Ethan cut through the bubble-wrap feeling, but not in the comforting way Chloe did. Now Matt felt exposed instead of protected. The sharpness of Ethan's gaze, maybe, or the way he always seemed to believe so strongly in whatever he was saying. 'Yeah?' Matt said warily.

Ethan grinned. 'Don't look so paranoid. It's a good thing. Every Vitale pledge is special, that's why they're chosen, but every year there's one who's even *more* special, who's a leader among leaders. I can see that, in this group, it's you, Matt.'

Matt cleared his throat. 'Really?' he said, flattered, not knowing quite what to say. No one had ever called him a leader before.

'I've got big plans for the Vitale Society this year,' Ethan said, his eyes shining. 'We're going to go down in history. We're going to be more powerful than we've ever been. Our futures are *bright*.'

Matt gave a half smile and nodded. When Ethan talked, his voice warm and persuasive, those golden eyes steady on his, Matt could see it, too. The Vitales leading not just the campus but, someday, the world. Matt himself would be transformed from the ordinary guy he knew he had always been into someone confident and clear-eyed, a leader among leaders, like Ethan said. He could picture it all.

'I want you to be my right-hand man here, Matt,' Ethan said. 'You can help me lead these pledges into greatness.'

Matt nodded again and, Ethan's eyes on his, felt a flush of pride, the first good thing he'd felt since Chris's death. He would help lead the Vitales, standing by Ethan's side. Everything would be better. The path was clear ahead.

Indeed, Keynes posited that economic activity was determined by aggregate demand. For the fifteenth time in half an hour, Stefan read the sentence without beginning to comprehend it.

It all just seemed so *pointless*. He'd tried to distract himself by investigating the murder on campus, but it had only made him more anxious that he couldn't be by Elena's side, seeing to it himself that she was safe. He closed the book and dropped his head into his hands.

Without Elena, what was he doing here?

He would have followed her anywhere. She was so beautiful it hurt him to look at her sometimes, the way it hurt to stare into the sun. She shone like that sun with her golden hair and lapis lazuli eyes, her delicate creamy skin that held just the faintest touch of pink.

But there was more to Elena than beauty. Her beauty alone wouldn't have held Stefan's attention for long. In fact, her resemblance to Katherine had nearly driven him away. But under her coolly beautiful exterior was a quicksilver mind that was always working, making plans, and a heart that was fiercely protective of everyone she loved.

Stefan had spent centuries searching for something to make him feel alive again, and he'd never felt as certain of anything as he did about Elena. She was *it*, the only one for him.

Why couldn't she be as sure of him? No matter what Elena said about Stefan being the one, the fact remained: the only two girls he'd loved in his long, long life both loved not just Stefan but his brother, too.

He closed his eyes and rubbed the bridge of his nose between his fingers, then shoved himself away from the desk. Maybe he was hungry. In a few quick strides, he crossed his white-painted room, through the mix of his own elegant possessions and the cheap school-issued furniture, and was out on the balcony. Outside, the night smelled of jasmine and car exhaust. Stefan reached tendrils of Power gently into the night, questing, feeling for . . . something . . . *there*. A tiny mind quickened in response to his.

His hearing, sharper than a human's, picked up the faint whine of sonar, and a small, furry bat landed on the balcony railing, drawn in by his Power. Stefan picked it up, keeping up a gentle thrum of Power between his mind and the bat's, and it gazed at him tamely, its little fox face alert.

He lowered his head and drank, careful not to take too much from the little creature. He grimaced at the taste and then released the bat, which flapped tentatively, a little dazed, then picked up speed and was lost again in the night.

He hadn't been terribly hungry, but the blood cleared his mind. Elena was so *young*. He had to remember that. She was still younger than he'd been when he became a vampire, and she needed time to experience life, for her path to lead her back to him. He could wait. He had all the time in the world.

But he missed her so much.

Gathering his strength, he leaped from the balcony and landed lightly on the ground below. There was a flower bed there, and he reached into it, feeling petals as soft as silk. A daisy, fresh and innocent. He plucked it and went back inside the dorm, using the front entrance this time.

Outside Elena's door, he hesitated. He could hear the slight sounds of her moving around in there, smell her distinctive, intoxicating scent. She was alone, and he was tempted to knock. Maybe she was longing for him, just as he longed for her. If they were alone, would she melt into his arms despite herself?

He shook his head, his mouth tight. He had to respect Elena's wishes. If she needed time apart, he could give her that. Looking at the white daisy, he slowly balanced it on top of Elena's doorknob. She would find the flower and know that it was from him.

Stefan wanted Elena to know that he could wait for her, if that was what she needed, but that he was thinking of her, always.

CHAPTER
15

As she headed for the door of her dorm room, Elena rummaged through her bag, checking off a mental list: *wallet, keys, phone, lip gloss, eyeliner, hairbrush, student ID*. As she swung the door open, something fluttered to the ground.

A perfect white daisy had fallen to the floor. She reached down and picked it up. Turning it in her hand, she felt a sudden sharp ache in her chest. *God, I miss Stefan*. She had no doubt the daisy was from him. It was just like him to let her know he was thinking of her while still respecting her space.

The ache in her chest was slowly replaced with a sweet glowing feeling. It seemed so silly and artificial to avoid talking to Stefan. She *loved* him. And, beyond that, he was one of her best friends. Elena pulled out her phone to call him.

And then she stopped. Taking a deep breath, she put the phone back in her bag.

If she talked to Stefan, she would want to see him. If she saw him, she would want to touch him. If she touched him, it would all be over. She would find herself falling into him, entangled in love. And then she would look up and see Damon's dark unfathomable eyes watching them and feel that pull towards him. And then the brothers would look at each other, and love and pain and fury would pass over their faces, and everything would start up again.

It had felt *good* to walk away from them for a while, even though it was heartbreaking and awful and terribly lonely, too. But, since then, Elena had felt a calm settle over her. She wasn't happy, exactly – it was as though she was covered with bruises, and if she wasn't careful, pain would flood over her as she remembered what she had done. But she also felt as if she had been holding her breath for weeks and now was able to exhale.

She knew that Stefan would be waiting for her when she was ready to face him again. Wasn't that what the daisy meant?

She tucked the flower inside her bag and set off down the hall, her heels clicking firmly. Elena was going to go out with her friends, she was going to have fun, and she wasn't going to think about Stefan, or

Damon. Or even the disappearances, or Christopher's death. She sighed under the weight of it all. For days, they had been mourning, and now Elena and her friends needed to embrace life again. They deserved an evening of freedom. They needed to remember what they were fighting for.

'There she is,' Elena heard Bonnie say as she entered the crowded bar. 'Elena! Over here!'

Bonnie, Meredith and a girl Elena didn't know were sitting at a small table near the dance floor. They had invited Matt to come out with them, but he'd said he had to study, his face politely closed off, and they knew he wasn't ready yet and that he needed some time alone.

Meredith, graceful and relaxed, gave Elena a cool smile in greeting and introduced her friend Samantha. Samantha was lean, bright eyed and alert. She seemed as if she had energy to spare, shifting from side to side, chatting without stopping.

Bonnie, too, was clearly *on* tonight and started talking as soon as Elena reached the table. Bonnie was brave, Elena thought. Christopher's death had shocked her, and she was as worried about Matt as any of them, but she would stick out her chin and smile and gossip and go on with life just as hard as she could, because they had decided that was what tonight would be about.

'I got you a Coke,' Bonnie said. 'They carded me, so

I couldn't get anything else. Guess what?' She paused dramatically. 'I called Zander, and he said he'd definitely try to make it here tonight. I can't wait for you guys to meet him!' Bonnie was practically bouncing out of her seat with excitement, red curls flipping everywhere.

'Who's Zander?' asked Samantha innocently.

Meredith gave Elena a sly glance. 'You know, I'm not sure,' she said with mock confusion. 'Bonnie, tell us about him.'

'Yes,' Elena added, smirking. 'I don't think you've mentioned him at all, have you?'

'Shut up, you guys,' Bonnie said amiably, and, leaning over the table to Samantha, started to extol all Zander's virtues to her fresh audience. Elena let her mind wander. She'd heard it all, night after night in their dorm lately: Zander's eyes, Zander's smile, Zander's bashful charm, Zander's very hot bod (Bonnie's words). How Zander and Bonnie studied together in a tucked-away corner of the library and how Zander brought Bonnie secret snacks even though it was *totally against the library rules*. The way they talked on the phone every night, the long velvety pauses when it seemed like he was on the verge of whispering something intimate, something no one but Bonnie could know, but then instead he would make a joke that made Bonnie laugh like crazy. There was something so *sweet* about Bonnie with a crush.

Elena really hoped this guy was worthy of her.

'He hasn't kissed me yet,' Bonnie added, eyes wide. 'Soon, though. I *hope*.'

'The very first kiss,' Samantha said, and wiggled her eyebrows. 'Maybe tonight?' Bonnie just giggled in response.

That ache was back in Elena's chest, and she pressed her hand against her sternum. During her first kiss with Stefan, the world had fallen away and there had been just the two of them, lips and souls touching. Everything had seemed so clear then.

She took a deep breath and willed away tears. She wasn't going to remember anything tonight; she was just going to have a good time with her friends.

Having Samantha there, Elena soon realised, was going to be a huge help with that. If it had been only Elena, Meredith and Bonnie, they would have ended up discussing Christopher's murder and the disappearances on campus, combing obsessively over the very few things they knew and theorising about everything they didn't. But with Samantha there, they had to keep the conversation light.

Somehow Bonnie got off the topic of wonderful Zander and on to palm reading. 'Look,' she said to Samantha. 'See the line that crosses down your palm, across the other three lines? That's a fate line, not everybody has that.'

'What does it mean?' Samantha said, gazing at her

own palm with great interest.

'Well,' Bonnie said, her brow furrowing, 'it changes direction a lot – see here? and here? – which means that your destiny is going to change because of outside forces influencing you.'

'Hmm,' Samantha said. 'How about love? Will I meet somebody amazing tonight?'

'No,' Bonnie said slowly, and her voice changed, taking on a flat, almost metallic tone. Elena glanced up quickly to see that Bonnie's pupils were dilated, her eyes looking away from Samantha's palm and into the distance. 'Not tonight. But there's someone waiting for you who will change everything. You'll meet him soon.'

'Bonnie,' Meredith said sharply. 'Are you OK?'

Bonnie blinked, and her eyes snapped back into focus. 'Of course,' she said, sounding confused. 'What do you mean?'

Elena and Meredith exchanged a glance – had Bonnie slipped into a vision? Before they could question her, a whole group of guys was suddenly at their table, laughing, shouting, swearing. Elena frowned up at them.

'Hey, gorgeous,' one said, staring down at Elena. 'Wanna dance?'

She started to shake her head, but another of the guys dropped into the seat next to Bonnie and threw his arm around her. 'Hey,' he said. 'Did you miss me?'

'Zander!' Bonnie exclaimed, her cheeks pink with delight.

So this was Zander, Elena thought, and watched him covertly as his three friends settled at the table, too, introducing themselves cheerfully, seeming to make the maximum amount of noise dragging chairs over and jockeying to sit next to the girls. Zander was cute, sure, she had to admit that. Pale blond hair and a gorgeous smile.

She didn't really like the way he was pulling Bonnie close, turning her head towards him, his hands running restlessly over her shoulders even as he talked over her head to his friends. It seemed really possessive for a guy who hadn't even kissed her yet. Elena looked over at Meredith to see if she was thinking the same thing. Meredith was listening, with an amused smile, to the guy next to her – Marcus, she thought his name was – Zander's friend with the shaggy brown hair, explaining his weight-lifting routine.

'Shots,' another friend of Zander's said succinctly, joining them with a tray full of shot glasses. 'Let's play quarters.'

Bonnie giggled. 'They're not allowed to serve us here. We're underage.'

The guy grinned. 'S'alright. I paid for them, not you.'

'Wanna dance?' Spencer, the one who had asked Elena a minute before, said again, asking Samantha this time.

'Sure!' she said, and jumped to her feet. The two were quickly lost in the crowd on the dance floor.

'God, I was so drunk last night,' the guy next to Elena, Jared, said, tipping his chair back on two legs and regarding her cheerfully. His friend on his other side gazed at him for a minute, then poured a shot into his lap.

'Hey!' In a moment, they were on their feet and shoving each other, the guy who had poured the drink laughing, Jared red-faced and angry.

'Knock it off, you guys,' Zander said. 'I don't want to get kicked out of here, too.'

Too? Elena raised her eyebrows. This guy and his friends were definitely too wild for innocent little Bonnie. Elena looked at Meredith again for confirmation, but she was still lost in jock world, now giving her opinion on the best weight training for martial arts.

Bonnie squealed with laughter and bounced a quarter directly into one of the shot glasses. All the guys cheered.

'Now what?' she said breathlessly, her eyes bright.

'Now you choose someone to drink it,' the guy who had brought the drinks said.

'Zander, of course,' Bonnie said, and Zander gave her a long, slow smile that even Elena had to admit was devastating. He drank, then winked at Bonnie as she laughed again.

Bonnie looked . . . really happy. Elena couldn't

remember the last time she had seen her laughing like this. It must have been at least a year ago, before things had gone crazy in Fell's Church.

Elena sighed and looked around the table. These guys were rowdy – tussling and shoving at one another – but they were friendly enough. And this was the kind of thing people did at college, wasn't it? If it made Bonnie happy, Elena ought to at least try to get along with them.

Samantha and Spencer came back to the table, both laughing, and Samantha collapsed in her seat. 'No more,' she said, raising her hands to fend him off. 'I need a water break. You're a madman, you know that?'

'Will *you* come and dance with me, then?' Spencer said pleadingly to Elena, widening big brown puppy-dog eyes at her.

'He'll try to lift you up,' Samantha warned. 'And dip you. And spin you around. But don't worry, I'll be back out on that floor in no time.'

'Pretty please?' Spencer said, making an even more pathetic face.

Bonnie laughed triumphantly as she bounced another quarter into the glass.

Dancing with a group of friends isn't betraying anyone, Elena thought. Besides, she was single now. Sort of, anyway. She should try to enjoy college, to embrace life. Wasn't that the whole point of tonight? She shrugged. 'Sure, why not?'

CHAPTER

16

When Stefan walked by Elena's room again, the daisy was gone, and the subtle scent of her citrusy shampoo lingered in the hallway.

No doubt she was out with Meredith and Bonnie, and he could depend on Meredith to protect her. He wondered if Damon was watching them, if he'd approach Elena. A bitter strand of envy curled in Stefan's stomach. It was hard being the good one sometimes, the one who would abide by the rules, while Damon did whatever he wanted.

He leaned back against the door to Elena's room. There was a window across the hall, and as he watched the cold crescent of the moon sailing high in the sky, he thought of his silent room, of the books of economics and philosophy waiting for him.

No. He wasn't going back there. He couldn't be with Elena, but he didn't have to be alone.

Outside, there was a chill in the air for the first time since college had started; the sultry heat of a Virginia summer was finally giving way to autumn. Stefan hunched his shoulders and tucked his hands into his jeans pockets.

Not really knowing where he was going, he headed off campus. Vague thoughts of hunting in the woods crossed his mind, but he wasn't hungry, just restless, and he turned away from the trail that led that way. Instead he wandered the streets of the small town around the college.

There wasn't much to do. There were a few bars hopping with college kids and a couple of restaurants, already closed up. Stefan couldn't imagine wanting to press into a hot and crowded bar right now. He wanted to be around people, maybe, but not too many, not too close, not close enough to sense the thrum of blood beneath their skins. When he was unhappy, like tonight, he could feel something hard and dangerous rising up inside him, and he knew he needed to be careful of the monster he carried within him.

He turned down another block, listening to the soft pad of his own steps against the sidewalk. Near the end of the street, a faint thud of music came from a dilapidated building whose buzzing neon sign read EDDIE'S BILLIARDS. None of the few cars in the parking lot had a Dalcrest parking sticker. Clearly a townie spot, not a student one.

If Stefan hadn't had this burning, angry loneliness inside him, he wouldn't have gone in. He looked like a student – he *was* a student – and this didn't look like a place that welcomed students. But the ugly thing inside him stirred at the thought of maybe having a reason to throw a punch or two.

Inside, it was well lit but dingy, the air thick and blue with smoke. An old rock song was playing on a jukebox in the corner. Six pool tables sat in the middle of the room, with small round tables around the sides, and a bar at the far end. Two of the pool tables and a few of the tables were occupied by locals, who let their eyes drift over him neutrally and then turn away.

At the bar, Stefan saw a familiar back, a sleek dark head. Even though he'd been sure Damon would be following Elena, he wasn't surprised to see him. Stefan had reined his Power in, concentrating on his own misery, but he'd always been able to sense his brother. If he had thought about it, he would have known Damon was there.

Damon, equally unsurprised, turned and tipped his glass to Stefan with a wry little grin. Stefan went over to join him.

'Hello, little brother,' Damon said softly when Stefan sat down. 'Shouldn't you be holed up somewhere, crying over your loss of the lovely Elena?'

Stefan sighed and slumped on the barstool. Propping his elbows on the bar, he rested his head on his hands. Suddenly, he was terribly tired. 'Let's not talk about Elena,' he said. 'I don't want to fight with you, Damon.'

'Then don't.' Patting him lightly on the shoulder, Damon was up and out of his seat. 'Let's play some pool.'

One thing about living for hundreds of years, Stefan knew, was that you had time to get really good at things. Versions of billiards had been around as long as he and Damon had, although he liked the modern version best – he liked the smell of the chalk and the squeak of the leather tip on the cue.

Damon's thoughts seemed to be running on the same track. 'Remember when we were kids and we used to play billiart on the lawns of Father's palazzo?' he asked as he racked up the balls.

'Different game, though, back then,' Stefan said. 'Go ahead and break.'

He could picture it clearly, the two of them fooling around when the adults were all inside, shoving the balls across the grass towards their targets with the heavy-headed maces, in a game that was a cross between modern pool and croquet. Back in those days, Damon was wild, prone to fights with stable boys and nights prowling the streets, but not yet as angry as he would be by the time they grew into young men. Back then, he let his adoring, more timid younger brother trail after him and have a share in his adventures.

Elena was right about one thing, he admitted to himself. He liked hanging out with Damon, being *brothers* again. When he'd spotted Damon at the bar just now, he'd felt a little lightening of the loneliness he was carrying around with him. Damon was the only person who remembered him as a child, the only person who remembered him alive.

Maybe they could be friends, without Katherine or Elena between them for a while. Maybe something good could come out of this.

Billiart, billiards or pool, Damon had always liked playing. He was better than Stefan, but, after hundreds of years of practice, Stefan was pretty good.

Which was why Stefan was so surprised when Damon's break sent balls spinning merrily all over the table, but none into the pockets.

'What's up?' he asked, cocking an eyebrow at Damon as he chalked his own cue.

I've been watching the locals, Damon said silently. *There are a couple of slick hustlers in here. I want to draw them over to us. Hustle them for a change.*

Come on, Damon added quickly when Stefan hesitated. *It's not wrong to hustle hustlers. It's like killing murderers, a public service.*

Your moral compass is seriously skewed, Stefan shot back at him, but he couldn't keep himself from smiling. What was the harm, really? 'Two ball in the corner pocket,' he added aloud. He made the shot and sank two more balls before intentionally stepping back to let Damon take his turn.

They went on like that, playing pretty well but not *too* well, careful to look like a couple of cocky college kids who knew their way around a pool cue but would be no challenge to a professional hustler. Damon's pretence of frustration when he missed a shot amused Stefan. Stefan had forgotten, it was *fun* to be part of Damon's schemes. Stefan won by a couple of balls, and Damon whipped out a wallet full of money.

'You got me, man,' he said in a slightly drunken voice that didn't sound quite like his own as he held out a twenty. Stefan blinked at him.

Take it, Damon thought at him. Something about the set of his jaw reminded Stefan again of the way Damon was when they were children, of the way he lied to their father about his misadventures, confident Stefan would back him up. Damon was trusting him without even thinking about it, Stefan realised.

Stefan smiled and slipped the note into his back pocket. 'Rack 'em up again?' he suggested, and noticed he was also pitching his voice a little younger, a little drunker than he normally would.

They played another game, and Stefan handed the twenty back. 'Another?' he asked.

Damon started to rack the balls, and then his hands slowed. He flicked a glance up at Stefan and then back down at the balls. 'Listen,' he said, taking a deep breath, 'I'm sorry for what's happening with Elena. If I—' He hesitated. 'I can't just stop feeling the way I do about her, but I didn't mean to make things harder for you. Or for her.'

Stefan stared at him. Damon *never* apologised. Was he serious? 'I – thank you,' he said.

Damon looked past him and his mouth twitched into his sudden, brilliant smile. *Bait taken*, he said silently. So much for the heartfelt brother moment.

Two guys were coming towards them. One was short and slight with sandy hair, the other big, bulky and dark.

'Hi,' the shorter one said. 'We wondered if you guys wanted to play teams, mix it up a little.' His smile was bright and easy, but his eyes were shrewd and watchful. The eyes of a predator.

Their names were Jimmy and David, and they were real pros. They kept the games close, waiting until after the third game to suggest raising the stakes to make things a little more interesting.

'A hundred?' Jimmy suggested casually. 'I can just about do it, if you want.'

'How about more?' Damon said, sounding drunk again. 'Stefan, you still got that five hundred in your wallet?'

Stefan didn't, nowhere near it, but he didn't think he'd need to pay up. He nodded but, at a glance from Damon, played reluctant. 'I don't know, Damon . . .' he said.

'Don't worry about it,' Damon said expansively. 'Easy money, right?'

Jimmy was watching them, his eyes alert. 'Five hundred it is,' he agreed, smiling.

'I'll break,' Damon said, and went into action. After a moment, Stefan rested his pool cue against the wall. He wasn't going to get a chance to shoot, none of them were; Damon was moving with clockwork precision to pocket one ball after another.

He wasn't making any effort to hide that he and Stefan had been running a hustle, and Jimmy's and David's faces darkened dangerously as the last few balls rattled into their pockets.

'Pay up,' Damon demanded sharply, setting down his cue.

Jimmy and David were moving towards them, scowling.

'You two think you're real smart, don't you?' David growled.

Stefan poised himself on both feet, ready to fight or run, whatever Damon wanted. They wouldn't have any trouble fending off these guys, but with the disappearances and attacks all over campus, he'd rather not call attention to themselves.

Damon, cool and relaxed, gazed at Jimmy and David, his hands open. 'I think you want to pay us the money you owe us,' he said calmly.

'Oh, that's what you think, do you?' Jimmy said

sarcastically. He shifted his grip on his pool cue and now he was holding it more like a weapon.

Damon smiled and unleashed a wave of Power into the room. Even Stefan, who was half expecting it, was chilled as Damon lifted his human mask for a moment, his black eyes cold and deadly. Jimmy and David staggered backwards as if they'd been shoved by invisible hands.

'OK, don't get upset,' Jimmy said, his voice shaking. David was blinking as if he had been slapped with a wet towel, clearly unsure of what had just happened. Jimmy opened his wallet and counted out five hundred dollars in fifties into Damon's hand.

'Now it's time for you to go home,' Damon said softly. 'Maybe you don't want to play pool for a while.'

Jimmy nodded and seemed unable to stop nodding, his head bobbing like it was on a spring. He and David backed away, moving quickly towards the door.

'Scary,' Stefan commented. There was a hollow place inside his chest still, an empty ache of missing Elena, but he felt better than he had since that day she walked out of the door alone. Tonight, he realised with a slight shock, he'd had *fun* with Damon.

'Oh, I'm a terror,' Damon agreed lightly, pocketing all the money. Stefan raised an eyebrow at him. He didn't care about the money, but it was typical of Damon to assume it was his. He grinned. 'Come on, little brother, I'll buy you a drink.'

CHAPTER

17

'That was amazing! Seriously,' Bonnie said happily, skipping along with her hand in Zander's. 'I am, like, the Queen of Quarters. Who knew I had this hidden talent?'

Laughing, Zander threw his arm around her shoulders and pulled her closer. 'You are pretty awesome,' he agreed. 'Drinking games, visions, astrology. Any other skills I should know about?'

Snuggling against him, Bonnie frowned in mock concentration. 'Not that I can think of. Just be aware of my general wonderfulness.' His T-shirt was soft and worn, and Bonnie tilted her head a bit to rest her cheek against it. 'I'm glad we got our friends together,' she said. 'I thought Marcus and Meredith really hit it off, didn't you? Not romantically, at all, which is good since

Meredith has a super-serious boyfriend, but it was like they shared the same secret jock language. Maybe we can all hang out in a group again sometime.'

'Yeah, Meredith and Marcus really bonded over their workouts,' Zander agreed, but there was a hesitation in his voice that made Bonnie stop walking and peer up at him sharply.

'Didn't you like my friends?' she asked, hurt. She and Meredith and Elena had always had what they privately called a 'velociraptor sisterhood'. Cross one of them and the other two would close in to protect her. Zander *had* to like them.

'No, I liked them a lot,' he assured her. He hesitated, then added, 'Elena seemed kind of . . . uncomfortable, though. Maybe we're not the kind of people she likes?'

Bonnie stiffened. 'Are you calling my best friend a snob?' she asked.

Zander stroked her back appeasingly. 'Sort of, I guess. I mean, *nice*, but just kind of a snob. The nicest kind of snob. I just want her to like me.'

'She's not a snob,' Bonnie said indignantly. 'And even if she was, she's got a lot to be a snob about. She's beautiful and smart and one of the best friends I've ever had. I'd do anything for her. And she'd do anything for me, too. So it doesn't matter if she's a snob,' she concluded, glaring at him.

'Come here,' Zander said. They were near the music building, and he pulled her into the lit alcove by the front door. 'Sit with me?' he asked, settling on the brick steps and tugging her hand.

Bonnie sat down, but she was determined not to snuggle up to him again. Instead, she kept a distance between them and stared stubbornly out at the night, her jaw firmly set.

'Listen, Bonnie,' he said, pushing a long strawberry-blonde curl out of her eyes. 'I'll get to know Elena better, and I'm sure I'll like her. I'll get her to like me, too. You know why I'm going to get to know her better?'

'No, why?' Bonnie said, reluctantly looking at him.

'Because I want to know *you* better. I'm planning on spending a lot of time with you, Bonnie McCullough.' He nudged her gently with his shoulder, and she melted.

Zander's eyes were so blue, blue like morning on the very first day of summer vacation. There was intelligence and laughter with just a touch of a wild longing in them. He leaned in closer, and Bonnie was sure he was about to kiss her, their first kiss at last.

She tilted her head back to meet his lips, her eyelashes fluttering closed.

After a moment of waiting for a kiss that didn't come, she sat up again and opened her eyes. Zander was staring past her, out into the darkness of the campus, frowning. Bonnie cleared her throat.

'Oh,' he said, 'sorry, Bonnie, I got distracted for a minute.'

'Distr*ac*ted?' she echoed indignantly. 'What do you mean you—'

'Hang on a sec.' He put a finger to her lips, shushing her.

'Do you hear something?' she asked, uneasy tingles creeping up her back.

Zander got to his feet. 'Sorry, I just remembered something I have to do. I'll catch up with you later, OK?' With a half-hearted wave, not even looking at her, he loped off into the darkness.

Bonnie's mouth dropped open. 'Wait!' she said, scrambling to her feet. 'Are you just going to leave me here –' Zander was gone – 'alone?' she finished in a tiny voice.

Great. She walked out to the middle of the path, looked around and waited a minute to see if there was any sign of Zander coming back. But there was no one in sight. She couldn't even hear his footsteps anymore.

There were pools of light beneath the street lamps on the path, but they didn't reach very far. A breeze rustled the leaves of the trees on the quad and she shivered. *No sense in standing here*, she thought, and started walking.

For the first few steps down the path towards her dorm, Bonnie was really angry, hot and humiliated. How could Zander have been such a flake? How could he leave her all alone in the middle of the night, especially after all the attacks and disappearances on campus? She kicked viciously at a pebble in her path.

A few steps further on, she stopped being so angry. She was too scared; the fear was pushing the anger out of her. She should have headed back to the dorm when Meredith and Elena did, but she'd assured them, gaily, that Zander would walk her back. How could he have just left her? She wrapped her arms around herself tightly and went as fast as she could without actually running, her stupid high-heeled going-out-dancing shoes pinching and making the balls of her feet ache.

It was really late; most of the other people who lived on campus must be tucked into their beds by now. The silence was unsettling.

When the footsteps began behind her it was even worse.

She wasn't sure she was really hearing them at first. Gradually, she became aware of a faint, quick padding in the distance, someone moving lightly and fast. She paused and listened, and the footsteps grew louder and faster still.

Someone was running towards her.

Bonnie sped up, stumbling over her feet in her haste. Her shoes skidded on a loose stone in the path and she fell, catching herself on her hands and one knee. The impact stung sharply enough to bring tears to her eyes, but she kicked off her shoes, not caring that she was leaving them behind. She scrambled up and ran faster.

The footsteps of her pursuer were louder now,

starting to catch up. Their rhythm was strange: loud periodic footfalls with quicker, lighter beats in between. Bonnie realised with horror that there was more than one person chasing her.

Her foot skidded again and she barely caught her balance, staggering sideways a few steps to keep from falling, losing more ground.

A heavy hand fell on her shoulder, and she screamed and whipped round, her fists raised in a desperate bid to defend herself.

'Bonnie!' Meredith gasped, clutching her shoulders. 'What are you doing out here by yourself?' Samantha came up beside them, carrying Bonnie's shoes, and doubled over, panting for breath.

'You are way too fast for me, Meredith,' she said.

Bonnie swallowed a sob of relief. Now that she was safe, she felt like sitting down and having hysterics. 'You scared me,' she said.

Meredith looked furious. 'Remember how we promised to stick together?' Her grey eyes were stormy. 'You were supposed to stay with Zander until you got home safely.'

Bonnie, about to respond heatedly that it hadn't been *her* choice to be out here alone, suddenly closed her mouth and nodded.

If Meredith knew that Zander had left Bonnie out here by herself, she would never, never forgive him. And Bonnie was mad at Zander for leaving her, but she wasn't quite that mad, not mad enough to turn Meredith against him. Maybe he had an explanation. And she still wanted that kiss.

'I'm sorry,' Bonnie said abjectly, staring down at her feet. 'You're right, I should have known better.'

Mollified, Meredith swung an arm over Bonnie's shoulders. Samantha silently handed Bonnie her shoes, and she pulled them back on. 'Let's walk Samantha back to her dorm, and then we'll go home together,' she said forgivingly. 'You'll be OK with us.'

Around the corner from her room, Elena sagged and leaned against the hallway wall for a moment. It had been a long, long night. There had been drinks, and dancing with the huge shaggy-haired Spencer who, as Samantha had warned her, did try to lift Elena up and swing her around.

Things got loud and aggravating, and the whole time her heart hurt. She wasn't sure she wanted to navigate the world without Stefan. *It's just for now*, she told herself, straightening up and plodding around the corner.

'Hello, princess,' said Damon. Elena stiffened in shock.

Lounging on the floor in front of her door, Damon somehow managed to look sleek and perfectly poised in what would have been an awkward position for anyone else. As she recovered from the shock of his being there at all, Elena was surprised by the burst of joy that rose up in her chest at the sight of him.

Trying to ignore that happy little hop inside her, she said flatly, 'I told you I didn't want to see you for a while, Damon.'

He shrugged and rose gracefully to his feet. 'Darling, I'm not here to plead for your hand.' His eyes lingered on her mouth for a moment, but then he went on in a dry and detached tone. 'I'm just checking in on you and the little redbird, making sure you haven't disappeared with whatever's gone sour on this campus.'

'We're fine,' Elena said shortly. 'Here I am, and Bonnie's new boyfriend is walking her home.'

'New boyfriend?' Damon asked, raising one eyebrow. He'd always had – something – some connection with Bonnie, Elena knew, and she guessed his ego might not be thrilled to have her moving past the little crush she'd focused on him. 'And how did you get home?' Damon asked acidly. 'I notice you haven't picked up a new boyfriend to protect you. Not yet, anyway.'

Elena flushed and bit her lip but refused to rise to the bait. 'Meredith just left to patrol around campus. I notice you didn't ask about her. Don't you want to make sure she's safe?'

Damon snorted. 'I pity any ghoul that goes after that one,' he said, sounding more admiring than anything else. 'Can I come in? Note that I'm being courteous again, waiting for you out *here* in this dingy hallway instead of comfortably on your bed.'

'You can come in for a minute,' Elena said grudgingly, and opened her bag to rummage for her keys.

Oh. She felt a sudden pang of heartache. At the top of her bag, rather crushed and wilted now, was the daisy she'd found outside her door at the beginning of the evening. She touched it gently, reluctant to push it aside in the hunt for her keys.

'A daisy,' Damon said dryly. 'Very sweet. You don't seem to be taking much care of it, though.'

Purposely ignoring him, Elena grabbed her keys and snapped the bag shut. 'So you think the disappearances and attacks are because of ghouls? Do you mean something supernatural?' she asked, unlocking the door. 'What did you find out, Damon?'

Shrugging, he followed her into the room. 'Nothing,' he answered grimly. 'But I certainly don't think the missing kids just freaked out and went home or to Daytona Beach or something. I think you need to be careful.'

Elena sat down on her bed, drew her knees up and rested her chin on them. 'Have you used your Power to try to figure out what's going on?' she asked. 'Meredith said she would ask you.'

Damon sat down next to her and sighed. 'Beloved, as little as I like to admit it, even my Power has limits,' he said. 'If someone is much stronger than me, like Klaus was, he can hide himself. If someone is much weaker, he doesn't usually make enough of an impression for me to find him unless I already know who he is. And for some ridiculous reason –' he scowled – 'I can never sense werewolves at all.'

'So you can't help?' Elena said, dismayed.

'Oh, I didn't say that,' he said. He touched a loose strand of her golden hair with one long finger. 'Pretty,' he said absently. 'I like your hair pulled back like this.' She twitched away from him and he dropped his hand. 'I'm looking into it,' he went on, his eyes gleaming. 'I haven't had a good hunt in far too long.'

Elena wasn't sure that she ought to find this comforting, but she did, in a kind of scary way. 'You'll be relentless, then?' she asked, a little chill going through her, and he nodded, his long black lashes half veiling his eyes.

She was so sleepy and felt happier now that she'd seen Damon, although she knew she shouldn't have let him in. She missed him, too. 'You'd better go,' she said, yawning. 'Let me know what you find out.'

He stood, hesitating by the end of her bed. 'I don't like leaving you alone here,' he said. 'Not with everything that's been happening. Where are those friends of yours?'

'They'll be here,' Elena said. Something generous in her made her add, 'But if you're that worried, you can sleep here if you want.' She'd missed him, and he was being a perfect gentleman. And she had to admit, she would feel safer with him there.

'I can?' He quirked a wicked eyebrow.

'On the floor,' Elena said firmly. 'I'm sure Bonnie and Meredith will be glad of your protection, too.' It was a lie. While Bonnie would be thrilled to see him, there was a decent chance Meredith would kick him on purpose as she crossed the room. She might even put on special pointy-toed boots to do it.

Elena got up and pulled down a spare blanket from her closet for him, then headed off to brush her teeth and change. When she came back, all ready for bed, he was lying on the floor, wrapped in the blanket. His eyes lingered for a minute on the curve of her neck leading down to her lacy white nightgown, but he didn't say anything.

Elena climbed into bed and turned out the light. 'Good night, Damon,' she said.

There was a soft rush of air. Then suddenly he whispered in her ear, 'Good night, princess.' Cool lips brushed her cheek and then were gone.

CHAPTER

18

The next morning, Elena woke to find Damon gone, his blanket folded neatly at the foot of her bed. Meredith was dressing for a morning workout, sleepy-eyed and silent, and she only nodded as Elena passed her; Elena had learned long ago that Meredith was useless for conversation before she'd had her first cup of coffee. Bonnie, who didn't have class until that afternoon, was only a lump under her covers.

Surely Meredith would have said something if she had noticed Damon on the floor, Elena thought as she dropped in at the cafeteria to grab a muffin before class. Maybe he hadn't stayed. Elena bit her lip, thinking about that, kicking little stones on her way to class. She'd thought he would stay, that he would want to try and keep her safe. Was it right that she *liked* it and that she felt more than a twinge of hurt at the idea that he had left?

She didn't *want* Damon to be in love with her, did she? Wasn't part of the reason she put her romance with Stefan on hold so that she and Damon could get each other out of their systems? But . . .

I am a lousy person, she realised.

Musing on her own lousiness took Elena all the way into her History of the South class, where she was doodling sadly in her notebook when Professor Campbell – James – came in. Clearing his throat loudly, he walked to the front of the class, and Elena reluctantly pulled her attention away from her own problems to pay attention to him.

James looked different. Unsure of himself, Elena thought. His eyes didn't seem quite as bright as usual, and he appeared to be somehow smaller.

'There's been another disappearance,' he said quietly. An anxious babble rose up from the rest of the class, and he held up his hand. 'The victim this time – and I think we can say at this point that we're talking about victims, not students simply leaving campus – is, unfortunately, a student in this class. Courtney Brooks is missing; she was last seen walking back to her dorm from a party last night.'

Scanning the class, Elena tried to remember who Courtney Brooks was. A tall, quiet girl with caramel-coloured hair, she thought, and spotted the girl's empty seat.

James raised his hand again to quell the rising clamour of frightened and excited voices. 'Because of this,' he said slowly, 'I think that today we must postpone continuing our discussion of the colonial period so that I can tell you a little bit about the history of Dalcrest College.' He looked around at the confused faces of the class. 'This is not, you see, the first time unusual things have happened on this campus.'

Elena frowned and, looking at her classmates, saw her confusion mirrored on their faces.

'Dalcrest, as many of you doubtlessly know, was founded in 1889 by Simon Dalcrest with the aim of educating the wealthy sons of the postwar Southern aristocracy. He said that he wanted Dalcrest to be considered the "Harvard of the South" and that he and his family would be at the forefront of intellectualism and academia in the soon-to-begin new century. This much is frequently featured in the official campus histories.

'It's less well known that Simon's hopes were dashed in 1895 when his wild twenty-year-old son, William Dalcrest, was found dead with three others in the tunnels underneath the college. It was what appeared to be a suicide pact. Certain materials and symbols found in the tunnels with the bodies suggested some ties to black magic. Two years later Simon's wife, Julia

Dalcrest, was brutally murdered in what is now the administration building; the mystery surrounding her death was never solved.'

Elena glanced around at her classmates. Had they known about this? The brochures mentioned when the college was founded and by who, but nothing about suicides and murders. *Tunnels underneath the college?*

'Julia Dalcrest is one of at least three distinct ghosts who are rumoured to haunt the campus. The other ghosts are those of a seventeen-year-old girl who drowned, again under mysterious circumstances, when visiting for a weekend dance in 1929. She is said to wander wailing through the halls of McClellan House, leaving dripping pools of water behind her. The third is a twenty-one-year-old boy who vanished in 1953 and whose body was found three years later in the library basement. His ghost has reportedly been seen coming in and out of offices in the library, running and looking backwards in terror, as if he's being pursued.

'There are also rumours of several other mysterious occurrences: a student in 1963 disappeared for four days and reappeared, saying he had been kidnapped by *elves*.'

A nervous giggle ran through the class, and James waved a reproving finger at his audience. He seemed to be perking up, swelling back to his usual self under the influence of the class's attention.

'The point is that Dalcrest is an unusual place.

Beyond elves and ghosts, there has been a plethora of documented strange occurrences, and rumours and legends of far more spring up around campus every year. Mysterious deaths. Secret societies. Tales of monsters.' He paused dramatically and looked around at them. 'I beg you, do not become part of the legend. Be smart, be safe and stick together. Class dismissed.'

The students glanced at one another uneasily, startled by this abrupt dismissal with still more than half an hour left of the class. Regardless, they started to gather their possessions together and trickle out of the room in twos and threes.

Elena grabbed her bag and hurried to the front of the room.

'Professor,' she said. '*James*.'

'Ah, Elena,' James said. 'I hope you were paying attention today. It's important that you young girls be on your guard. The young men, too, really. Whatever affects this campus does not seem to discriminate.' Up close, he looked pale and worried, older than he had at the beginning of the semester.

'I was very interested in what you said about the history of Dalcrest,' Elena said. 'But you didn't talk about what's happening *now*. What do you think is going on here?'

Professor Campbell's face creased into even grimmer lines, and his bright eyes gazed past her. 'Well, my dear,' he said, 'it's hard to say. Yes, very hard.' He licked his lips nervously. 'I've spent a lot of time at this college, you know, years and years. There's not a lot I wouldn't believe at this point. But I just don't know,' he said softly, as if he was talking to himself.

'There was something else I wanted to ask you,' Elena said, and he looked at her attentively. 'I went to see the picture you told me about. The one of you and my parents when you were students here. You were all wearing the same pin in the picture. It was blue and in the shape of a V.'

She was close enough to James that she felt his whole body jolt with surprise. His face lost its grim thoughtfulness and went blank. 'Oh, yes?' he said. 'I can't imagine what it was, I'm afraid. Probably something Elizabeth made. She was always very creative. Now, my dear, I really must run.' He slipped past Elena and made his escape, hurrying out of the classroom despite a few other students trying to stop him with questions.

Elena watched him go, feeling her eyebrows going up in surprise. James knew more than he was saying, that was for sure. If he wouldn't tell her – and she wasn't giving up on him just yet – she'd find out somewhere else. Those pins were significant, his reaction proved that.

What kind of mystery could be tied to a pin? Had James said something about *secret societies*?

* * *

'After my parents died,' Samantha told Meredith, 'I went to live with my aunt. She came from a hunter family, too, but she didn't know anything about it. She didn't seem to want to know. I kept on doing martial arts and everything I could learn by myself, but I didn't have anyone to train me.'

Meredith shone her flashlight into the dark bushes over by the music building and waved the beam around. Nothing to see except plants.

'You did a good job teaching yourself,' she told Samantha. 'You're smart and strong and careful. You just need to keep trusting your instincts.'

It had been Samantha's idea to patrol the campus together after sundown, to check out the places where the missing girl, Courtney, had been spotted last night, to see if they could find anything.

Meredith had felt powerful at the beginning of the evening, poised to fight, with her sister hunter beside her. But now, even though it was interesting to patrol with Samantha, to see the hunter life through her eyes, it was starting to feel like they were just wandering around at random.

'The police found her sweater somewhere over here,' Samantha said. 'We should look around for clues.'

'OK.' Meredith restrained herself from saying that the police had already been through here with dogs, looking for clues themselves, and there was a good chance they had already found anything there was to find. She scanned the flashlight over the grass and path. 'Maybe we'd be better off doing this during the day, when we can see better.'

'I guess you're right,' Samantha said, flicking her own flashlight on and off. 'It's good that we're out here at night, though, don't you think? If we're patrolling, we can protect people. Keep things from getting out of control. We walked Bonnie home last night and kept her safe.'

Meredith felt a flicker of anxiety. What if they *hadn't* come along? Could Bonnie have been the one who disappeared, instead of Courtney?

Samantha looked at Meredith, a little smile curling up the corners of her mouth. 'It's our destiny, right? What we were born for.'

Meredith grinned back at her, forgetting her momentary anxiety. She loved Samantha's enthusiasm for the hunt, her constant striving to improve, to fight the darkness. 'Our destiny,' she agreed.

Across the quad, someone screamed.

Snapping into action without even thinking about it, Meredith began running. Samantha was a few steps behind her, already struggling to keep up. *She needs to work on her speed*, coolly commented the part of Meredith that was always taking notes.

The scream, shrill and frightened, came again, slightly to the left. Meredith changed direction and sped towards it.

Where? She was close now, but she couldn't see anything. She scanned her flashlight over the ground, searching.

There. Nearby, two dark figures lay, one pinning the other down.

Everyone froze for a moment, and then Meredith was racing towards them, shouting 'Stop it! Get off! Get off!' and a second later, the figure that had been pinning the other down was up and running into the darkness.

Black hoodie, black jeans, the note taker said calmly. *Can't tell if it's a guy or a girl.*

The person who'd been pinned was a girl, and she flinched and screamed as Meredith ran past her, but Meredith couldn't stop. Samantha was behind her so she could help the girl. Meredith had to catch the fleeing figure. Her long strides ate up the ground, but she wasn't fast enough.

Even though she was going as fast as she could, the person in black was faster. There was a glimpse of paleness as the figure looked back at her and then melted into the darkness. Meredith ran on, searching, but there was nothing to be found.

Finally, she halted. Panting, trying to catch her breath, she swept the beam of the flashlight over the ground, looking for some clue. She couldn't believe she had failed, that she had let the attacker get away.

Nothing. No trace. They had got so *close*, and still, all

she knew was that the person who attacked this girl owned black clothes and was an insanely fast runner. Meredith swore and kicked at the ground, then pulled herself together.

Approximating calmness, she headed back towards the victim. While Meredith was chasing the attacker, Samantha had helped the girl to her feet, and now she was huddled close to Samantha's side, wiping her eyes with a tissue.

Shaking her head at Meredith, Samantha said, 'She didn't see anything. She thinks it was a man, but she didn't see his face.'

Meredith clenched her fists. 'Dammit. I didn't see anything either. He was so fast . . .' Her voice trailed off as a thought struck her.

'What is it?' Samantha asked.

'Nothing,' Meredith said. 'He got away.' In her mind, she replayed that momentary glimpse of pale hair she'd seen as the attacker looked back at her. That shade of pale – she had seen it somewhere very recently.

She remembered Zander, his face turned towards Bonnie's. His white-blond hair was that same unusual shade. It wasn't enough to go on, not enough to tell anyone. A momentary impression of a colour didn't mean anything. Meredith pushed the thought away, but, as she gazed off into the darkness again, she wrapped her arms around herself, suddenly cold.

CHAPTER

19

Nobody was going to lie to Elena Gilbert and get away with it.

Elena marched along the path to the library, indignation keeping her head high and her steps sharp. So James thought he could pretend he didn't remember anything about those V-shaped pins? The way his eyes had skipped away from hers, the faint flush of pink in his plump cheeks, everything about him had shouted that there was something there, some secret about him and her parents that he didn't want to tell her.

If he wasn't going to tell her, she would find out for herself. The library seemed like a logical place to start.

'Elena,' a voice called, and she stopped. She was so focused on her mission that she almost walked right past Damon, leaning against a tree outside the library. He smiled up at her with an innocently enquiring expression, his long legs stretched in front of him.

'What are you doing here?' she said abruptly. It was so *weird*, just seeing him here in the daylight on campus, like he was part of one picture superimposed on another. He didn't belong in this part of her life, not unless she brought him in herself.

'Enjoying the sunshine,' Damon said dryly. 'And the scenery.' The wave of his hand encompassed the trees and buildings of the campus as well as a flock of pretty girls giggling on the other side of the path. 'What are *you* doing here?'

'I go to this college,' Elena said. 'So it's not weird for *me* to be hanging around the library. See my point?'

He laughed. 'You've discovered my secret, Elena,' he said, getting to his feet. 'I was here hoping to see you. Or one of your little friends. I get so lonely, you know, even your Mutt would be a welcome distraction.'

'Really?' she asked.

He shot her a look, his dark eyes amused. 'Of course I always want to see you, princess. But I'm here for another reason. I'm supposed to be looking into the disappearances, remember? So I have to spend some time on the campus.'

'Oh. OK.' Elena considered her options. Officially, she shouldn't be hanging around Damon at all. The terms of her break-up – or just *break*, she corrected herself – with Stefan were that she wasn't going to see either of the Salvatore brothers, not until they worked out their own issues and this *thing* between the three of them had time to cool off. But she'd already violated that by letting Damon sleep on the floor of her room, a much bigger deal than going to the library together.

'And what are you up to?' he asked her. 'Anything I can assist with?'

Really, a trip to the library ought to be innocent enough. Elena made up her mind. She and Damon were supposed to be *friends*, after all. 'I'm trying to find out some information about my parents,' she said. 'Want to help?'

'Certainly, my lovely,' he said, and took her hand. She felt a slight frisson of unease. But his fingers were reassuringly firm in hers, and she pushed her hesitation away.

The ancient tennis-shoed librarian in charge of the archive room explained how to search the database of college records and got Elena and Damon set up in the corner on a computer.

'Ugh,' Damon said, poking disdainfully at a key. 'I don't mind computers, but books and pictures ought to be *real*, not on a *machine*.'

'But this way everyone can see them,' Elena said patiently. She'd had this kind of conversation with Stefan. The Salvatore brothers might look college-aged, but there were some things about the modern world they just couldn't seem to get their heads around.

Elena clicked on the photo section of the database and typed in her mother's name, Elizabeth Morrow.

'Look, there are a bunch of pictures.' She scanned through them, looking for the one she'd seen hanging in the hall. She saw a lot of cast and crew pictures from various theatrical productions. James had told her that her mother was a star on the design side, but it looked like she was in some productions, too. In one, Elena's mother was dancing, her head flung back, her hair going everywhere.

'She looks like you.' Damon was contemplating the picture, his head tilted to one side, dark eyes intent. 'Softer here, though, around the mouth –' one long finger gestured – 'and her face is more innocent than yours.' His mouth twisted teasingly, and he shot a sidelong glance at Elena. 'A nicer girl than you, I'd guess.'

'I'm nice,' she said, hurt, and quickly clicked on to find the picture she was looking for.

'You're too clever to be *nice*, Elena,' he said, but she was barely listening.

'Here we are,' she said. The photograph was just as she remembered it: James and her parents under a tree, eager and impossibly young. She zoomed in on the image, focusing on the pin on her father's shirt. Definitely a *V*. It was blue, a deep dark blue, she could see that now, the same shade as the lapis lazuli rings Damon and Stefan wore to protect themselves from sunlight.

'I've seen one of those pins before,' Damon said abruptly. He frowned. 'I don't remember where, though. Sorry.'

'You've seen it recently?' Elena asked, but he just shrugged. 'James said my mother made the pins for all of them,' she said, zooming closer so that all she could see on the screen was the grainy image of the V. 'I don't believe him, though. She didn't make jewellery, that wasn't her kind of thing. And it doesn't look handmade, not unless it was made by someone with an actual jewellery studio. That's some kind of enamelling on the V, I think.' She typed V in the search engine, but it came back with nothing. 'I wish I knew what it stood for.'

With a graceful one-shouldered shrug, Damon reached for the mouse and zoomed in and out on different parts of the picture. Behind them, the librarian thunked a book down, and Elena glanced back at her to find the woman's eyes fixed on them with disconcerting intensity. Her mouth tightened as her eyes met Elena's and she looked away, walking a little further along the aisle. But Elena was left with the creepy feeling that the librarian was still watching and listening to them.

She turned to whisper something to Damon about it but was caught again by the sheer unexpectedness of him, of him *here*. He just didn't fit in the drab and ordinary library computer station – it was like finding a wild animal curled up on your desk. Like a dark angel making porridge in your kitchen.

Had she ever seen him under fluorescent lights before? Something about the lighting brought out the clean paleness of his skin, cast long shadows along his cheekbones and fell without reflection into the black velvet of his hair and eyes. A couple of his shirt buttons were undone, and Elena found herself almost mesmerised by the subtle shifts of the long muscles in his neck and shoulders.

'What would a Vital Society be?' he asked suddenly, breaking her out of her reverie.

'What?' she asked, confused. 'What are you talking about?'

Damon clicked the mouse and shifted the zoom, focusing this time on the notebook in her mother's lap. Her mother's hands – pretty hands, Elena noticed, prettier than her own, which had slightly crooked pinkies – were splayed over the open book, but between the fingers, Elena could read: *Vit l Soci y*

'I assume that's what it says,' he said. 'Since you're looking for something that starts with V. It could say something else, of course. Vital Socially, maybe? Was your mother a social queen bee like you?'

She ignored the question. 'The Vitale Society,' she said slowly. 'I always thought it was a myth.'

'*Leave the Vitale Society alone.*' The hiss came from behind them, and Elena whipped round.

The librarian seemed curiously impressive framed against the bookshelves despite her tennis shoes and pastel sweater set. Her hawklike face was tense and focused on Elena, her body tall and, Elena felt instinctively, threatening.

'What do you mean?' Elena asked. 'Do you know something about them?'

Confronted by a direct question, the woman seemed to shrink from the almost menacing figure she had been a second before to an ordinary, slightly dithering old lady. 'I don't know anything,' she muttered, frowning. 'All I can say is that it's not safe to mess with the Vitales. Things happen around them. Even if you're careful.' She started to wheel her book cart away.

'Wait!' Elena said, half rising. 'What kind of things?' What had her parents been involved in? They wouldn't have done anything *wrong*, would they? Not Elena's parents. But the librarian only walked faster, the wheels of her cart squeaking as she rounded the corner into another aisle.

Damon gave a low laugh. 'She won't tell you anything,' he said, and Elena glared at him. 'She doesn't know anything, or she's too scared to say what she *does* know.'

'That's not helpful, Damon,' she said tightly. She pressed her fingers against her temples. 'What do we do now?'

'We look into the Vitale Society, of course,' he said. Elena opened her mouth to object, and he shushed her, drawing one cool finger over her mouth. His touch was soft on her lips, and she half raised a hand towards them. 'Don't worry about what a foolish old woman has to say,' he told her. 'But if we really want to find out the secrets of this society of yours, we probably need to look somewhere other than the library.'

He got to his feet and held out his hand. 'Shall we?' he asked. Elena nodded and took his hand in hers. When it came to finding out secrets, digging up what people wanted to keep concealed, she knew she could put her faith in Damon.

'Pick up, Zander,' Bonnie muttered into the phone.

The ringing stopped and a precise mechanical voice informed her that she was welcome to leave a message. She hung up. She had already left a couple of voicemails, and she didn't want Zander thinking she was any crazier or more clueless than he inevitably would when he saw his missed-call list.

Bonnie was pretty sure she was going through the Five Stages of Being Ditched. She was almost done with Denial, where she was convinced something had happened to him, and was moving quickly into Anger. Later, she knew, she would slide into Bargaining, Depression and eventually (she hoped) Acceptance.

Apparently her psych class was already coming in handy.

It had been *days* since he had abruptly run off, leaving her all alone in front of the music building. When she found out that a girl disappeared that same night, at first she was angry and scared for herself. Zander had left her alone. What if *Bonnie* had been the one to vanish? Then she began to worry about Zander, to be afraid that he was in trouble. He seemed so sweet, and so into her, that it was almost impossible for her to believe he was avoiding her all of a sudden.

Wouldn't his friends have sounded the alarm if Zander was missing, though? And when she thought that, Bonnie realised that she didn't know how to contact any of those guys; she hadn't seen any of them around campus since that night.

She stared at her phone as fresh tendrils of worry grew and twisted inside her. Really, she was having a very tough time moving on to Anger when she was still not quite sure that Zander was safe.

The phone rang.

Zander. It was *Zander*.

Bonnie snatched up her phone. 'Where have you been?' she demanded, her voice shaking.

There was a long pause on the other end of the line. She was almost ready to hang up when Zander finally spoke. 'I'm so sorry,' he said. 'I didn't mean to freak you out. Some family stuff came up, and I've had to be out of touch. I'm back now.'

She knew that Elena or Meredith would have said something pithy and cutting here, something to let him know exactly how little they appreciated being forgotten about, but she couldn't bring herself to. He sounded rough and tired, and there was a break in his voice when he said he was sorry that made her want to forgive him.

'You left me outside alone,' she said softly. 'A girl disappeared that night.'

Zander sighed, a long sad sound. 'I'm sorry,' he said again. 'It was an awful thing to do. But I knew you would be OK. You have to believe that. I wouldn't have left you in danger.'

'How?' Bonnie asked. 'How could you know?'

'Just trust me, Bonnie,' he said. 'I can't explain it now, but you weren't in danger that night. I'll tell you about it when I can, OK?'

She shut her eyes and bit her lip. Elena and Meredith would never have settled for this kind of half explanation. Not even half an explanation, just an apology and an evasion. But she wasn't like them, and Zander sounded sincere, so desperate for her to believe him. It was her choice, she knew: trust him, or let him go.

'OK,' she said. 'OK, I believe you.'

He let out another sigh, but it sounded like one of relief this time. 'Let me make it up to you,' he said. 'Please? How about I take you out this weekend, anywhere you want to go?'

Bonnie hesitated, but she was starting to smile despite herself. 'There's a party at Samantha's dorm on Saturday,' she said. 'Want to meet there at nine?'

'There's something peculiar going on at the library,' Damon said, and Stefan twitched in surprise at his sudden appearance.

'I didn't see you there,' he said mildly, looking out onto his dark balcony, where Damon leaned against the railing.

'I just landed,' Damon said, and smiled. 'Literally. I've been flying around campus, checking things out. It's a wonderful feeling, riding the breezes as the sun sets. You should try it.'

Stefan nodded, keeping his face neutral. They both knew that one of the few things Stefan envied about Damon was his ability to change into a bird. It wasn't worth it, though – he would have to drink human blood regularly to have Power as strong as Damon's.

Elena's face rose up in his mind's eye, and he pushed her image away. She was his salvation, the one who connected him to the world of humans, who kept him from sinking into the darkness. Believing that their separation was only temporary was what was keeping him going.

'Don't you miss Elena?' Stefan asked, and Damon's face immediately closed off, becoming hard and blank.

Stefan sighed inwardly. Of course Damon didn't miss Elena, because he was undoubtedly seeing her all the time. He'd *known* his brother wouldn't abide by the rules.

'What's the matter?' Damon asked him. His voice was almost concerned, and Stefan wondered what his own face looked like to get that kind of reaction from Damon. Damon who had probably just seen Elena.

'Sometimes I'm a fool,' Stefan told him dryly. 'What do you want?'

Damon smiled. 'I want you to come and do some detective work with me, little brother. Really, anything's better than seeing this sulking, forehead-wrinkling brooding expression on your face.'

Stefan shrugged. 'Why not?' He leaped down from the balcony with perfect grace, and Damon followed swiftly behind.

As Damon led the way to their destination, he filled Stefan in on the details. Or rather, the vague scenario Stefan could gather from his explanation. Damon never was one for full disclosure. All Stefan knew was that some research at the library had prompted a sketchy warning from an old librarian. Stefan inwardly chuckled at the thought of a frail old woman squaring up against Damon over library fines.

'What were you looking at?' Stefan asked, trying to get more substantial information. 'What did she want you to stay away from?' He shifted on the rough branch of the oak tree they were both sitting on, trying to get comfortable. Damon had a habit of sitting in trees, Stefan realised. It must be a side effect of spending so much time as a bird. They were on a stakeout outside the librarian's home, but what exactly they were looking for Stefan wasn't sure.

'Just some old photographs from the college's history,' Damon said. 'It doesn't matter. I just want to make sure she's human.' He peered through the window nearest their tree, where an elderly woman was sipping tea and watching television.

Stefan noted with irritation that Damon seemed a lot more at ease in the tree than he did. Damon was leaning forward, resting gracefully on one knee, and Stefan could sense his sending questing strands of Power at the woman, trying to find out whether there was anything unusual about her.

His balance seemed awfully precarious, and he was completely focused on the old woman. Stefan inched towards Damon on the branch, stretched out a hand and suddenly shoved him.

It was extremely satisfying. Damon, his composure shaken for once, let out a muffled yelp and fell out of the tree. In mid-air, he turned into a crow and flew back up, perching on a branch above Stefan and eyeing him with a baleful glare. He cawed his annoyance at Stefan loudly.

Stefan glanced through the window again. The woman didn't seem to have heard Damon's shout or the crow's caw – she was just flipping channels. When he looked back at Damon, his brother had regained his usual form.

'I would think playing a trick like that would go against your precious moral code,' Damon said, fastidiously smoothing his hair.

'Not really,' Stefan said, grinning. 'I couldn't help myself.'

Damon shrugged, seeming to accept Stefan's playfulness as good-natured, and looked through the librarian's window again. She had got up to make herself another cup of tea.

'Did you sense anything from her?' Stefan asked.

Damon shook his head. 'Either she's brilliantly hiding her true nature from us or she's just a peculiar librarian.' He pushed himself off the branch and leaped, landing lightly on the grass far below. *Either way, I've had enough*, he added silently.

Stefan followed, landing beside him at the bottom of the tree. 'You didn't need me for any of that, Damon,' he said. 'Why did you ask me to come with you?'

Damon's smile was brilliant in the darkness. 'I just thought you could use some cheering up,' he said simply. Clearly, it wasn't the librarian Stefan should be worried about acting peculiarly.

CHAPTER

20

This is way worse than the obstacle course, Matt thought. And building a house out of newspaper. And the firewalk. This is definitely the worst pledge event yet.

He twisted the toothbrush in his hand to really get into the little niche running along the bottom of the panelling on the Vitale Society's pledge room walls. The toothbrush came out black with ancient dirt and dangling cobwebs, and Matt grimaced in disgust. His back was already sore from hunching over.

'How's it going, soldier?' Chloe asked, squatting down next to him, a dripping sponge in one hand.

'Honestly, I'm not sure how scrubbing out this room is going to help us develop honour and leadership and all the stuff Ethan keeps talking about,' Matt said. 'I think this might just be a way to save a couple of bucks on a cleaning service.'

'Well, they say cleanliness is next to godliness,' she reminded him. Chloe laughed. He really liked her laugh. It was sort of bubbly and silvery.

Internally, he gave himself a little eye roll. *Bubbly and silvery*. She had a nice laugh, that was all he meant.

They'd been spending a lot of time together since Christopher's death. Matt had felt like nothing could be as bad as living with all of Christopher's stuff when Christopher himself was gone, but then Chris's parents came and packed it up, gently patting Matt on the back as if *he* deserved some kind of sympathy when *they* had lost their only son. And with just empty space where Christopher's things had been, everything was a million times worse.

Meredith, Bonnie and Elena had tried to comfort him. They wanted so badly for him to be OK again that he'd felt guilty he wasn't, making it harder for him to be around them.

Chloe had taken to coming by the room, hanging out with him or getting him to come to the cafeteria or wherever with her, keeping him in touch with the world when he felt like locking himself away. There was something so easy about her. Elena, the only girl he'd ever loved – *before now*, part of him whispered – was much more *work* to be around. Inside, he flinched at his own disloyalty to Elena, but it was true.

Now he was starting to wake up and take an interest in things again. And he kept noticing with fresh surprise the cute dimples Chloe had in her cheeks, or how shiny her curly dark hair was, or how graceful and pretty her hands were despite the fact they were often stained with paint.

So far, though, they were just friends. Maybe . . . maybe it was time to change that.

Chloe snapped her fingers in front of his face, and Matt realised he had been staring at her. 'You all right, buddy?' she asked, a little frown wrinkling her forehead, and Matt had to restrain himself from kissing her right then.

'Yeah, just spacing out,' he said, feeling a flush creep over his cheeks. He was smiling like a goof, he knew. 'Want to help with these walls?'

'Sure, why not?' Chloe answered. 'I'll soap down the wall part, and you keep doing whatever you're doing there with that little toothbrush.'

They worked companionably together for a while, Chloe now and then accidentally-on-purpose dripping soapy water onto the top of Matt's head.

As they worked further along the panelling, the niche under the baseboard got deeper, until it was not so much a niche as a gap. Matt slid the toothbrush underneath to scrub – *man*, but it got grimy down there – and felt something shift.

'There's something under here,' he told Chloe,

pressing his hand flat against the floor and working his fingers into the gap. He slid his hands and the toothbrush around, trying to shimmy whatever was down there towards them, but he couldn't quite get a grip on it.

'Look,' said Chloe after a moment, 'I think the panelling might slide up here.' She wiggled the section of wood until it gave a raucous screech and she was able to work it up. 'Huh,' she said, puzzled. 'Wow, it's like a secret compartment. Seems like it hasn't been opened for a while, though.'

Once she managed to ease the panelling up, they could see the space behind it was small, only around half a metre or so in height and width and a few cenimetres deep. It was full of cobwebs. Inside was something rectangular, wrapped in a cloth that had probably once been white but was now grey with dust.

'It's a book,' Matt said, picking it up. The grime on the outside of the cloth was thick and soft and came away on his hands. Unwrapping it, he found the book inside was clean.

'Wow,' Chloe said softly.

It looked old, really old. The cover was flaking dark leather, and the edges of the pages were rough as if they'd been hand cut instead of by a machine. Tilting the book a little, Matt could see the remains of gilt that must have once been the title, but it was worn away now.

He opened it to the middle. Inside, it was handwritten, black ink inscribing neat strong strokes. And totally indecipherable.

'I think it's Latin. Maybe?' he said. 'Do you know Latin at all?'

Chloe shook her head. Matt flipped back to the first page, and one word popped out at him. *Vitale*.

'Maybe it's a history of the Vitale Society,' she said. 'Or ancient secrets of the founders. Cool! We should give it to Ethan.'

'Yeah, sure,' Matt said, distracted. He turned a few more pages, and the ink changed from black to a dark brown. *It looks like dried blood*, he thought, and shuddered, then pushed the image away. It was just some kind of old ink, faded brown with time.

One word he recognised, written three – no, four – times on the page: *Mort*. That meant death, didn't it? He traced the word with his finger, frowning. Creepy.

'I'll show it to Ethan,' Chloe said, jumping up and taking the book from him. She crossed the room and interrupted Ethan's conversation with another girl. From the other side of the room, Matt watched Ethan's face break into a slow smile as he took the book.

After a few minutes, Chloe returned, grinning. 'Ethan was really excited,' she said. 'He said he'll tell us all about it after he gets someone to translate the book.'

Matt nodded. 'That's terrific,' he said, pushing the last of his unease away. This was *Chloe*, lively, laughing

Chloe, and he would try not to think about death or blood or anything morbid around her. 'Hey,' he said, pushing away the dark thoughts, focusing on the golden highlights in her dark hair. 'Are you going to the party at McAllister House tonight?'

Maybe not pulled back, Elena thought, looking critically at herself in the mirror. She tugged the clip out of her hair and let her golden locks tumble, sleek and straightened, down around her shoulders. *Much better*.

She looked good, she noted, running her eyes dispassionately over her reflection. Her strappy short black dress accentuated her rose-petal skin and pale hair, and her dark blue eyes seemed huge.

Without Stefan, though, what did it matter how she looked?

She watched her mouth tighten in the mirror as she pushed the thought away. However much she missed the feeling of Stefan's hand in hers, his lips on hers, however much she wanted to be with him, it was impossible for now. She couldn't be Katherine. And her pride wouldn't let her just mope around, either. *It's not forever*, she told herself grimly.

Bonnie came up and threw her arm around Elena's shoulders, regarding them both in the mirror. 'We scrub up nice, don't we?' she asked cheerfully. 'Ready to go?'

'You do look amazing,' Elena said, looking at Bonnie

with affection. The shorter girl was practically glowing with excitement – eyes sparkling, smile bright, cheeks flushed, mane of red hair flying out seemingly with a life of its own – and her short blue dress and strappy high-heeled shoes were adorable. Bonnie's smile got bigger.

'Let's get going,' Meredith said, all business. She was sleek and practical in jeans and a soft fitted grey shirt that matched her eyes. It was hard to know what Meredith was thinking, but Elena had overheard her murmuring to Alaric on the phone late at night. She figured that Meredith, at heart, might not be into the party either.

Outside, people walked quickly in large, silent groups, glancing around nervously as they went. No one lingered, no one was alone.

Meredith stopped mid-stride and stiffened, suddenly aware of a potential threat. Elena followed her gaze. She was wrong: one person lingered alone. Damon was sitting on a bench outside their dorm, his face tipped towards the sky as if he was basking in the sun despite the darkness of the evening.

'What do you want, Damon?' Meredith said, warily. Her voice wasn't actually rude – they'd got past that, working together this summer – but it wasn't friendly, and Elena could feel her bristling beside her.

'Elena, of course,' Damon said lazily, rising and smoothly taking Elena's arm.

Bonnie looked back and forth between them, puzzled. 'I thought you weren't going to spend time with either of them for a while,' she said to Elena.

Damon spoke quietly into Elena's ear. 'It's about the Vitale Society. I've got a lead.'

Elena hesitated. She hadn't told her friends about the hints she and Damon had found that the Vitale Society might be more than a myth, or that they might be connected to her parents in some way. There wasn't really anything much to go on yet, and she didn't feel quite ready to talk about the possibility that her parents might have been mixed up in some kind of dark secret or how she felt, seeing the images of them when they were young.

Making up her mind, she turned to Meredith and Bonnie. 'I've got to go with Damon for a minute. It's important. I'll explain it to you guys later. See you at the party in a little bit.'

Meredith frowned but nodded, and she steered Bonnie towards McAllister House. As they went, Elena could hear Bonnie saying, 'But wasn't the whole point . . .'

Keeping his hand tucked firmly under Elena's arm, Damon led her in the opposite direction. 'Where are we going?' she asked, feeling too aware of the softness of his skin and the strength of his grip.

'I saw a girl wearing one of those pins from the photo,' Damon answered. 'I followed her to the library, but once she got inside, she just disappeared. I looked everywhere for her. Then, an hour later, she came out of the library doors again. Remember when I said we needed to look for answers somewhere other than the library?' He smiled. 'I was wrong. There's something going on in there.'

'Maybe you just didn't see her?' Elena wondered aloud. 'It's a big library, she could have been tucked away in a study cubicle or something.'

'I would have found her,' Damon said briefly. 'I'm *good* at finding people.' His teeth shone white for a moment under the streetlights.

The problem was that the library was so *normal*. Once they were inside, Elena looked around at the grey-carpeted floors, the beige chairs, the rows and rows of bookshelves, the buzzing fluorescent lights. It was a place to study. It didn't look like any secrets were hidden here.

'Upstairs?' she suggested.

They took the stairs rather than the elevator and worked their way down from the top floor. Going from floor to floor, they found . . . nothing. People reading and taking notes. Books, books and more books. In the basement, there was a room of vending machines and small tables for study breaks. Nothing unexpected.

Elena paused in a hallway of administrative offices near the vending machines. 'We're not going to find anything,' she told Damon. His face twisted in frustration, and she added, 'I believe you that there's something going on here, I do, but without any leads, we don't even know what we're looking for yet.'

The door behind her, marked Research Office, opened, and Matt came out.

He looked tired, and Elena felt a quick flash of guilt. After Christopher's death, she and Meredith and Bonnie had meant to stick close to Matt. But he was always busy with football or class and didn't seem to want them around. She realised with a shock that she hadn't talked to him in days.

'Oh, hey, Elena,' Matt said, looking startled. 'Are you going to the party tonight?' He greeted Damon with an awkward nod.

'Mutt,' Damon acknowledged, giving a half-smile, and Matt rolled his eyes.

As they chatted about the party and classes and Bonnie's new semi-boyfriend, Elena catalogued her impressions of Matt. Tired, yes – his eyes were a little bloodshot, and there was grimness to his lips that hadn't been there a few weeks ago. But why did he smell so strongly of soap? It wasn't like he was particularly clean, she thought, inspecting a grubby trail tracing down Matt's cheek to his neck. It looked like something had been dripped on his head. It was almost like he had been cleaning something. Something really dirty.

Struck by a new thought, she glanced at his chest.

Surely he wouldn't be wearing one of the *V* pins? As if aware of what she was wondering, Matt pulled his jacket more tightly around him.

'What were you doing in that office?' she asked him abruptly.

'Uh.' His face was blank for half a second, and then he glanced up at the door, at the sign saying Research Office. 'Research, of course,' he said. 'I've got to go,' he added. 'I'll catch you at the party later, OK, Elena?'

He had half turned away, when she impulsively put out her hand to catch his arm. 'Where have you been, Matt?' she asked. 'I've hardly seen you lately.'

He grinned, but he didn't quite meet her eyes. 'Football,' he said. 'College ball's a big deal.' He gently pulled away from her restraining hand. 'Later, Elena. Damon.'

They watched him walk away, and then Damon nodded towards the door Matt had come out of. 'Shall we?' he said.

'Shall we what?' Elena asked, puzzled.

'Oh, like *that* wasn't suspicious,' he said. He put his hand on the knob, and Elena heard the lock snap as he forced it open.

Inside was a very boring room. A desk, a chair, a small rug on the floor.

Maybe a little *too* boring?

'A research office without books? Or even a computer?' Elena asked. Damon cocked his head to one side, considering, then, with a swift movement, pulled aside the rug.

Below it was the clear outline of a trapdoor. 'Bingo,' Elena breathed. She stepped forward, already bending down to try and pry it open, but Damon pulled her back.

'Whoever is using this could still be down there,' he said. 'Matt just left, and I doubt he was alone.'

Matt. Whatever was going on, Matt knew about it. 'Maybe I should talk to him,' Elena said.

Damon frowned. 'Let's wait until we know what we're dealing with,' he said. 'We don't know what Matt's involvement is. This could be dangerous for you.' He had taken hold of her arm again and was pulling her gently, steadily out of the room. 'We'll come back later.'

Elena let him lead her away, grappling with what he'd said. *Dangerous?* she thought. Surely Matt wouldn't be doing anything that would be a danger to Elena?

CHAPTER
21

'What's taking so long?' Bonnie asked, bouncing on the balls of her feet.

'Stop being so hyper,' Meredith said absently, craning her neck to see over the crowd outside McAllister. There was some kind of bottleneck by the entrance to the dorm that was slowing everyone down. She shivered in her thin top; it was starting to get cold at night.

'Security's at the door,' Bonnie said as they got closer to the entrance. 'Are they *carding* people to get in?' Her voice was shrill with outrage.

'They're just checking that you have a student ID,' someone in the crowd told her, 'to make sure you're not a crazed killer from off campus.'

'Yeah,' his friend said. 'Only on-campus killers allowed.'

A couple of people laughed nervously. Bonnie fell silent, biting her lip, and Meredith shivered again, this time for reasons that had nothing to do with the cold.

When they finally got to the front of the queue, the security guards glanced quickly at their IDs and waved them through. Inside, it was crowded and music was pumping, but no one really seemed to be in a partying mood. People stood in small groups, talking in undertones and glancing around nervously. The presence of the security guards had reminded everyone of the danger lurking unseen on campus. Anyone could be responsible, even someone in the room at that very moment.

As she thought about that, Meredith's view of the room shifted, the other students around her changing from innocent to sinister. That curly-headed frat boy in the corner – was he eyeing his pretty companion with something more than simple lust? The faces of strangers twisted viciously and Meredith took a deep breath, calming herself until everyone looked normal again.

Samantha was coming towards her, a red plastic cup in her hand. 'Here,' she said, handing Meredith a soda. 'Everyone's on edge tonight, it's creepy. We'd better stay alert and not drink,' she said, already on the same wavelength as Meredith.

Bonnie squeezed Meredith's arm in farewell and took off into the crowd to look for Zander. Meredith sipped her drink and warily eyed the strangers surrounding her.

Despite the general malaise hanging over the party, some people were so wrapped up in each other that they were managing to have a good time anyway. She watched a couple kiss, as fully focused on each other as if there was no one else in the world who mattered. They weren't worrying about the attacks and disappearances on campus, and Meredith found herself feeling a sharp pang of envy. She *missed* Alaric, missed him with a bone-deep longing that stayed with her, even when she wasn't consciously thinking about him.

'The killer could be right here at this party,' Samantha said unhappily. 'Shouldn't we be able to *sense* something? How can we protect anyone if we don't know who we're up against?'

'I know,' said Meredith. The crowd parted, and she saw a face she hadn't expected: Stefan, leaning against the far wall. His eyes lit up when he saw her, and he glanced past her with a hopeful half-smile already forming on his lips.

Poor guy. No matter what Meredith thought about Elena's decision to take a break – and, for the record, Meredith thought that Elena was doing the right thing; her entanglement with *both* Salvatore brothers meant that they had all been heading for trouble – she couldn't help pitying him. Stefan had the look of someone who was experiencing the same sharp pang of loneliness and desire as Meredith did when she thought of Alaric. It must be worse for him, because Elena was so close and because she chose to separate herself from him against his wishes.

'Excuse me for a second,' she said to Samantha, and went to Stefan.

He greeted her politely and asked about her classes and her hunter training, although she could tell that he was burning to talk about Elena. He had such good *manners*, always.

'She's not here yet, but she's definitely coming,' she told him, interrupting one of his pleasantries. 'She had something to do first.' His face bloomed into a smile of grateful relief, and then he frowned.

'Elena's coming here alone?' he asked. 'After all the attacks?'

'No,' Meredith reassured him. She hadn't thought of this, and she didn't think she should tell him Elena was with Damon. 'She's with other people,' she settled for saying and was glad that her answer seemed to satisfy him.

Meredith sipped her drink and hoped grimly that Elena had the sense not to bring Damon to the party.

Matt spotted Chloe from across the room. Tonight was the night, he decided. Enough playing around, enough exchanging glances and gentle, platonic hugs and hand squeezes. He wanted to know if she felt the same way he did, if she felt like maybe there was something between them worth exploring.

She was talking to someone, a guy he recognised from Vitale, and her curly brown hair shone softly in the light from overhead. There was so much *life* in Chloe: the way she laughed, the way she listened to what the guy was saying, attentive and involved, her face focused.

Matt wanted to kiss her, more than anything.

So he started working his way across the room towards her, nodding at people he knew as he passed them. He didn't want to look too uncool and eager, not as though he was making a beeline for her, but he didn't want to stop and lose her in the crowd, either.

Matt.

Matt jerked as if he'd been stung as the silent greeting hit him. Twisting around to see where it was coming from he found Stefan standing right behind him and frowned irritably at him. He *hated* it when Stefan got into his head like that.

'You could have just said hi,' he told Stefan, as mildly as he could. 'You know, out loud.'

Stefan ducked his head apologetically, his cheeks flushing. 'I'm sorry,' he said. 'That was rude of me, but I just wanted to get your attention. It's so loud in here.' He gestured around, and Matt wondered, as he sometimes had before, how the life of a modern teenager seemed to the vampire. Stefan had experienced more than Matt probably ever would, but the loud rock music and the press of bodies all around him seemed to make him uncomfortable, showing the cracks in his disguise as someone *young*. He tried hard, for Elena's sake, Matt knew.

'I'm waiting for Elena,' Stefan said. 'Have you seen her?' The lines of his face were anxious, and, just like that, Matt's picture of Stefan as someone too old, too out of place here, snapped. Stefan looked achingly young, lonely and worried.

'Yeah,' Matt said. 'I just saw her at the library. She said she was coming here later.' He bit his tongue to keep from adding that he'd seen her there with *Damon*, of all people. Matt wasn't quite sure what was going on between Elena and the brothers, but he figured Stefan didn't need to know that Elena and Damon were together.

'I'm supposed to be staying away from her,' Stefan confided sadly. 'She feels like she's coming between Damon and me, and she wants some time for us all to work things out before the two of us can be together again.' He glanced up at Matt, almost beseechingly. 'But I thought since there are so many people here, it isn't like we'd be alone.'

Matt took a swallow of his beer, his mind working furiously. Now he *knew* he'd been right not to mention that Damon and Elena had been together. What game was Elena playing now?

It was a shock, too, to realise how far out of the loop he was. When did all this happen? Since Christopher's death, he'd been avoiding his friends, spending so much time focused on the Vitale Society that he'd missed this big development in their lives. What else was he missing?

Stefan was still looking at him as if he was seeking some kind of approval, and Matt rubbed the back of his neck thoughtfully, then offered, 'You should talk to her. Let her know how unhappy you are without her. Love is worth taking the chance.'

As Stefan nodded, considering, Matt's eyes sought out Chloe in the crowd again. The guy she'd been talking to was gone, and she was alone for the moment, biting her lip as she looked around the room. He was about to excuse himself and head towards her when another voice spoke in his ear.

'Hi, Matt, how's it going?' Ethan came up beside him, his golden brown eyes focused on Matt's. Matt felt himself straightening up and pulling back his shoulders, trying to look loyal and honourable, a promising candidate, everything the Vitale wanted him to be. Matt saw this reaction to Ethan in the other pledges as well: whatever Ethan wanted them to be or do, they wanted, too. Some people were just natural leaders, he guessed.

They chatted for a minute, not about the Vitale Society, of course, not in front of Stefan, but simple, friendly stuff about football and classes and the music that was playing, and then Ethan turned the warmth of his smile on Stefan. 'Oh, uh, Ethan Crane, Stefan Salvatore,' Matt introduced them, adding, 'Stefan and I went to high school together.'

Stefan and Ethan started making conversation, and Matt looked for Chloe again. She wasn't in the last place he had seen her, and he started to panic, until he found her again in the crowd, moving to the music.

'I can't help noticing just a slight accent, Stefan,' Ethan was saying. 'Are you from Italy originally?'

Stefan smiled shyly. 'Most people don't hear it anymore,' he said. 'My brother and I, we left Italy a long time ago.'

'Oh, does your brother go here, too?' Ethan asked, and Matt decided the two of them seemed happy enough together and that it was OK for him to leave now.

'I'll catch up with you guys later,' he said. Taking another swallow of beer, Matt strode through the crowd, straight towards Chloe. Her eyes were shining, her dimples were showing, and he knew the time was right. Like he had told Stefan, love was worth taking the chance.

CHAPTER
22

Bonnie knew the minute that Zander and his friends came into the party, because the noise level went *way* up. Honestly, Zander was calmer than his friends, sort of, at least around Bonnie, but as a group, they were definitely wild.

It was kind of irritating, actually.

But when Zander appeared next to her – hip-checking Marcus into a wall on his way – and gave her his long, slow smile, her toes curled inside her high-heeled shoes and she forgot all about being annoyed.

'Hi!' she said. 'Is everything OK?' He cocked an eyebrow at her enquiringly. 'I mean, you said something came up with your family, and that's why you've been . . . busy.'

'Oh, yeah.' Zander bent his head down to talk to her,

and his warm breath ghosted across Bonnie's neck as he sighed. 'My family's pretty complicated,' he said. 'I wish sometimes that things were easier.' He looked sad, and she impulsively took his hand, twining her fingers through his.

'Well, what's wrong?' she asked, striving for a tone of understanding and reliability. A dependable girlfriend tone. 'Maybe I can help. You know, a fresh ear and all that.'

Zander frowned and bit his lip. 'I guess it's like . . . I have responsibilities. My whole family is in a position where there are promises we've made and sort of things we have to take care of. And sometimes what I want to do and what I have to do don't line up.'

'Could you be any more vague?' Bonnie asked teasingly, and he huffed a half laugh. 'Seriously, what do you mean? What do you have to do? What don't you want to do?'

Zander looked down at her for a moment and then his smile widened. 'Come on,' he said, tugging her hand. Bonnie went with him, weaving their way through the party and up the stairs. He seemed to know where he was going; he turned a couple of corners, then pushed open a door.

Inside was a dorm common room: a couple of ratty couches, an old table. Someone's art project, a large canvas covered with splotches of paint, leaned against the wall.

'Do you live in this dorm?' she asked.

'No,' he said, his eyes on her mouth. He pulled her towards him and rested his hands on her hips. And then he kissed her.

It was the most amazing kiss Bonnie had ever experienced. Zander's lips were so soft yet firm, and there were little fireworks going off all over her body. She lifted her hand and cupped it against his cheek, feeling the strong bones of his face and the slight scratch of stubble against her palm.

Once again, she felt as she had during their first date, standing on the roof, when it had felt like she was flying. So free, and with a wild kind of joy zinging through her. She slid her hand to the back of his neck, feeling his fine pale blond hair brush softly against her fingers.

When the kiss ended, neither of them spoke for a moment, they just leaned against each other, breathing hard. Their faces were so close, and Zander's brilliant blue eyes were fixed on hers, warm and intent.

'Anyway, that's what I *want* to do, since you asked. Do you –' his voice cracked – 'do you want to go back to the party now?'

'No,' said Bonnie, 'not yet.' And this time, she kissed him.

'Oh, thank God,' Chloe said when Matt came up to her. 'I was beginning to feel like the biggest wallflower.'

She crinkled her nose appealingly at him. Her nose, which tilted up just a little, was spattered with freckles, and she had a pretty cupid's bow of a mouth. He wanted to tug gently on the soft brown ringlets of her curls, just to see them straighten and then spring back into shape.

'What do you mean?' he said, pulling himself back together, although he was painfully aware that he sounded half-witted. 'A wallflower?'

'Oh, just . . .' She waved one hand vaguely at the crowd. 'There's hardly anyone I know here besides you and Ethan. This whole party's completely stuffed with freshmen.'

Matt's heart sank. He had forgotten that Chloe was a junior. It shouldn't be a big deal, really, should it? But she sounded like she thought freshmen were beneath her, or something. Disdainful, that was the word he was looking for to describe her tone.

'I thought the party seemed OK,' he said weakly.

Chloe pursed her lips teasingly, then socked him gently on the arm. 'Well,' she said softly, 'there's only enough room for *one* freshman in my life. Right, Matt?'

That was more of a hopeful sign. The problem was, Matt realised, that his only dating experience had been in asking out girls who he either didn't really care about, but was just thinking of as potential dates for dances or whatever, or who were Elena. Who he cared tremendously about, but who he'd known well enough to tell she was going to say yes.

Still, he thought he could see an opening here.

'Chloe,' he said, 'I was wondering if you would—'

He broke off as Ethan joined them, smiling widely. For the first time, Matt felt a flash of irritation towards him. Ethan was so smart with people. Couldn't he see he was interrupting a *moment* here?

'I liked your friend Stefan,' Ethan told Matt. 'He seemed very sophisticated for a freshman, very well spoken. Do you think it's because he's European?'

Matt only shrugged in response, and Ethan turned to Chloe.

'Hey, sweetheart,' he said, putting an arm around her and kissing her lightly on the lips.

And yeah, wow, maybe Ethan *had* realised he was interrupting a moment. It wasn't a long kiss, but there was definitely a possessive air about it, and about his arm flung across Chloe's shoulders. When it ended, Chloe smiled up at Ethan, breathless, and Ethan's eyes flicked to Matt, just for a second.

Matt wanted to fold right over and sink into the sticky, beer-stained floor beneath his feet. But instead he eked out a smile of his own and tipped his beer to Ethan.

Because Chloe – adorable, sweet, funny, easygoing Chloe – had a boyfriend. He ought to have anticipated that he wouldn't be the only one who saw how amazing she was. And Matt would have backed off no matter who Chloe's boyfriend was. He didn't want to be that guy who sleazed all over other people's relationships; he never had been.

But since Chloe's boyfriend was Ethan? Ethan, the Vitale Society leader, the one who had made Matt feel like he was special, like he could be the best? Since it was Ethan, Matt was just going to have to grit his teeth and ignore that hollow feeling in his chest. He was going to be strong and keep himself from even thinking about what he wished could have been with Chloe.

There were some lines he just couldn't cross. Ever.

CHAPTER

23

'I don't know how it got so *late*,' Elena said for the third time as they hurried down the path by the quad. 'Bonnie and Meredith are probably worried about me.'

'They know you're with me,' Damon said, pacing along unruffled beside her.

'I don't think they'll find that comforting,' she said, and bit her tongue as he shot her an expressive look.

'After all the time we've spent fighting side by side, they still don't trust me?' he said silkily. 'I'd be terribly hurt. If I cared what they thought.'

'I don't mean that they think you'd hurt me,' Elena said. 'Not anymore. Or that you wouldn't protect me. I guess they worry that you might . . . might make a pass at me. Or something.'

Damon stopped and looked at her. Then he picked

up her hand and held it, running one finger down the inside of her arm, tracing the vein that led from her wrist to her elbow. 'And what do you think?' he asked, smiling gently.

Elena snatched her hand back, glaring at him. 'Clearly they have a point,' she said. 'Knock it off. Just friends, remember?'

Sighing deeply, he started walking again, and she hurried to catch up.

'I'm glad you decided to come to the party with me,' she said eventually. 'It'll be fun.' He shot her a velvet-black glance through his lashes but said nothing.

It was always fun to be with Damon, Elena thought, listening to the clicking of her heels and watching her shadow grow and disappear as they walked beneath the streetlights. Or at least, it was always fun when Damon was in a good mood *and* nothing was trying to kill them, two circumstances she wished coincided more often.

Stefan, sweet, darling Stefan, was the love of her life. She had no doubts about that. But Damon made her feel breathless and excited, swept up in something bigger than herself. Damon made her feel like she was special.

And he was more easygoing than usual tonight. After Matt left, they'd searched the library some more, and then Damon treated her to crisps and soda in the basement vending-machine room. They sat at one of the little tables and talked and laughed. It wasn't anything fancy or elegant, nothing like the parties he'd escorted her to in the Dark Dimension, but it was comfortable and fun, and when she looked at her phone, she was startled to see that more than an hour had passed.

And now Damon even volunteered to come to a college keg party. Maybe he was trying to get along with her friends. Maybe *they* could really be friends, once things somehow worked out between Stefan and him.

Elena had reached this point in her musings when she suddenly got the unmistakable creepy-crawly feeling that she was being watched. The little hairs on the back of her neck stood up.

'Damon,' she said softly. 'There's someone watching us.'

His pupils dilated as he sniffed the air. Elena could tell that he was sending out questing tendrils of Power, searching for an answering surge, for someone focusing on them.

'Nothing,' he said after a moment. He tucked his hand under her arm, pulling her closer. 'It could just be your imagination, princess, but we'll be careful.'

The leather of his jacket was smooth against her side, and she held tightly onto him as they stepped out into the road that divided the campus.

Just across from them, a car that had been idling at

the curb gunned its engine. Its headlights blazed on, blinding her. Damon's arms locked around her waist, squeezing the breath out of her.

The car's tyres squealed and it shot towards them. Elena panicked – *oh God, oh God*, she thought helplessly – and froze. Then she was sailing through the air, Damon holding her so tightly that it hurt.

When they hit the grass on the other side of the road, he paused for a moment, adjusting his grip on Elena, and she peered back at the car, which had passed where they were standing a moment before and skidded back around in a U-turn. She couldn't make out anything, not what kind of car it was nor anything about the driver; behind the bright lights, it was just a hulking dark shape.

A hulking dark shape that was veering onto the grass and coming back after them. Damon swore and yanked her onwards, running rather than flying now, her feet barely touching the ground. Her heart was pounding. She could tell Damon was hampered from using his full speed by keeping her close. They dodged around the corner of a building and leaned against its wall, surrounded by bushes.

The car hurtled by, then turned, its wheels leaving long skid marks, and lumbered back to the road.

'We lost him,' Elena whispered, panting.

'Annoy anyone lately, princess?' Damon asked, his eyes sharp.

'I should be asking *you* that,' she retorted. Then she wrapped her arms around herself. She was so cold suddenly. 'Do you think it could have been because of the Vitale Society?' she asked, her voice quavering. 'Something about them and my parents?'

'We don't know who or what could have been on the other side of that trapdoor,' he replied sombrely. 'Or maybe Matt . . .'

'Not Matt,' Elena said firmly. 'Matt would never hurt me.'

Damon nodded. 'That's true. He's ridiculously honourable, your Matt.' He gave her a little wry sideways smile. 'And he loves you. Everyone loves you, Elena.' He shrugged out of his jacket and draped it over her shoulders. 'One thing's certain, though. If the driver of that car thought I was human before, he knows differently now.'

Elena pulled the jacket more tightly around herself. 'You saved me,' she said in a tiny voice. 'Thank you.'

Damon's eyes were soft as he put his arms around her. 'I will always save you, Elena,' he promised. 'Don't you know that by now?' His pupils dilated, and he pulled her closer. 'I can't lose you,' he murmured.

Elena felt like she was falling. The world was being swallowed up in Damon's midnight eyes, and she was being drawn along with it, into the darkness. A tiny part of her said *no*, but despite it she leaned towards him and met his mouth with hers.

* * *

Stefan tapped his fingers against the wall behind him, looked around at all the people jammed too close together: talking, laughing, arguing, drinking, dancing. His skin was crawling with anxiety. Where was she? Matt said he'd seen her at the library more than an hour ago, that she'd had been planning on coming to the party then.

Making up his mind, Stefan began to push his way towards the exit. Maybe Elena didn't want him in contact with her right now, but people were dying and disappearing. It would be worth it to have her angry with him, as long as he knew that she was OK.

He passed Meredith, deep in conversation with her friend, and said, 'I'm going to find Elena.' He had the quick impression of her faltering, starting to reach out a hand to stop him, but he left her behind. He pushed open the door and stepped out into the cool night air. Campus security was still by the door checking IDs, but they let him pass without comment, only interested in people trying to come into the party.

Outside, the wind was rushing through the trees overhead and a crescent moon rode high and white above the buildings around him. Stefan sent his Power out around him, feeling for the distinct traces of Elena.

He couldn't sense anything, not yet. There were too many people too close together here, and Stefan could only feel the tangled traces of hundreds of humans, their emotions and life force mixing together in one great underlying buzz from which it was impossible for him, at this distance, to pick out any particular individual, even one as singular as Elena.

If he had fed on human blood recently, it would have been easier. He couldn't help thinking longingly of the way that Power had surged through him when he drank regularly from his friends. But that was when Fell's Church needed his best defence against the kitsune. He wouldn't drink human blood just for pleasure or convenience.

Stefan started walking quickly across the quad, still sending out questing fingers of Power around and ahead of himself. If he couldn't locate Elena that way, he would head for where she was last seen. He hoped that, as he got closer to the library, his Power would pick up some hint of her.

His whole body was thrumming anxiously. What if Elena had been attacked, what if she mysteriously vanished and never returned, leaving him with this strange distance as their last memory of each other? He walked faster.

He was halfway to the library when the distinctive sense of *Elena* hit him like a punch. Somewhere nearby.

He scanned left and right and then he saw her. A terrible pain shot through his chest, as if he could actually feel his heart breaking. She was kissing Damon. They were half hidden in the shadows, but their light skin and Elena's blonde hair shone. They were focused only on each other, so much so that, despite his Power, Damon wasn't aware of Stefan's presence, not even when he walked right up to them.

'Is this why you wanted to take some time apart, Elena?' Stefan asked, his voice sounding hollow and distant. Finally noticing him, they broke away from each other, Elena's face pale with shock.

'Stefan,' she said. 'Please, Stefan, no, it's not what it looks like.' She reached out a hand towards him, then drew it back uncertainly.

Everything seemed so far away to Stefan; he was aware that he was shaking, his mouth was dry, but it felt almost as if he was watching someone else in pain. 'I can't do this,' he said. 'Not again. If I fight for you, I'll just end up destroying us all. Just like with Katherine.'

Elena was shaking her head back and forth, her hands stretched out towards him imploringly again. 'Please, Stefan,' she said.

'I can't,' he said again, backing away, his voice thin and desperate.

Then, for the first time, he looked at Damon, and a red-hot rage slammed into him, overriding the numb distance instantly. 'All you do is take,' Stefan told him bitterly. 'This is the last time. We're not brothers anymore.'

Damon's face opened for a split second in dismay, his eyes widening, as if he was about to speak, and then he hardened again, his mouth twisting scornfully, and he jerked his head at Stefan. *Very well*, that gesture indicated, *then get lost*.

Stefan stumbled backwards, and then he turned and ran, moving with all the supernatural grace and speed at his command, leaving them far behind even as Elena screamed, '*Stefan!*'

CHAPTER

24

Giggling, Bonnie tripped on her way down the stairs, her foot coming right out of her high-heeled shoe.

'Here you go, Cinderella,' Zander said, picking up the shoe and kneeling in front of her. He helped slip her foot back into it, his fingers warm and steady against her instep. Bonnie gave a mock curtsy, muffling her laughter. 'Thank you, m'lord,' she said flirtatiously.

She felt fabulous, so silly and happy. It was almost as if she was drunk, but she'd only had a few sips of beer. No, she was drunk. Drunk on Zander, on his kisses, his gentle hands and his big blue eyes. She took his hand, and he smiled down at her, that long slow smile, and Bonnie just absolutely *quivered*.

'Seems like the party's wrapping up,' she said, as they hit the ground floor. It was really getting late, almost two o'clock. There were only a few groups of hard-core partiers left: a bunch of frat boys by the keg, some theatre-department girls dancing with great wide swoops of their arms, a couple sitting hand in hand at the bottom of the stairs in deep conversation. Meredith, Stefan, Samantha and Matt had disappeared, and if Elena had ever shown up, she had left, too. Zander's friends had gone, or been kicked out.

'Goodbye, goodbye,' Bonnie carolled to the few people who remained. She hadn't really got a chance to talk to any of them, but they all looked perfectly nice. Maybe next time she went to a party, she'd stay longer and really bond with people she hadn't met before.

Look at all the new friends her friends had made on campus. Bonnie gave a special wave to a couple of people she'd seen Matt with lately – a shortish guy whose name she thought was Ethan and that girl with the dark curls and dimples. Not freshmen. She loved everyone tonight, but they deserved it most, because they had seen what a wonderful guy Matt was. They waved back at her, a little hesitantly, and the girl smiled, her dimples deepening.

'They seem really nice,' Bonnie told Zander, and he glanced back at them as he opened the door.

'*Hmmm*,' he said non-committally, and the look in his eyes, just for a minute, made Bonnie shiver.

'Aren't they?' she said nervously. Zander looked away from them, back towards her, and his warm brilliant smile spread across his face. Bonnie relaxed; the coldness she'd seen in his eyes must have been just a trick of the light.

'Of course they are, Bonnie,' he said. 'I just got distracted for a sec.' He wrapped his arm around her shoulders, pulling her close, and dropped a kiss on the top of her head. She sighed contentedly, cuddling up against his side.

They walked together companionably for a while. 'Look at the stars,' Bonnie said softly. The night was clear and the stars hung bright in the sky. 'It's because it's starting to get colder at night that we can see them so well.'

Zander didn't answer, only made a *hmming* sound deep in his throat again, and Bonnie glanced up at him through her eyelashes. 'Do you want to get breakfast with me in the morning?' she asked. 'On Sundays, the cafeteria does make-your-own waffles, with lots of different toppings. Delicious.'

He was staring off into the distance with that same half-listening expression he had the last time they walked across campus together. 'Zander?' Bonnie asked cautiously, and he frowned down at her, biting his lip thoughtfully.

'Sorry,' he said. He took his arm off her shoulders and backed away a few steps, smiling stiffly. His whole body was tense, as if he was about to take off running.

'Zander?' she asked again, confused.

'I forgot something,' he said, avoiding her eyes. 'I have to go back to the party.'

'Oh. I'll come with you,' she offered.

'No, that's OK.' He was shifting from foot to foot, glancing over her shoulder as if, suddenly, he'd rather be anywhere than with her. Abruptly, he surged forward and kissed her awkwardly, their teeth knocking together, and then he stepped backwards and turned, walking in the other direction. His strides lengthened, and soon he was running away from her, disappearing into the night. Again. He didn't look back.

Bonnie, suddenly alone, shivered and looked around, peering into the darkness on all sides. She had been so happy a minute ago, and now she felt cold and dismayed, as if she had been hit with a splash of freezing water. 'You have *got* to be kidding me,' she said aloud.

Elena was shaking so hard that Damon was afraid she might just shake herself apart. He wrapped his arms around her comfortingly, and she glanced up at him without really seeming to see him, her eyes glassy.

'Stefan . . .' she moaned softly, and Damon had to fight down a sharp stab of irritation. So Stefan was overreacting. What else was new? Damon was *here*, Damon was with her and supporting her, and Elena needed to realise that. He was tempted to grab her firmly by the chin and make her really *look* at him.

In the old days, he would have done just that. Hell, in the old days, he would have sent a blast of Power at her until she was docile in his hands, until she didn't even remember Stefan's name. His canines prickled longingly just thinking of it. Her blood was like *wine*.

Not that expecting Elena to give in to his Power meekly had ever worked particularly well, he admitted to himself, his mouth curling into a smile.

But he wasn't like that anymore. And he didn't want her that way. He was trying so hard, although he hated to admit it even to himself, to be worthy of Elena. To be worthy of Stefan, even, if it came right down to it. It had been comforting to finally have his baby brother looking at him with something other than hatred and disgust.

Well, that was over. The tentative truce, the beginnings of friendship, the brotherhood, whatever it had been between him and Stefan, was gone.

'Come on, princess,' he murmured to Elena, helping her up the stairs towards her door. 'Just a little further.'

He couldn't be sorry they'd kissed. She was so beautiful, so alive and vibrant in his arms. And she tasted so good.

And he loved her, he did, as far as his hard heart was capable of it. His mouth curled again, and he could taste his own bitterness. Elena was never going to be his, was she? Even when Stefan turned his back on her, the self-righteous idiot, he was all she thought about.

Damon's free hand, the one that wasn't cupping Elena's shoulder protectively, tightened into a fist.

They'd reached her room, and he fished in her bag for her keys, unlocking the door for her.

'Damon,' she said, turning in the doorway to look him straight in the eyes for the first time since Stefan had caught them kissing. She looked pale still, but resolute, her mouth a straight line. 'Damon, it was a mistake.'

His heart dropped like a stone, but he held her gaze. 'I know,' he said, his voice steady. 'Everything will work out in the end, princess, you'll see.' He forced his lips to turn up in a reassuring, supportive smile. The smile of a friend.

Then Elena was gone, the door to her room shutting firmly behind her.

He spun in his tracks, cursing, and kicked at the wall behind him. It cracked, and he kicked it again with a sour satisfaction at the feeling of the plaster splitting.

There was a muted grumbling from behind the other doors on the floor, and Damon could hear footsteps approaching, someone coming to investigate the noise. If he had to deal with anyone now, he'd probably kill them. That wouldn't be a good idea, no matter how much he might enjoy it for the moment, not with Elena right here.

Launching himself towards an open hall window, he smoothly transitioned to a crow in mid-air. It was a relief to stretch his wings, to pick up the rhythm of flying and feel the breeze against his feathers, lifting and supporting him. He flew through the window with a few strong beats of his wings and flung himself out into the night. Catching the wind, he soared recklessly high despite the darkness of the night. He needed the rush of the wind against his body, needed the distraction.

CHAPTER

25

*D*ear Diary,

I can't believe what a fool I am, what a faithless, worthless fool.

I should never have kissed Damon, or let him kiss me.

The look on Stefan's face when he found us was heartbreaking. His features were so stiff and pale, as if he was made of ice, and his eyes were shining with tears. And then it seemed like a light went out inside him, and he looked at me like he hated me. Like I was Katherine. No matter what happened between us, Stefan never looked at me like that before.

I won't believe it. Stefan could never hate me. Every beat of my heart tells me that we belong together, that nothing can tear us apart.

I've been such a fool, and I've hurt Stefan, although that was the one thing I never wanted to do. But this isn't the end for us. Once I apologise and explain what a moment of madness he witnessed, he'll forgive me. Once I can touch him again, he'll see how sorry I am.

It was only the adrenaline from coming so close to death, from that car chasing after us. Neither Damon nor I really wanted the other one, that kiss was just us clinging hard to life.

No. I can't lie. Not here. I have to be honest with myself, even if I pretend with everyone else. I wanted to kiss Damon. I wanted to touch Damon. I always have.

But I don't have to. I can stop myself, and I will. I don't want to cause Stefan any more pain.

Stefan will understand that, will understand that I'll do anything I can to make him happy again, and then he'll forgive me.

This can't be the end. I won't let it be.

Elena closed her journal and dialled Stefan's number once more, letting the phone ring until it went to voicemail and then hanging up. She'd called him several times last night, then over and over again this morning. He could see her calling, she knew. He always kept his phone on. He always answered, too; he seemed to feel some obligation to be available since he had the phone with him.

The fact that he wasn't answering meant he was avoiding her on purpose.

Elena shook her head fiercely and dialled again. Stefan was going to listen to her. She wasn't going to *let* him turn her away. Once she explained and he forgave her, everything could go back to normal. They could end this separation that was making them both so unhappy – clearly, it hadn't worked out the way she intended.

Except, what exactly was she going to say? Elena sighed and flopped down backwards onto her bed, her heart sinking. Adrenaline from the car's pursuit aside, all she could really say was that she hadn't meant for the kiss with Damon to happen, that she didn't want him, not really. She wanted Stefan. All she could tell him was that it wasn't something she had expected or planned. That *Damon* wasn't the one she wanted. Not truly. That she would always choose Stefan.

That would have to be enough. She dialled again.

This time, Stefan picked up.

'Elena,' he said flatly.

'Stefan, please listen to me,' she said in a rush. 'I'm so sorry. I never—'

'I don't want to talk about this,' he said, cutting her off. 'Please stop calling me.'

'But, please, Stefan—'

'I love you, but . . .' His voice was soft but cold. 'I don't think we can be together. Not if I can't trust you.'

The line went dead. Elena pulled the phone away from her ear and stared at it for a moment, puzzled, before she realised what had happened. Stefan, dear, darling Stefan who had always been there for her, who loved her no matter what she did, had hung up on her.

Meredith pulled one foot up behind her back, held it in both hands, breathed deep and slowly pulled the foot higher, stretching her quadriceps muscle.

It felt good to stretch, to get a little blood flowing after her late night. She was looking forward to sparring with Samantha. There was a new move Meredith had figured out, a little something kickboxing inspired, that she thought Sam was going to *love*, once she got over the shock of being knocked down by Meredith once again. Samantha had been getting faster and more sure of herself as they kept working out together, and Meredith definitely wanted to keep her on her toes.

That was, it would be terrific to spar with Samantha, if Samantha ever actually arrived. Meredith glanced at her watch. Sam was almost twenty minutes late.

Of course, they'd been out late the night before. But still, it wasn't like Samantha not to show up when she said she was going to. Meredith turned on her phone to see if she had a message, then called Samantha. No answer.

She left a quick voicemail, then hung up and went back to stretching, trying to ignore the faint quiver of unease running through her. She circled her shoulders, stretched her arms behind her back.

Maybe Samantha just forgot and had her phone turned off. Maybe she'd overslept. Samantha was a *hunter*; she wasn't in danger from whoever – or whatever – was stalking the campus.

Sighing, Meredith gave up on her workout routine. She wasn't going to be able to focus until she checked on Samantha, even though she was probably fine. Undoubtedly fine. Scooping up her backpack, she headed for the door. She could get in a run on the way over.

The sun was shining, the air was crisp, and Meredith's feet pounded the paths in a regular rhythm as she wove between people wandering around campus. By the time she reached Samantha's dorm, she was thinking that maybe Sam would want to go for a nice long run with her instead of sparring today.

She tapped on Samantha's door, calling, 'Rise and shine, sleepyhead!' The door, not latched, drifted open a little.

'Samantha?' she said, pushing it open further.

The smell hit her first. Like rust and salt, with an underlying odour of decay, it was so strong Meredith staggered backwards, clapping a hand over her nose and mouth.

Despite the smell, she couldn't at first understand what was all over the walls. *Paint?* she wondered, her brain feeling sluggish and slow. *Why would Samantha be painting?* It was so red. She walked through the door slowly, although something in her was starting to scream. *No, no, get away.*

Blood. Bloodbloodbloodblood. Meredith wasn't feeling slow and sluggish anymore: her heart was pounding, her head was spinning, her breath was coming hard and fast. There was death in this room.

She had to see. She had to see Samantha. Despite every nerve in her body urging her to run, to fight, Meredith kept moving forward.

Samantha lay on her back, the bed beneath her soaked red with blood. She looked like she had been ripped apart. Her open eyes stared blankly at the ceiling, unblinking.

She was dead.

CHAPTER

26

'**A**re you sure you don't want us to call your parents, Miss?' The campus security officer's voice was gruff but kind, and his eyes were worried.

For a second, Meredith let herself picture having the kind of parents he must be imagining: ones who would swoop in to rescue their daughter, wrap her up and take her home until the horrible images of her friend's death faded. *Her* parents would just tell her to get on with the job. Tell her that any other reaction was a failure. If she let herself be weak, more people would die.

More so because Samantha had been a hunter, from a family of hunters, like Meredith. She knew exactly what her father would have said if she had called him. *'Let this be a lesson to you. You are never safe.'*

'I'll be OK,' she told the security guard. 'My room-mates are upstairs.'

He let her go, watching her climb the stairs with a distressed expression. 'Don't worry, Miss,' he called. 'The police will get this guy.'

Meredith bit back her first reply, which was that he seemed to be putting a lot of faith in a police force that had yet to find any clues as to the whereabouts of the missing people or to solve Christopher's murder. He was only trying to comfort her. She nodded to him and gave a little wave.

She hadn't been any more successful than the police, not even with Samantha's help. She hadn't been trying hard enough, had been too distracted by the new place, the new people.

Why now? Meredith wondered suddenly. It hadn't occurred to her before, but this was the first death, attack ōr disappearance that had taken place in a dorm room instead of out on the quad or paths of the campus. Whatever this was, it came after Samantha specifically.

Meredith remembered the dark figure she'd chased away after it attacked a girl, a girl who said she didn't remember anything. Meredith recalled the flash of pale hair as the figure turned away. Did Samantha die because they got too close to the killer?

Her parents were right. No one was ever safe. She needed to work harder, needed to get on with the job and follow up on every lead.

Upstairs, Bonnie's bed was empty. Elena looked up from where she was lying, curled on her bed. Part of Meredith noted that Elena's face was wet with tears and knew that usually she would have dropped everything to comfort her friend, but now she had to focus on finding Samantha's killer.

Meredith crossed to her closet, opened it and pulled out a heavy black satchel and the case for her hunter's stave.

'Where's Bonnie?' she asked, tossing the satchel onto her bed and unbuckling it.

'She left before I got up,' Elena answered, her voice shaky. 'I think she had a study group this morning. Meredith, what's going on?'

Meredith flipped the satchel open and began to pull out her knives and throwing stars.

'What's going on?' Elena asked again, more insistently, her eyes wide.

'Samantha's dead,' Meredith said, testing the edge of a knife against her thumb. 'She was murdered in her bed by whatever's been stalking this campus, and we need to stop it.' The knife could be sharper – Meredith had been letting her weapons maintenance slide – and she dug in the bag for a whetstone.

'*What?*' Elena said. 'Oh, no, oh, Meredith, I'm so sorry.' Tears began to run down her face again, and Meredith looked over at her, holding out the bag with the stave in it.

'There's a small black box in my desk with little bottles of different poison extracts inside it,' she said. 'Wolfsbane, vervain, snake venoms. We don't know what we're dealing with exactly, so you'd better fill the hypodermics with a variety of things. Be careful,' she added.

Elena's mouth dropped open, and then, after a few seconds, she closed it firmly and nodded, wiping her cheeks with the backs of her hands. Meredith knew that her message – *mourn later, act now* – had been received and that Elena, as always, would work with her.

Elena put the stave on her bed and found the box of poisons in Meredith's desk. Meredith watched as Elena figured out how to fill the tiny hypodermics inset in the ironwood of the stave, her steady fingers pulling them out and working them cautiously open. Once she was sure Elena knew what she was doing, Meredith went back to sharpening her knife.

'They must have come after Samantha on purpose. She wasn't a chance victim,' Meredith said, her eyes on the knife as she drew it rhythmically against the whetstone. 'I think we need to assume that whoever this is knows we're hunting him, and that therefore we're in danger.' She shuddered, remembering her friend's body. 'Samantha's death was brutal.'

'A car tried to run me and Damon down last night,'

Elena said. 'We'd been trying to investigate something weird in the library, but I don't know if that's why. I couldn't get a look at the driver.'

Meredith paused in her knife sharpening. 'I told you that Samantha and I chased away someone attacking a girl on campus,' she said thoughtfully, 'but I didn't tell you one thing, because I wasn't sure. I'm still not sure.' She told Elena about her impressions of the black-clad figure, including the momentary impression of paleness below the hoodie, of almost white hair.

Elena frowned, her fingers faltering on the stave. 'Zander?' she asked.

They both looked at Bonnie's unmade bed.

'She really likes him,' Meredith said slowly. 'Wouldn't she know if there was something wrong with him? You know . . .' She made a vague gesture around her head, trying to indicate Bonnie's history of visions.

'We can't count on that,' Elena said, frowning. 'And she doesn't remember the things she sees. I don't think he's right for Bonnie,' she continued. 'He's so – I mean, he's good-looking, and friendly, but he seems off somehow, doesn't he? And his friends are jerks. I know it's a long way from having terrible friends to being dangerous enough to do something like this, but I don't trust him.'

'Can you ask Stefan to watch him?' Meredith asked. 'I know you're taking a break from dating, but this is important, and a vampire would be the best one to keep an eye on him.' Stefan looked so *sad* the other night, she thought distantly. Why shouldn't Elena call him? Life was short. She felt the blade of the knife against her thumb again. Better. Putting the sharpened knife down, she reached for another.

Elena wasn't answering, and Meredith looked up to see her staring hard at the stave, her mouth trembling. 'I – Stefan isn't talking to me,' she said in a little burst. 'I don't think – I don't know if he'd help us.' She closed her mouth firmly, clearly not wanting to talk about it.

'Oh,' Meredith said. It was hard to imagine Stefan not doing what Elena wanted, but it was also clear that Elena didn't want to ask him. 'Should I call Damon?' she suggested reluctantly. The older vampire was a pain, and she didn't really trust him, but he was certainly good at being *sneaky*.

Elena sucked in a breath and then nodded briskly, her mouth set. 'No, I'll call him,' she said. 'I'll ask Damon to investigate Zander.'

Meredith sighed and leaned back against the wall, letting the knife drop onto her bed. Suddenly, she was terribly tired. Waiting for Samantha in the gym that morning seemed like a million years ago, but it still wasn't even lunchtime. She and Elena both looked at Bonnie's bed again.

'We have to talk to her about Zander, don't we?' Elena asked quietly. 'We have to ask her whether he was with her all last night. And we have to warn her.'

Meredith nodded and closed her eyes, letting her head rest against the coolness of the wall, then opened them again. Tired as she was, she knew the images of Samantha's death would come back to her if she let herself pause for even a moment. She didn't have time to rest, not while the killer was out there. 'She's not going to be happy about it.'

CHAPTER
27

Bounce
  Bounce
  Bounce
  Swish
  Catch
  Bounce
  Bounce
  Swish
  Catch

Stefan stood on the free-throw line of the empty basketball court, mechanically dribbling and throwing the ball through the net. He felt empty inside, an automaton making perfect identical shots.

He didn't really love basketball. For him, it lacked both the satisfying contact of football and the mathematical precision of pool. But it was something to do. He'd been up all night and all morning, and he couldn't stand the endless pacing of his own feet around the campus, or the sight of the four walls of his room.

What was he going to do now? There didn't seem to be much point to going to college without Elena beside him. He tried to block out his memories of the centuries of wandering the world alone, without her, without Damon, that preceded his coming to Fell's Church. He was shutting down his emotions as hard as he could, forcing himself numb, but he couldn't help dimly wondering if centuries of loneliness were in store for him again.

'Quite a talent you got there,' a shadow said, stepping away from the bleachers. 'We should have recruited you for the basketball team, too.'

'Matt,' Stefan acknowledged, making another basket, then tossing the ball to him.

Matt lined up carefully to the basket and shot, and it circled the rim before dropping through.

Stefan waited while Matt ran to get the ball, then turned to him. 'Were you looking for me?' he asked, carefully *not* asking if Elena had sent him.

Looking surprised, Matt shook his head. 'Nah. I like to shoot baskets when I've got some thinking to do. You know.'

'What's going on?' Stefan asked.

Matt rubbed the back of his neck, embarrassed. 'There was this girl who I kind of liked, who I've been thinking about for a while, wanting to ask out. And, uh, it turns out she already has a boyfriend.'

'Oh.'. After a few moments, Stefan realised he ought to respond with something more. 'I'm sorry to hear that.'

'Yeah.' Matt sighed. 'She's really special. I thought – I don't know, it would be nice to have something like what you and Elena have. Someone to love.'

Stefan winced. It felt like Matt had twisted a knife in his gut. He flung the ball at the basket, not aiming this time, and it bounced back at them hard off the backboard. Matt jumped to catch it, then moved towards him, holding out a hand. 'Hey, hey, Stefan. Take it easy. What is it?'

'Elena and I aren't seeing each other anymore,' Stefan said flatly, trying to ignore the stab of pain from saying the words. 'She – I saw her kissing Damon.'

Matt looked at Stefan silently for what felt like a long time, his pale blue eyes steady and compassionate. Stefan was struck sharply by the memory that Matt had loved Elena, too, and that they had been together before Stefan came into the picture.

'Look,' Matt said finally. 'You can't control Elena. If there's one thing I know about her – and I've known her for our whole lives – it's that she's always going to do what she wants to do, no matter what gets in her way. You can't stop her.' Stefan began to nod, hot tears burning behind his eyes. 'But,' Matt added, 'I also know that, in the end, you're the one for her. She's never felt the way she does about you for anyone else. And, y'know, I'm starting to discover that there are other girls out there, but I don't think you're going to. Whatever's going on with Damon, Elena will come back to you. And you'd be an idiot not to let her, because she's the only one for you.'

Stefan rubbed the bridge of his nose. He felt breakable, like his bones were made of glass. 'I don't know, Matt,' he said tiredly.

Matt grinned sympathetically. 'Yeah, but I do.' He tossed Stefan the ball and Stefan caught it automatically. 'Want to play Horse?'

He was tired and heartsick, but, as he dribbled the ball, thinking that he'd have to take it a tiny bit easy to give Matt a chance, Stefan felt a stirring of hope. Maybe Matt was right.

'Are you *crazy*?' Bonnie shouted. She had always thought that 'seeing red' was just a metaphor, but she was so angry that she actually *was* seeing the faintest scarlet touch on everything, as if the whole room had been dipped in blood-tinged water.

Meredith and Elena exchanged glances. 'We're not saying there is anything wrong with Zander,' Meredith said gently. 'It's just that we want you to be careful.'

'Careful?' Bonnie gave a mean, bitter little laugh and shoved past them to grab a duffel bag out of her closet. 'You're just jealous,' she said without looking at them. She unzipped the bag and started to throw in some clothes.

'Jealous of what, Bonnie?' Elena asked. '*I* don't want Zander.'

'Jealous because I'm finally the one who has a boyfriend,' Bonnie retorted. 'Alaric is back in Fell's Church, and you broke up with *both* your boyfriends, and you don't like seeing me happy when you're miserable.'

Elena shut her mouth tightly, white spots showing on her cheekbones, and turned away. Eyeing Bonnie carefully, Meredith said, 'I told you what I saw, Bonnie. It's nothing definite, but I'm afraid that the person who attacked that girl might have been Zander. Can you tell me where he was after you two left the party last night?'

Focusing on stuffing her favourite jeans into what was already starting to seem like an overcrowded bag, Bonnie didn't answer. She could feel an annoying telltale flush spreading up her neck and over her face. Fine, this was probably enough clothes. She could grab her toothbrush and moisturiser from the bathroom on her way down the hall.

Meredith came towards her, hands open and outstretched placatingly. 'Bonnie,' she said gently, 'we do want you to be happy. We really do. But we want you to be safe, too, and we're worried that Zander might not be everything you think he is. Maybe you could stay away from him, just for a little while? Until we check things out?'

Bonnie zipped up her bag, threw it over her shoulder and headed for the door, brushing past Meredith without a glance. She was planning to just walk out but, at the last minute, wheeled round in the doorway to face them again, unable to bite back what she was thinking.

'What's killing me here,' she said, 'is what hypocrites you two are. Don't you remember when Mr Tanner was murdered? Or the tramp who was almost killed under Wickery Bridge?' She was actually shaking with fury. 'Everyone in the whole town thought Stefan was responsible. All the evidence pointed to him. But Meredith and I didn't think so, because Elena told us she *knew* Stefan couldn't have done it, that he *wouldn't* have done it. And we believed you, even though you didn't have any proof to give us,' she said, staring at Elena, who dropped her eyes to the floor. 'I would have thought you could trust me the same way.' She looked back and forth between them. 'The fact that you're suspecting Zander even though I'm standing here, telling you he would never hurt anybody, makes it clear that you don't respect me,' she said coldly. 'Maybe you never did.'

Bonnie stomped out of the room, hitching the strap of the duffel bag higher on her shoulder.

'*Bonnie*,' she heard behind her and turned to look back one more time. Meredith and Elena were both reaching after her, identical expressions of frustration on their faces.

'I'm going to Zander's,' Bonnie told them curtly. *That* would show them what she thought about their suspicions of him.

She slammed the door behind her.

CHAPTER
28

'Of course Bonnie's upset,' Alaric said. 'This is her first real boyfriend. But the three of you have been through a lot together. She'll come back to you, and she'll listen to you, once she gets a chance to cool down.' His voice was deep and loving, and Meredith squeezed her eyes shut and held the phone more tightly to her ear, picturing his grad-student apartment with the cosy brown couch and the milk-crate bookshelves. She had never wished so hard that she was there.

'What if something happens to her, though?' Meredith said. 'I can't wait around for Bonnie to get over being mad at me if she's in danger.'

Alaric made a thinking noise into the phone, and Meredith could picture his forehead scrunching in that cute way it did when he was analysing a problem from different angles.

'Well,' he said at last, 'Bonnie's been spending a lot of time with Zander, right? A lot of time alone? And she's been fine so far. I think we can conclude that, even if Zander is the one behind the attacks on campus, he's not planning to hurt Bonnie.'

'I think your reasoning is sort of specious there,' Meredith said, feeling oddly comforted by his words nevertheless.

Alaric gave a small huff of surprised laughter. 'Don't call my bluff,' he said. 'I have a reputation for being logical.' Meredith heard the creak of his desk chair on the other end of the line and imagined him leaning back, phone tucked into his shoulder, hands behind his head. 'I'm so sorry about Samantha,' he said, voice sobering.

Meredith nestled further into her bed, pressing her face against the pillow. 'I can't talk about it yet,' she said, closing her eyes. 'I just have to figure out who killed her.'

'I don't know if this is going to be useful,' Alaric said, 'but I've been doing some research on the history of Dalcrest.'

'Like the ghosts and weird mysteries around campus Elena's professor was talking about in class?'

'Well, there's even more to the history of the college than he told them about,' Alaric said. Meredith could hear him shuffling papers, probably flicking through the pages of one of his research notebooks. 'Dalcrest appears to be something of a paranormal hot spot. There have been incidents that sound like vampire and werewolf attacks throughout its history, and this isn't the first time there's been a string of mysterious disappearances on campus.'

'Really?' Meredith sat up. 'How can the college stay open if people disappear all the time?'

'It's not all the time,' Alaric replied. 'The last major wave of disappearances was during the Second World War. There was a lot of population mobility at the time, and, although the missing students left worried friends and families behind, the police assumed that the young men who disappeared had run off to enlist and the young women to marry soldiers or to work in munitions factories. The fact that the students never turned up again seems to have been disregarded, and the cases weren't viewed as related.'

'*Super* work on the police department's part,' Meredith said acidly.

'There's a lot of weird behaviour on campus, too,' Alaric said. 'Sororities in the 1970s practising black magic, that kind of thing.'

'Any of those sororities still around?' she asked.

'Not those specific ones,' Alaric said, 'but it's something to keep in mind. There might be something about the campus that makes people more likely to experiment with the supernatural.'

'And what is that?' she asked, flopping down on her back again. 'What's your theory, Professor?'

'Well, it's not *my* theory,' Alaric said, 'but I found someone online who suggested that Dalcrest may be somewhere with a huge concentration of crossing ley lines, the same way that Fell's Church is. This whole part of Virginia has a lot of supernatural power, but some parts even more than others.'

Meredith frowned. Ley lines, the strong lines of Power running beneath the surface of the earth, shone like beacons to the supernatural world.

'And some people theorise that, where there are ley lines, the barriers between our world and the Dark Dimensions are thinner,' Alaric continued. Wincing, Meredith remembered the creatures she, Bonnie and Elena had faced in the Dark Dimension. If they were able to cross over, to come to Dalcrest as the kitsune had come to Fell's Church, everyone was in danger.

'We don't have any proof of that, though,' Alaric said reassuringly, hurrying to fill up the silence between them. 'All we know is that Dalcrest has a history of supernatural activity. We don't even know for sure if that's what we're facing now.'

An image of Samantha's blank dead eyes filled Meredith's mind. There had been a smear of blood across her cheek below her right eye. The murder scene had been so gruesome, and Samantha had been killed so horrifically. Meredith believed in her heart of hearts that Alaric's theories must be correct: there was no way Samantha had been murdered by a human being.

CHAPTER 29

'You should be proud.' The Vitale Society pledges were lined up in the underground meeting room, just like they had been the first day when they removed their blindfolds. Under the arch in front of them, the Vitales in black masks watched quietly.

Ethan paced among the pledges, eyes bright. 'You should be proud,' he repeated. 'The Vitale Society offered you an opportunity. The chance to become one of us, to join an organisation that can give you great power, help you on your road to success.'

He paused and gazed at them. 'Not all of you were worthy,' he said seriously. 'We watched you, you know. Not just when you were here, or doing pledge events, but all the time. The candidates who couldn't cut it, who didn't merit joining our ranks, were eliminated.'

Matt looked around. It was true, there were fewer of them now than there had been at their first meeting. That tall bearded senior who was some kind of biogenetics whiz was gone. A skinny blonde girl who Matt remembered doggedly grinding her way through the run wasn't there either. There were only ten pledges left.

'For those of you who remain,' Ethan lifted his hands like he was giving them some kind of benediction, 'at last it is time for you to be initiated, to fully become members of the Vitale Society, to learn our secrets and walk our path.'

Matt felt a little swell of pride as Ethan smiled at them all. It felt like Ethan's eyes lingered longer on Matt than on the others, like his smile for Matt was just a bit warmer. Like Matt was, among all these exceptional pledges, *special*.

Ethan started to walk through the crowd and talk again, this time about the preparations that needed to be made for their initiation. He asked a couple of pledges to bring roses and lilies to decorate the room – it sounded like he was expecting them to buy out a couple of flower stores – others to find candles. One person was assigned to buy a specific kind of wine. Frankly, it reminded Matt of Elena and the other girls planning a high school dance.

'OK,' Ethan said, indicating Chloe and a long-haired girl named Anna, 'I'd like you two to go to the herb store and get yerba mata, guarana, hawthorn, ginseng, chamomile and danshen. Do you want to write that down?'

Matt perked up a little. Herbs were slightly more mystical and mysterious, befitting a secret society, although ginseng and chamomile just reminded him of the tea his mum drank when she had a cold.

Ethan moved on from the girls, his eyes fixed on Matt, and Matt prepared to be sent in search of punch or ranch dip.

But Ethan, locking eyes with Matt, inclined his head a little, indicating that Matt should join him a little apart from the rest of the group. Matt jogged over to meet him, slightly intrigued. What couldn't Ethan say in front of the others?

'I've got a special job for you, Matt,' Ethan said, rubbing his hands together in obvious pleasure at the prospect. 'I want you to invite your friend Stefan Salvatore to join us.'

'Sorry?' Matt said, confused.

'To be a Vitale Society member,' Ethan explained. 'We missed him when we selected candidates at the beginning of the year, but now that I've met him, I think – we think –' and he waved a hand at the quietly watching masked figures on the other side of the room – 'that he would be an ideal fit for us.'

Matt frowned. He didn't want to look like an idiot in front of Ethan, but something struck him as off about this.

'But he hasn't done any of the pledge stuff. Isn't it too late for him to join this year?'

Ethan smiled slightly, just a thin tilting of his lips. 'I think we can make an exception for Stefan.'

'But—' Matt began to protest, then instead smiled back at Ethan. 'I'll call him and see if he's interested,' he promised.

Ethan patted him lightly on the back. 'Thank you, Matt. You're a natural for Vitale, you know. I'm sure you can convince him.'

As Ethan walked away, Matt watched him, wondering why the praise felt sour this time.

It was because it didn't make *sense*, Matt decided, walking back to his dorm after the pledge meeting. What was so special about Stefan that Ethan had decided they had to have him pledge the Vitale Society now instead of just waiting till next year? OK, yes: *vampire* – that was special about Stefan, but no one knew that. And he was handsome and sophisticated in that ever-so-slightly European way that had all the girls back in high school falling at his feet, but he wasn't *that* handsome, and there were plenty of foreign students on campus.

Matt stopped stock-still. Was he *jealous*? It wasn't fair, maybe, that Stefan could just waltz in and be immediately offered something that Matt had worked for, that Matt had thought was only his.

But so what? It wasn't Stefan's fault if Ethan wanted

to give him special treatment. Stefan was hurting after his break-up with Elena; maybe it would do him good to join the Vitale. And it would be fun to have one of his friends in the Society. Stefan deserved it, really: he was brave and noble, a leader, even if there was no way Ethan and the others could have known that.

Firmly pushing away any remaining niggle of *not fair*, Matt pulled out his mobile phone and called Stefan.

'Hey,' he said. 'Listen, do you remember that guy Ethan?'

'I guess I don't understand,' Zander said. His arm around Bonnie's shoulder was strong and solidly reassuring, and his T-shirt, where she had buried her face against him, smelled of clean cotton and fabric softener. 'What were you and your friends fighting about?'

'The point is, they don't trust my judgment,' Bonnie said, wiping her eyes. 'If it had been either of them, they wouldn't have been so quick to jump to conclusions.'

'Conclusions about what?' he asked, but she didn't answer. After a moment, he reached out and ran one finger gently along her jawline and over her lips, his eyes intent on her face. 'Of course you can stay here as long as you want to, Bonnie. I'm at your service,' he said in an oddly formal tone.

Bonnie looked around Zander's room with interest.

She'd never been here before; in fact, she'd had to call him to find out which dorm he lived in, and how weird was that for a girlfriend to not know? But if she'd tried to picture what his room would be like, she would have assumed it would be messy and very guyish: old pizza boxes on the floor, dirty laundry, weird smells. Maybe a poster with a half-naked girl on it. But, in fact, it was just the opposite. Everything was very bare and uncluttered: nothing on top of the school-issued dresser and desk, no pictures on the walls or rug on the floor. The bed was neatly made.

The *single* bed. That they were both sitting on. Her and her boyfriend.

Bonnie felt a flush rise up over her face. She silently cursed her habit of blushing – she was sure that even her ears were bright red. She'd just asked her boyfriend if she could *move into* his room. And sure, he was gorgeous and lovely and kissing him was probably the most amazing experience of her life so far, but she'd just started *kissing* him last night. What if he thought she was suggesting something more?

He was eyeing her thoughtfully as she blushed. 'You know,' he said, 'I can sleep on the floor. I'm not – um – expecting—' He broke off and now he was blushing, too.

The sight of flustered Zander immediately made her feel better. She patted him on the arm. 'I know,' she said. 'I *told* Meredith and Elena you were a good guy.'

He frowned. 'What? Do they think I'm not?' When she didn't answer, he slowly released her, leaning back to take a close look at her face. 'Bonnie? When you had this big fight with your friends, were you fighting about *me*?'

She shrugged, wrapping her arms around herself.

'OK. Wow.' Zander ran a hand through his hair. 'I'm sorry. I know Elena and I didn't really hit it off, but I'm sure we'll get along better when we get to know each other. This will all blow over then. It's not worth it to stop being friends with them.'

'It's not—' Tears sprang into Bonnie's eyes. Zander was being so sweet, and he had *no* idea how Elena and Meredith had wronged him. 'I can't tell you,' she said.

'Bonnie?' He pulled her closer. 'Don't cry. It can't be that bad.' She began to cry harder, tears streaming down her cheeks, and he held on to her. 'Just tell me,' he said.

'It's not that they just don't like you, Zander,' she said between sobs. 'They think you might be the killer.'

'*What? Why?*' He recoiled, almost leaping across the bed away from her, his face white and shocked.

Bonnie explained what Meredith thought she saw, her impression of Zander's hair beneath the hoodie of the attacker she'd chased off. 'Which is so unfair,' she finished, 'because even if she did see what she thought she saw, it's not like you're the only person with really light blond hair on campus. They're being ridiculous.'

Zander sucked in a long breath, his eyes wide, and sat still and silent for a few seconds. Then he reached out and put a gentle hand under her chin, turning her face so they were gazing straight into each other's eyes.

'I would never hurt you, Bonnie,' he said slowly. 'You know me, you see me. Do you think I'm a killer?'

'No,' she said, her eyes filling with tears. 'I don't. I never did.'

Zander leaned forward and kissed her, his lips soft against hers, as if they were sealing some kind of pact. Bonnie closed her eyes and leaned into the kiss.

She was falling in love with him, she knew. And, despite the fact that he had run off so suddenly last night, just before Samantha's murder, she was sure he could never be a killer.

CHAPTER
30

'Cappuccino and a croissant?' the waitress said, and, at Elena's nod, set them down on the table. Elena pushed her notebooks aside to make room. Midterms were coming up, on top of everything else that was happening. Elena had tried studying in her room but was too distracted by the sight of Bonnie's empty bed. She and Meredith were all *wrong* without Bonnie.

She hadn't got much done here at the café, either, despite getting one of the prime big outdoor tables that she could spread her books out on. She'd tried, but her mind kept circling back to Samantha's death.

Samantha was such a nice girl, Elena thought. Elena remembered how her eyes lit up when she laughed and the way she bounced on the balls of her feet as if she was bursting to move, run, dance, too full of energy to sit still. Meredith didn't make new friends that easily, but the wary coolness she usually wore with strangers had relaxed around Samantha.

When Elena had left the dorm, Meredith was on the phone with Alaric. Maybe he would know what to say, how to comfort her. Unwilling to break into their conversation, Elena left her a note indicating where she would be if Meredith needed her.

Stirring her coffee, Elena looked up to see Meredith coming towards her. The taller girl sat down across from Elena and fixed her with her serious grey eyes. 'Alaric says Dalcrest is a hot spot for paranormal activity,' she said. 'Black magic, vampires, werewolves, the whole package.'

Elena nodded and added more sugar to her cup. 'Just as Professor Campbell hinted,' she said thoughtfully. 'I get the feeling he knows more than he's saying.'

'You need to push him,' Meredith said tightly. 'If he liked your parents so much, he'll feel as though he has to tell you the truth. We don't have time to waste.' She reached out and broke off a piece of Elena's croissant. 'Can I have this? I haven't had anything to eat today, and I'm starting to feel dizzy.'

Looking at the strained lines on Meredith's face, the dark shadows under her eyes, Elena felt a sharp stab of sympathy. 'Of course,' she said, pushing the plate towards her. 'I just called Damon to come and meet me.' She watched as Meredith decimated the croissant, stirring still more sugar into her coffee. Elena felt in need of comfort.

It wasn't long before they saw Damon sauntering down the street towards them, his hair sleek and perfect, his all-black clothes casually elegant, sunglasses on. Heads turned as he walked by, and Elena distinctly saw one girl miss her footing and fall off the curb.

'That was fast,' Elena said, as Damon pulled out a chair and sat down.

'*I'm* fast,' he answered, 'and you said it was important.'

'It is,' Elena said. 'Our friend Samantha is dead.'

Damon jerked his head in acknowledgment. 'I know. The police are all over campus. As if they'll be able to do anything.'

'What do you mean?' Meredith asked, glaring at him.

'Well, these killings don't exactly fall under the police's agency, do they?' Damon reached out and plucked Elena's coffee cup from her hand. He took a sip, then made a small moue of distaste. 'Darling, this is far too sweet.'

Meredith's hands were balling into fists, and Elena thought she'd better speed things up. 'Damon, if you know something about this, please tell us.'

He handed back her cappuccino and signalled the

waitress to bring him one of his own. 'To tell you the truth, darling, I don't know much about Samantha's death, or that of Mutt's roommate, whatever his name was. I couldn't get close enough to the bodies to have any real information. But I've found definite evidence that there are other vampires on campus. Sloppy ones.' His face twisted into the same expression he'd made after tasting Elena's coffee. 'Probably newly made, I'd guess. No technique at all.'

'What kind of evidence?' Meredith asked.

Damon looked surprised. 'Bodies of course. Very poorly disposed of bodies. Shallow graves, bonfires, that kind of thing.'

Elena frowned. 'So the people who have disappeared were killed by vampires?'

He wagged a finger at her teasingly. 'I didn't say that. The bodies I examined – and let me tell you, digging *up* a shallow grave was really a first for me – were *not* the same ones that vanished from campus. I don't know if your missing students were killed by vampires or not, but somebody else was. Several somebodies. I've been trying to find these vampires, but I haven't had any luck. Yet.'

Meredith, who normally would have jumped on Damon's comment about this being his first time digging *up* a grave, looked thoughtful. 'I saw Samantha's body,' she said hesitantly. 'It didn't look like a typical vampire attack to me. And from the way

Matt described Christopher's body, I don't think his did, either. They were –' she took a deep breath – '*mauled*. Torn apart.'

'It could be a pack of really *angry* vampires, or messy ones,' Damon said. 'Or werewolves might be vicious like that. It's more their style.' The waitress appeared with his cappuccino, and he thanked her graciously. She retreated, blushing.

'There's another thing,' Elena said once the waitress was out of hearing range. She glanced enquiringly at Meredith, who nodded at her. 'We're worried about Bonnie and her new boyfriend.' Quickly, she outlined the reasons they had for being suspicious of Zander and Bonnie's reaction to their concerns.

Damon raised one eyebrow as he finished his drink. 'So you think the little redbird's suitor might be dangerous?' He smiled. 'I'll look into it, princess. Don't worry.'

Dropping a few dollars on the table, he rose and sauntered across the street, disappearing into a grove of maples. A few minutes later, a large black crow with shining iridescent feathers rose above the trees, flapping its wings powerfully. It gave a raucous caw and flew away.

'That was surprisingly helpful of him,' Meredith said. Her face was still tired and drawn, but her voice was interested.

Elena didn't have to look up to know that her friend

was watching her speculatively. Eyes demurely downwards, feeling her cheeks flush pink, she took another sip of her cappuccino. Damon was right. It was much too sweet.

CHAPTER
31

*W*hy *do they always want to be on top of buildings?* Bonnie thought irritably. *Inside. Inside is nice. No one falls to their death if they're inside a building. But here we are.*

Stargazing from the top of the science building while on a date with Zander was romantic. Bonnie would be all for another little night-time picnic, just the two of them. But partying on a different roof with a bunch of Zander's friends was *not* romantic, not even slightly.

She took a sip of her drink and moved out of the way without even looking as she heard the smack of bodies hitting the ground and the grunts of guys wrestling. After two days of living with Zander, she was beginning to get the names of his friends straight: Tristan and Marcus were the ones rolling around on the floor with

Zander. Jonah, Camden and Spencer were doing something they called parkour, which mostly seemed to involve running around like idiots and almost falling off the roof. Enrique, Jared, Daniel and Chad were all playing an elaborate drinking game in the corner. There were a few more guys who hung around sometimes, but this was the core group.

She liked them, she really did. Most of the time. They were boisterous, sure, but they were always very nice to her: getting her drinks, immediately handing her their jackets if she was cold, telling her that they had no idea what she saw in a loser like Zander, which was clearly their *guy* way of declaring how much they loved him and that they were happy he had a girlfriend.

She looked over at Zander, who was laughing as he held Tristan in a headlock and rubbed his knuckles over the top of his head. 'Do you give in?' he said, and grunted in surprise as Marcus, whooping joyfully, tackled them both.

It would have been easier if there were other girls around that she could get to know. If Marcus (who was very cute in a giant shaggy-haired yeti kind of way) or Spencer (who had the kind of preppy rich-boy elegance that some girls found extremely attractive) had a regular girlfriend, Bonnie would have someone to exchange wry glances with as the guys acted like doofuses.

But, even though a girl would occasionally appear clinging to the arm of one of the guys, Bonnie would never see her again after that night. Except for Bonnie, Zander seemed to travel in an almost exclusively masculine world. And, after two days of following the macho parade around town, Bonnie was starting to get sick of it. She missed having girls to talk to. She missed Elena and Meredith, specifically, even though she was still mad at them.

'Hey,' she said, making her way over to Zander. 'Want to get out of here for a while?'

Zander wrapped his arm around her shoulders. 'Um. Why?' he asked, leaning down to kiss her neck.

Bonnie rolled her eyes. 'It's kind of loud, don't you think? We could go for a nice quiet walk or something.'

He looked surprised but nodded. 'Sure, whatever you want.'

They made their way down the fire escape, followed by a few shouts from Zander's friends, who seemed to think he was going on a food run and would shortly return with hot wings and tacos.

Once they were a block away from the rooftop party, the noise faded and it was peaceful, except for the distant sound of an occasional car on the roads nearby. Bonnie knew she ought to feel creeped out, walking around at night on campus, but she didn't. Not with Zander's hand in hers. 'This is nice, isn't it?' she said happily, gazing up at the half-moon overhead.

'Yeah,' he said, swinging her hand between them. 'You know, I used to go on long walks – runs, really – with my dad at night. Way out in the country, in the moonlight. I love being outside at night.'

'Aw, that's sweet,' Bonnie said. 'Do you guys still do that when you're home?'

'No.' Zander hesitated and hunched his shoulders, his hair hanging in his face. Bonnie couldn't read his expression. 'My dad . . . he died. A while ago.'

'I'm so sorry,' she said sincerely, squeezing his hand.

'I'm OK,' he said, still staring at his shoes. 'But, y'know, I don't have any brothers or sisters, and the guys have sort of become like a family to me. I know they can be a pain sometimes, but they're really good guys. And they're important to me.' He glanced at Bonnie out of the corner of his eyes.

He looked so apprehensive, she felt a sharp pang of affection for him. It was sweet that Zander and his friends were so close – that must have been the family stuff he had to deal with the other night. He was loyal, that much she knew. '*Zander*,' she said. 'I know they're important to you. I don't want to take you away from your friends, you goof.' She reached up to wrap her arms around his neck and kissed him gently on the mouth. 'Maybe just for an hour or two sometimes, but not for long, I promise.'

He returned the kiss with enthusiasm, and Bonnie tingled all the way down to her toes.

Clinging to each other, they made their way to a bench by the side of the path and sat down to kiss some more. Zander just felt so *good* under her hands, all sleek muscles and smooth skin, and she ran her fingers across his shoulders, along his arms, down his sides.

At her touch, he suddenly winced.

'What's the matter?' she said, lifting her head away from his.

'Nothing,' he said, reaching for her. 'I was just messing around with the guys, you know. They play rough.'

'Let me see,' Bonnie said, grabbing at the hem of his shirt, half concerned and half wanting to just check out his abs. He had turned out to be surprisingly modest, considering they were sharing a room.

Wincing again, he sucked his breath in through his teeth as she lifted his shirt. She gasped. His whole side was covered with ugly black-and-purple bruises.

'Zander,' Bonnie said horrified, 'these look really bad. You don't get bruises like that just messing around.' *They look like you were fighting for your life – or someone else was*, she thought, and pushed away the words.

'They're nothing. Don't worry,' he said, tugging his shirt back down. He started to wrap his arms around her again, but she moved away, feeling vaguely sickened.

'I wish you'd tell me what happened,' she said.

'I did,' he said comfortingly. 'You know how crazy those guys get.'

It was true, she'd never known guys so rowdy. He

reached for her again, and this time she moved closer to him, turning her face up for his kiss. As their lips met, she remembered him saying to her, '*You know me. You see me.*'

She did know him, Bonnie told herself. She could trust Zander.

Across the street, Damon stood in the shadow of a tree, watching Bonnie kiss Zander.

He had to admit he felt a little pang, seeing her in the arms of someone else. There was something so sweet about Bonnie, and she was brave and intelligent under that cotton-candy exterior. The witchy angle added a little touch of spice to her, too. He'd always thought of her as his.

Then again, didn't the little redbird deserve someone of her own? As much as Damon liked her, he didn't love her, he knew that. Seeing the lanky boy's face light up in response to her smile, he thought maybe this one would.

After making out for a few more minutes, Bonnie and Zander stood up and wandered, hand in hand, towards what Damon knew was Zander's dorm. Damon trailed them, keeping to the shadows.

He huffed out a breath of self-mocking laughter. *I'm getting soft in my old age*, he thought. Back in the old days he would have *eaten* Bonnie without a second thought, and here he was worrying about her love life.

Still, it would be nice if the little redhead could be happy. If her boyfriend wasn't a threat.

Damon fully expected the happy couple to disappear into the dorm together. Instead, Zander kissed Bonnie goodbye and watched as she went inside, then headed back out. Damon followed him, keeping hidden, as he went back to the party where they'd been before. A few minutes later, Zander came down again, trailed by his pack of noisy guys.

Damon twitched in irritation. *God save me from college boys*, he thought. They were probably going to gorge themselves on greasy bar food. After a couple of days of watching Zander, he was ready to go back to Elena and report that the boy was guilty of nothing more than being uncouth.

Instead of heading towards the nearest bar, though, the boys jogged across campus, quick and determined, as if they had an important destination in mind. Reaching the edge of campus, they headed into the woods.

Damon gave them a few seconds and then followed.

He was *good* at this, he was a predator, a natural hunter, and so it took him a few minutes of listening, of sending his Power out, of racing through the woods, black branches snapping before him, to realise that Zander and his boys were gone.

Finally, Damon stopped and leaned against a tree to catch his breath. The woods were silent except for the innocent sound of various woodland creatures going about their business and his own ragged panting. That pack of noisy, obnoxious *children* had escaped him, disappearing without the slightest trace. He gritted his teeth and tamped down his anger at being evaded, until it was mostly curiosity about how they'd done it.

Poor Bonnie, Damon thought as he fastidiously smoothed and adjusted his clothing. One thing was abundantly clear: Zander and his friends weren't entirely human.

Stefan twitched. This was all just kind of *strange*.

He was sitting in a velvet-backed chair in a huge underground room, as college students roamed around arranging flowers and candles. The room was impressive, Stefan would give them that: cavernous yet elegant. But the little arrangements of flowers seemed chintzy and false somehow, like a stage set in the Vatican. And the black-masked figures lurking in the back of the room, watching, were giving him the jitters.

Matt had called him to tell him about some kind of college secret society that he'd joined, and that the leader wanted Stefan to join, too. Stefan agreed to meet him and talk about it. He never was much of a joiner, but he liked Matt, and it was something to do.

It would take his mind off Elena, he'd thought. Lurking around campus – and it felt like lurking, when he saw Elena, with the way his eyes were irresistibly drawn to her even as he hurried out of sight – he'd watched her. Sometimes she was with Damon. Stefan's fingernails bit into his palms. Consciously relaxing, he turned his attention back to Ethan, who was sitting at a small table opposite him.

'The members of the Vitale Society hold a very special place in the world,' he was saying, leaning forward, smiling. 'Only the best of the best can hope to be tapped, and the qualities we look for I think are very well exemplified in you, Stefan.'

Stefan nodded politely and let his mind drift again. Secret societies were something he actually knew a little about. Sir Walter Raleigh's School of Night in Elizabethan England wrestled with what was then forbidden knowledge: science and philosophy the Church declared out of bounds. *Il Carbonari* back home in Italy worked to encourage revolt against the government of the various city-states, aiming for a unification of Italy. Damon, Stefan knew, toyed with the members of the Hellfire Club in London for a few months in the 1700s, until he got bored with their posturing and childish blasphemy.

All those secret societies, though, had some kind of purpose. Rebelling against conventional morality, pursuing truth, revolution.

Stefan leaned forward. 'Pardon me,' he said politely, 'but what is the *point* of the Vitale Society?'

Ethan paused mid-speech to stare at him, then wet his lips. 'Well,' he said slowly, 'the real secrets and rituals of the Society can't be unveiled to outsiders. None of the pledges know our true practices and purposes, not yet. But I can tell you that there are innumerable benefits to being one of us. Travel, adventure, power.'

'None of the pledges know your real purpose?' Stefan asked. His natural inclination to stay away was becoming more resolute. 'Why don't you wear a mask like the others?'

Ethan looked surprised. 'I'm the face of the Vitale for the pledges,' he said simply. 'They'll need someone they know to guide them.'

Stefan made up his mind. He didn't want to be guided. 'I apologise, Ethan,' he said formally, 'but I don't think I would be an appropriate candidate for your organisation. I appreciate the invitation.' He started to rise.

'Wait,' Ethan said. His eyes were wide and golden and had a hungry, eager expression in them. 'Wait,' he said, licking his lips again. 'We . . . we have a copy of Pico della Mirandola's *De hominis dignitate*.' He stumbled over the words as if he didn't quite know what they were. 'An old one, from Florence, a first edition. You'd get to read it. You could *have* it if you wanted.'

Stefan stiffened. He had studied Mirandola's work on reason and philosophy with enthusiasm back when he was still alive, when he was a young man preparing for university. He had a sudden visceral longing to feel the old leather and parchment, see the blocky type from the first days of the printing press, so much more *right* somehow than the modern computer-set books. There was no way Ethan should have known to offer him that specific book. His eyes narrowed.

'What makes you think I'd want that?' he hissed, leaning across the table towards him. He could feel Power surging through him, fuelled by his rage, but Ethan wouldn't meet his eyes.

'I . . . you told me you like old books, Stefan,' he said, and gave a little false laugh, gazing down at the tabletop. 'I thought you would be interested.'

'No, thank you,' Stefan said, low and angry. He couldn't force Ethan to look him in the eye, not with all these people around, so after a moment, he stood. 'I refuse your offer,' he told him shortly. 'Goodbye.'

He walked to the door without looking back, holding himself straight and tall. As he reached the door he glanced at Matt, who was talking to another student, and, when Matt met his eyes, gave him a shrug and a shake of the head, trying to telegraph an apology. Matt nodded, disappointed but not arguing.

No one tried to stop Stefan as he left the room. But he had a nervous feeling in the pit of his stomach. There was something wrong here. He didn't know enough to dissuade Matt from joining, but he decided to keep tabs on the Vitale Society. As he shut the door behind him, he could sense Ethan watching him.

CHAPTER
32

Moonlight shone in the window, illuminating a long swathe of Elena's bed. Meredith had tossed and turned for a while, but now Elena could hear her steady breathing. It was good that Meredith was sleeping. She was exhausting herself: working out constantly, patrolling every night, making sure all her weapons were in prime condition, wild with frustration that they weren't able to find any solid clues as to the killer's identity.

But it was lonely being the only one awake.

Elena stretched her legs under the sheets and flipped over her pillow to rest her head on the cooler side. Branches tapped against the window, and she wiggled her shoulders against the mattress, trying to calm her busy mind. She wished Bonnie would come home.

The tapping on the window came again, then again, sharp peremptory raps.

Slowly, it dawned on Elena, a little late, that there weren't any trees whose branches touched that window. Heart pounding, she sat up with a gasp.

Eyes black as night peered in the window, skin as pale as the moonlight. It took Elena's brain a minute to start working again, but then she was out of bed and opening the window. He was so quick and graceful that by the time she shut the window and turned round, Damon was seated on her bed, leaning back on his elbows and looking totally at ease.

'Some vampire hunter she is,' he said coolly, looking over at Meredith as she made a soft whuffling sound into her pillow. His gaze, though, was almost affectionate.

'That's not fair,' Elena said. 'She's exhausted.'

'Someday her life might depend on her staying alert even when she's exhausted,' he said pointedly.

'OK, but today is not that day,' Elena said. 'Leave Meredith alone and tell me what you've found out about Zander.' Sitting down cross-legged on the bed next to him, she leaned forward to give Damon her full attention.

He took her hand, slowly interlacing his fingers with hers. 'I haven't learned anything definite,' he said, 'but I have suspicions.'

'What do you mean?' Elena said, distracted. He was

stroking her arm lightly with his other hand, feather touches, and she realised he was watching her closely, waiting to see if she would object. Inwardly, she shrugged a little. What did it matter, after all? Stefan had left her; there was no reason now to push Damon away. She glanced over at Meredith, but the dark-haired girl was still deeply asleep.

Damon's eyes glittered in the moonlight. He seemed to sense what she was thinking, because he leaned closer to her on the bed, pulling her snugly against him. 'I need to investigate a little more,' he said. 'There's definitely something off about him and those boys he runs around with. They're too fast, for one thing. But I don't think Bonnie's in any immediate danger.'

Elena stiffened in his arms. 'What proof do you have of that?' she asked. 'And it's not just Bonnie. If anyone's in danger, they have to be our top priority.'

'I'll watch them, don't worry.' He chuckled, a dry, intimate sound. 'He and Bonnie are certainly getting close. She seems besotted.'

Elena twisted away from his careful hands, feeling anxious. 'If he could be dangerous, if there's anything *off* about him the way you say, we have to warn her about him. We can't just sit by *watching* and waiting for him to do something wrong. By then, it might be too late.'

Damon pulled her back to him, his hand flat and

steady against her side. 'You already tried warning Bonnie, and that didn't work, did it? Why would she listen to you now that she's spent more time with him, bonding with him, and nothing bad's happened to her?' He shook his head. 'It won't work, princess.'

'I just wish we could *do* something,' Elena said miserably.

'If I'd seen the bodies,' Damon said thoughtfully, 'I might have more of an idea of what could be behind this. I suppose breaking into the morgue is out of the question?'

Elena considered this. 'I think they've probably released the bodies by now,' she said doubtfully, 'and I'm not sure where they'd take them next. Wait!' She sat up straight. 'The campus security office would have something, wouldn't they? Records, or maybe even pictures of Christopher's and Samantha's bodies? The campus officers were all over the crime scenes before the police got there.'

'We can check it out tomorrow, certainly,' he said casually. 'If it will make you feel better.'

His voice and expression were almost disinterested, provokingly so, and once again, Elena felt the strange mixture of desire and irritation that Damon often sparked in her. She wanted to shove him away and pull him closer at the same time.

She had almost decided on shoving him away when he turned to look her full in the face. 'My poor Elena,' he said in a soothing murmur. He ran a soft hand up her arm, shoulder and neck, coming to rest gently against her jawline. 'You can't get away from the dark creatures, can you, Elena? No matter how you try. Come to a new place, find a new monster.' He stroked her face with one finger. His words were almost mocking, but his voice was gentle and his eyes shone with emotion.

She pressed her cheek against his hand. Damon was elegant and clever, and something in him spoke to the dark, secret part of her. She couldn't deny that she was drawn to him – that she'd always been drawn to him, even when they first met and he scared her. And Elena had loved him since that winter night when she awoke as a vampire and he cared for her, protected her and taught her what she needed to know.

Stefan had left her. There was no reason why she shouldn't do this. 'I don't always want to get away from the dark creatures, Damon,' she said.

He was silent for a moment, his hand stroking her cheek automatically, and then he kissed her. His lips were like cool silk against hers, and Elena felt as if she had been wandering for hours in a desert and had finally been given a cold drink of water.

She kissed him harder, letting go of his hand to twine her fingers through his soft hair.

Pulling away from her mouth, Damon kissed her neck gently, waiting for permission. Elena dropped her head back to give him better access. She heard his breath hiss through his teeth, and he looked into her eyes for a moment, his face soft and more open than she'd ever seen it, then he lowered his mouth to her neck again.

The twin wasp stings of his fangs hurt for a moment, and then she was sliding through darkness, following a ribbon of aching pleasure that led her through the night, led her to Damon. She felt his joy and wonder at having her in his arms without guilt, without reserve. In return she let him feel her happiness in him and her confusion over wanting him and still loving Stefan, her pain at Stefan's absence. There was no guilt, not now, but there was a huge Stefan-shaped hole in her heart, and she let Damon see it.

It's all right, Elena, she felt from him, not quite in words, but in a complete contentment, like the purr of a cat. *All I want is this.*

CHAPTER

33

Ethan was, Matt observed, totally freaking out. The guy's usual cheerful composure had worn off, and he was supervising the initiation arrangements with the intensity of a drill sergeant.

'No!' he snarled from across the room. He darted over and slapped the leg of a girl who was standing on a chair and weaving roses through the welded metal V at the top of the central arch.

'Ouch!' she yelled, dropping the roses to the floor. 'Ethan, what is your problem?'

'We don't put anything on the V, Lorelai,' he told her coldly, and bent to pick up the flowers. 'You must respect the symbols of the Vitale Society. It's a matter of honour. When our leader finally joins us, we must demonstrate to him that we are disciplined, that we are capable.' He shoved the roses back into her hands. 'We don't do that by draping *garbage* all over the symbol of our organisation.'

Lorelai stared at him. 'I'm sorry. But I thought you were the leader of the Vitale Society, Ethan.'

Everyone had stopped working to watch Ethan's meltdown. Noticing that he was the centre of attention, he breathed deeply, clearly trying to regain his composure.

Finally he addressed them all, biting off his words sharply. 'I am trying to prepare you all, and to prepare this chamber, for the initiation ceremony. For *you*.' His voice was steadily rising as he glared around at them. 'And this is when I learn that, despite all your promise, you're a bunch of incompetents. You can't even place a candle or mix some herbs without my help. We're running out of time, and I might just as well be doing everything myself.'

Matt glanced around at the other pledges. Their faces were shocked and wary. Like him, all along they had been looking up to Ethan and were flattered and encouraged by his praise. Now their role model had turned on them, and no one seemed to know how to react. Chloe, setting out candles by the arch, was anxious, her lips pressed together tightly. She looked quickly at Matt and then away, back towards Ethan.

'Just tell us what you want us to do, Ethan,' Matt said, stepping forward. He tried to keep his voice level and soothing. 'We'll do our best to make everything perfect.'

Ethan glowered at him. 'You couldn't even get your friend Stefan to join us,' he said bitterly. 'One simple task, and you failed.'

'Hey,' Matt said, offended. 'That's not fair. I got Stefan to come and talk to you. If he's not interested, that's his decision. He doesn't have to join us.'

'I question your commitment to the Vitale Society, Matt,' Ethan said flatly. 'And the conversation with Stefan Salvatore is *not* over.' He walked straight past Matt, glancing briefly at the rest of the pledges gathered around him. 'There's not much time, everyone. Get back to work.'

Matt could feel the beginnings of a headache starting at his temples. For the first time, he wondered if maybe he didn't want to join the Vitale Society after all.

'I could have this door open in a single second,' Damon said irritably. 'Instead we stand here, waiting.'

Meredith sighed and carefully wiggled the hairgrip in the lock. 'If you force the door open, Damon, they'll know right away that someone broke into the campus security office. By picking the lock instead, we can keep a low profile. OK?' The hairgrip caught on something, and she carefully slid it upwards, trying to turn it to catch the pins of the lock so she could move the tumbler. Then the hairgrip bent, and she lost the angle. She groaned and dug into her bag for another one. 'Twenty-seven weapons,' she grumbled. 'I brought twenty-seven separate weapons to college and not a single lock pick.'

'Well, you couldn't be prepared for *everything*,' Elena said. 'What about using a credit card?'

'Being prepared for everything is sort of my job description,' Meredith muttered. She sat back on her heels and stared at the door. The lock was pretty flimsy: not only Damon, but both she and Elena could easily have forced it open. And yes, a credit card or something similar probably would work just fine. Dropping the hairgrip into her open bag, she took out her wallet instead and found her student ID.

The ID slid right into the crack between the door and the jamb, she gave it a careful little wiggle, and, bingo, she was easily able to slide the lock back and pull the door open. Meredith smiled over her shoulder at Elena, arching one eyebrow. 'That was strangely satisfying,' she said.

Once they were inside and the door was locked again behind them, Meredith checked to make sure the windows were covered, then flicked on the lights.

The security office was simply furnished: white walls, two desks, each with a computer, one with a forgotten half cup of coffee on top, and a filing cabinet. There was a dying plant on the windowsill, its leaves dry and browning.

'We're sure that none of the officers are going to show up and catch us?' Elena asked nervously.

'I told you, I checked their routine,' Meredith answered. 'After eight o'clock, all but one of the security guards on duty is patrolling the campus. The one who isn't is sitting in the downstairs lobby of the administration building, keeping in radio contact with the others and helping students who lock themselves out of their dorms and stuff.'

'Well, let's get it over with,' Damon said. 'I don't particularly relish the idea of spending the whole evening in this dismal little hole.'

His voice sounded both well bred and bored, as usual, but there was something different about him. He was standing very close to Elena, so close that his arm was brushing against hers, and, as Meredith watched, his hand came up to touch Elena's back very lightly, just with his fingertips. There was a slight secretive curve to his mouth, almost as if Damon was even more pleased with himself than usual.

'Well?' he asked, gazing back at Meredith. 'What now, hunter?'

Elena stepped away from him and knelt in front of the filing cabinet before Meredith could answer, sliding the top drawer open. 'What was Samantha's last name? Her file's probably under that.'

'Dixon,' Meredith told her, pushing away the little shock she kept getting whenever anyone referred to

Samantha in the past tense. It was just . . . she'd been so full of life. 'And Christopher's was Nowicki.'

Elena rifled through the files in both drawers, pulling out first one thick folder and then a second. 'Got them.' She opened Samantha's folder and made a sick little sound in her throat. 'They're . . . worse than I thought,' she said, her voice shaking as she looked at pictures from the murder scene. She turned over a few pages. 'And here's the coroner's report. It says she died from blood loss.'

'Let me see,' Meredith said. She took the file and made herself study the crime scene pictures to see if she had missed anything when she was there. Her eyes kept flinching away from Sam's poor defenceless body, so she swallowed hard and focused on the areas away from the body, the floor, the walls of Samantha's room. 'Blood loss because she was killed by a vampire? Or because there's so much blood everywhere else?' She was proud of how steady her own voice was, steadier than Elena's anyway. She held out the folder towards Damon. 'What do you think?' she asked.

He took the folder and studied the photos dispassionately, flipping a few pages to read the coroner's report. Then he held out his hand to Elena for Christopher's file and looked through that one as well.

'I can't tell anything for certain,' he said after a few minutes. 'Just like with the bodies I found, they could have been killed by werewolves, who are primitive like this. Or it could have been sloppy vampires. Demons, easily. Even humans could do this, if they were sufficiently motivated.' Elena made a soft sound of denial, and Damon flashed his brilliant sudden grin at her. 'Oh, don't forget that humans can come up with far more creative means of violence than some simple hungry monsters do, sweetheart.' Serious again, he looked down at the photographs once more. 'I can tell you, though, that more than one creature – or person – was responsible.'

His finger traced a line across one of the pictures, and Meredith forced herself to look. Bloodstains were spattered in wide arcs across the room, beyond Samantha's outstretched arms. 'See the way the blood sprayed here?' Damon asked. 'Someone held her hands and someone else held her feet, and at least one other, maybe more, killed her.' He flipped open Christopher's folder again. 'Same thing. This might be evidence that werewolves are the culprits, since they like to travel in packs, but it isn't firm proof. You can get groups of almost anything. Even vampires: they're not all as self-sufficient as I am.'

'Matt saw only one person – or whatever – near Chris's body, though,' Elena pointed out. 'And he got there really soon after Christopher screamed.'

Damon waved a disparaging hand. 'So they were fast,' he said. 'A vampire could do it before a human had time to even react to the scream. Almost anything supernatural could. Speed comes with the package.'

Meredith shuddered. 'A whole pack of something,' she said numbly. 'One would have been bad enough.'

'A pack's *much* worse,' Damon agreed. 'Are you ready to go now?'

'We'd better check and see if there's anything else and then clean up,' Elena said. 'Do you want to stand guard outside? I feel like we're really tempting fate by staying here so long. You could give some kind of signal if you see someone coming or use your Power to get rid of them. Please?'

Damon smiled at her flirtatiously. 'I'll be your watchdog, princess, but only because it's you.'

Meredith waited until he left before saying dryly, 'Speaking of dogs, remember when Damon killed Bonnie's pet pug?'

Elena opened the top file drawer again and started going through it methodically. 'I don't want to talk about this, Meredith. It was Katherine who killed Yangtze, anyway.'

'I just don't think you realise what you're getting into here,' Meredith said. 'Damon's not terrific relationship material.'

Elena's hands faltered in their efficient progress. 'I don't . . . it's not like that,' she said. 'It's not a relationship, I don't want a relationship with anyone but Stefan.'

Meredith frowned, confused. 'Well, then, what—'

'It's complicated,' Elena said. 'I care about Damon, you know that. I'm seeing where things might go with him. There's something between us, there always has been. With Stefan gone –' her voice cracked – 'I have to give it a chance. Just . . . just let it alone for now, OK?' She picked up Samantha's folder to put it back in the drawer. Her lips were trembling, and Meredith was about to pursue the subject: she *wasn't* going to let it alone. Not when Elena was upset and somehow involved – *more* involved than she had been before – with Damon the dangerous vampire. But Elena interrupted her. 'Huh,' she said. 'What do you think this means?'

Meredith craned to see what she was talking about, and Elena pointed. On the inside front of Samantha's file was written a large black *V*. She picked up Christopher's file. 'This one, too,' she said, showing Elena.

'Vampires?' Elena asked. 'The Vitale Society? What else starts with *V* and might have to do with these murders?'

'I don't know,' Meredith started to say, when they suddenly heard the rumble of a car engine pulling up outside the building. A raucous caw came through the window.

'That's Damon,' Elena said, shoving Christopher's file back into the cabinet. 'If we don't want him to have to compel the whole security force, we'd better get out of here fast.'

CHAPTER

34

'I like your place,' Elena told Damon, looking around.

She'd been mildly surprised when he invited her to dinner. A conventional date wasn't something she ever associated with Damon, but on her way over she had been tingling with excitement and curiosity. Despite having lived in the same palace as Damon in the Dark Dimension, she had never seen a home he'd made for himself. For all his brashness, she realised, he was oddly private.

She would have expected his apartment to be gothically decorated in blacks and reds, like the vampire manors she'd visited in the Dark Dimension. But it wasn't like that at all. Instead, it was minimalist, sleek and elegant in its simplicity, with clean pale walls, lots of windows, furniture in glass and metal and soft cool colours.

It suited him somehow. If you didn't look too deeply into his dark, ancient eyes, he could have been a handsome young model or architect, clad in fashionable black, firmly rooted in the modern world.

But not entirely modern. Elena paused in the living room to admire the view over the town: stars sparkled in the sky above the muted lights of houses and car headlights on the roads. On a glass-and-chrome table below the window, something else sparkled just as brightly.

'What's this?' she asked, picking it up. It looked like a golden ball overlaid with a tracery of diamonds, just the right size to fit comfortably in her palm.

'A treasure,' Damon said, smiling. 'See if you can find the catch on the side.'

She felt the sphere with careful fingers, finally finding a cleverly concealed catch and pressing it. The ball unfolded in her hands, revealing a small golden figure. A hummingbird, Elena saw, holding it up to inspect it, the gold chased with rubies, emeralds and sapphires.

'Wind the key,' he said, coming to stand behind her, one cool hand on each of her sides. She found the small key low on the back of the bird and turned it. The bird arched its neck and spread its wings, moving slowly and smoothly, as a delicate tune began to play.

'It's beautiful,' she said.

'Made for a princess,' Damon told her, his eyes fixed on the bird. 'A dainty little toy, from Russia before the Revolution. They had craftsmen there in those days. A fun place to be, too, if you weren't a peasant. Palaces, feasts and riding through the snow in sleighs piled with furs.'

'You were in Russia during the Revolution?' Elena asked.

He laughed, a dry sharp little sound. 'I was there before the Revolution, darling. "Get out before things go bad," that's always been my motto. I never cared enough to stay and see things through till the end. Before I met you, anyway.'

As the music stopped playing, Elena half turned, wanting to see Damon's face. He smiled at her and reached to take her hand, closing the bird back into its sphere. 'Keep it,' he said. She tried to protest – it was surely priceless – but he just shrugged. 'I want you to have it,' he said. 'Besides, I have a lot of treasures. You tend to accumulate things when you live several lifetimes.'

He ushered her into the dining room, where the table was set for one. 'Are you hungry, princess?' he asked. 'I had food brought in for you.'

He served her an amazing soup – something she didn't recognise that was smooth and velvety on her tongue, with just a hint of spice – followed by a tiny roast bird, which Elena dissected carefully with her fork, its small bones cracking. Damon didn't eat, he never ate, but he sipped a glass of wine and watched her, smiling as she told him about her classes, nodding seriously as she told him about the toll that patrolling every night was taking on Meredith.

'This was wonderful,' she said at last, still picking at the rich flourless chocolate tart he'd brought out for dessert. 'I think it's the best meal I've ever had.'

He smiled. 'I want to give you the best of everything,' he said. 'You should have the world at your feet, you know.'

Something in Elena stirred. She put her fork down and rose, walking over to the window to gaze out at the stars again. 'You've been everywhere, haven't you, Damon?' she asked. She pressed her palm against the glass.

He came up close behind her and pulled her to face him, gently stroking her hair. 'Oh, Elena,' he said. 'I *have* been everywhere, but the thing about the world is that it keeps changing, so it's always new and exciting. There are so many places I want to show you, to see them through your eyes. There's so much out there, so much life to live.'

He kissed her neck, his canines pushing gently against the vein on the side of her throat, then put his hands on her hips, turning her back towards the window, where a spread of stars glowed against the night. 'Most people never even see a tenth of what the human world holds,' he murmured in her ear. 'Be extraordinary with me, Elena.' His breath was warm on her throat. 'Be my dark princess.'

She leaned against him, trembling.

Dear Diary,

I don't know who I am anymore.

Tonight, with Damon, I could almost picture my life if I took what he offered me, became his 'dark princess'. The two of us, hand in hand, strong and beautiful and free. Everything I wanted without having to lift a finger, from jewels to clothes to wonderful food. A life above the concerns I used to have, somewhere far away. Experiencing and seeing wonders I can't even imagine.

It would have to be a world without Stefan, though. He's shut me out, utterly. But seeing me with Damon – not just kissing, but being who Damon wants me to be – would hurt him, I know. And I can't stand to do that anymore.

It's like there are two paths in front of me. One goes into the daylight, and it's the ordinary girl I thought I wanted to be: parties and classes and eventually a job and a house and a normal life. Stefan wants to give me that. The other is in the darkness, with Damon, and I'm just starting to realise how much that world has to offer, and how much I want to experience everything it holds.

I always thought Stefan would be with me on the daylit path. But now I've lost him, and that path seems so lonely. Maybe the dark path really is my future. Maybe Damon is right, and I belong with him, in the night.

'I can't wait to see my surprise.' Bonnie giggled as she and Zander crossed the lawn by the science building hand in hand. 'You're so romantic. Wait till I tell the guys.'

He brushed a feather-light kiss across her cheek, his lips warm. 'They already know I've lost all my cool guy points for you. I sang *karaoke* with you last night.'

Bonnie snickered. 'Well, after I introduced you to *Dirty Dancing*, we had to sing the big duet, right? I can't believe you'd never seen that movie before.'

'It's because I used to be manly,' Zander admitted. 'But now I've seen the error of my ways.' He gave her one of his slow smiles, and Bonnie's knees nearly buckled. 'It was a cute movie.'

They reached the bottom of the fire escape, and he boosted her up and then climbed after her. When they got to the roof, he gestured expansively at the scene before them. 'For our six-week anniversary, Bonnie, a recreation of our first date.'

'Oh! That's so sweet!' She looked around. There was the ragged army blanket, covered with the pizza box and sodas. The stars shone overhead, just as they had six weeks ago. It was sweet; it was a romantic idea even if their first date hadn't been all that amazing. Then she corrected herself: it had actually been a pretty amazing date, even though it had been simple.

She took a seat on the blanket, then peeked into the pizza box and involuntarily grinned. Olive, sausage and mushroom. Her favourite. 'At least one improvement in the recreation, though, I see.'

He sat next to her and slipped his arm around her shoulders. 'Of course I know what you like on your pizza now,' he said. 'Got to pay attention to my girl.'

She snuggled up under his arm, and they shared the pizza, gazing at the stars and talking cosily about this and that. When the pizza was all gone, Zander wiped his greasy hands carefully with a napkin, then took both of Bonnie's hands in his. 'I need to talk to you,' he said seriously, his sky-blue eyes intent on hers.

'OK,' she said nervously, a flash of panic starting in her stomach. Surely Zander wouldn't have brought her all the way up here and recreated their first date if he was planning to dump her, would he? No, that was a ridiculous idea. But he looked so solemn and worried. 'You're not sick, are you?' she asked, horrified by the idea.

The corner of his mouth twitched up into a smile.

'You're so funny, Bonnie,' he said. 'You just say whatever pops into your head. That's one of the reasons why I love you.' Bonnie's heart leaped into her throat, and she felt her cheeks flush. Zander *loved* her?

He got serious again. 'I mean it,' he said. 'I know it's really early, and you don't have to feel like you need to say something back, but I wanted you to know that I'm falling in love with you. You're amazing. I've never felt like this before. Never.'

Tears of happy surprise sprang into Bonnie's eyes, and she sniffed, squeezing Zander's hands tightly. 'I feel it, too,' she said in a tiny voice. 'These last few weeks have been amazing. I mean, I don't think I've ever had as much fun as I do with you. We get each other, you know?'

They kissed, a long, slow, sweet kiss. She leaned against him and sighed contentedly. She'd never been so comfortable. Then he pulled away.

She reached out for him, but he took her hands again and gazed into her eyes. 'It's because I'm falling in love with you,' he said slowly, 'that I have to tell you something. You have the right to know.' He squeezed his eyes closed tightly for a moment, then opened them again, looking at her as if he wanted to climb into her head and find out how she was going to react to what he said next. 'I'm a werewolf,' he said flatly.

Bonnie sat frozen for a minute, her mind scrambling to understand. Then she shrieked and pulled her hands away from him, jumping to her feet. 'Oh no,' she gasped. 'Oh my *God*.' Images were rushing through her mind: Tyler Smallwood's face twisting, grotesquely lengthening into a muzzle, his newly yellow and slit-pupiled eyes glaring at her with vicious, bloodthirsty hatred. Meredith crumpled on her bed like an abandoned doll, blank-eyed as she told them how Samantha's body had been mauled. The flash of white-blond hair Meredith had seen when she chased a dark-clad figure away from a screaming girl. The black bruises on Zander's side.

'Meredith and Elena were right,' she said, backing away from him.

'*No!* No, it's not like that, Bonnie, please,' Zander said, scrambling to his feet so that they stood facing each other. His face was white and strained. 'I'm a good werewolf, I swear, I don't . . . we don't hurt people.'

'Liar!' she shouted, furious. 'I've *known* werewolves, Zander. To become one, you have to be a *killer*!' With that, she was off, scrambling down the fire escape to the relative safety of the ground. *Don't look back, don't look back*, hammered inside her head. *Get away, get away*.

'*Bonnie!*' Zander called from the top of the fire escape, and she heard him clattering down after her.

She jumped the last few feet from the bottom of the fire escape and landed hard, stumbling. She straightened up and started to run immediately. She had to get inside, had to find somewhere she wouldn't be alone.

Out of the corner of her eye, she glimpsed

movement in the shadows of the building. Jared and Tristan and, oh no, big muscular Marcus. *Werewolves*, she realised, just like Zander, part of his pack. Bonnie thought she was moving as quickly as she could, but, as they came into the light, she found a fresh spurt of speed.

'Bonnie!' Jared called hoarsely, and they came after her.

She was running faster than she ever had, breathless sobs torn from her chest, but it wasn't nearly fast enough. They were close behind her; she could hear their heavy footsteps catching up to her.

'We just want to talk to you, Bonnie,' Tristan called, his voice level and calm. He didn't even sound out of breath.

'Stop,' Marcus said. 'Wait for us,' and *oh God*, he was coming up beside her now, and Tristan on her other side, cutting her off. They were moving in closer, penning her in.

She stopped, her hands on her knees, panting for breath. Hot tears ran down her face and dripped off her chin. They had caught her. She had run and run, as fast as she could, but she hadn't been able to get away. The three guys were pacing around her, hemming her in, their faces wary.

They'd pretended to be her friends, but now they looked like hunters, circling her. They'd lied, all of them.

'*Monsters,*' she muttered like a curse, and pulled herself upright, still panting. They had caught her, but they hadn't defeated her yet. She was a witch, wasn't she? She clenched her hands into fists and began to chant under her breath the charms Mrs Flowers had taught her for protection and defence. She didn't think she could beat three werewolves, not without the time to make a magic circle, without any supplies, but maybe she could *hurt* them.

'Guys, wait. Stop.' Zander was coming now, running across the college lawn towards them. Even through the hot tears clouding her vision, Bonnie could see how beautiful he was, how graceful and natural a runner, his long legs eating up the distance, and her heart ached just a little more. She had loved him so much. She went on chanting, feeling the power building up inside her like the pressure in a shaken can of soda, ready to pop.

Zander came to a halt when he reached them, clasping Marcus's shoulder with one hand. The other three looked at him.

'She ran away from us,' Tristan said, and he sounded baffled and resentful.

'Yeah,' Zander said. 'I know.' Tears were running down his face, too, Bonnie realised, and he was making no move to wipe them away. He just looked at her, those beautiful blue eyes wide open, heartbreakingly sad. 'Back off, guys,' he said without looking away from Bonnie. Speaking to her, he added, 'You do what you have to do.'

She stopped chanting, letting the built-up power drain away. She took a harsh gasp of air, and then, quick as an arrow, her heart pounding as if it would burst out of her chest, she ran.

CHAPTER

35

Initiation night for the newest members of the Vitale Society had arrived at last. The cavernous room was lit only by golden candlelight from long tapers placed around the space and by the fire of high-flaming torches against the walls. In the flickering light, the animals carved in the wood of the pillars and arches almost seemed to be moving. Matt, dressed in a dark hooded robe like the other initiates, gazed around proudly. They'd worked hard, and the room looked *amazing*.

At the front of the room, beneath the highest arch, a long table had been placed, draped in a heavy red satin cloth and looking like some kind of altar. In the centre of the table sat a huge deep stone bowl, almost like a baptismal font, and around it roses and orchids were set. More flowers had been scattered on the floor, and the scent of the crushed blossoms underfoot was so strong it was dizzying. The pledges were lined up, evenly spaced, before the altar.

As if she'd picked up on his pride at how everything had turned out, Chloe pushed her dark hood back a bit and leaned towards him to mutter, 'Pretty fabulous, huh?' Matt smiled at her. So what if she was dating someone else? He still *liked* her. He wanted to stay friends, even if that was all there could be between them.

He tugged at his robe self-consciously; the fabric was heavy, and he didn't like the way it blocked his peripheral vision.

The current masked members of the Vitale Society wove silently among the pledges, handing out goblets full of some kind of liquid. Matt sniffed his and smelled ginger and chamomile as well as less familiar scents: so this was where the herbs had been used.

He smiled at the girl who gave it to him, but got no response. Her eyes behind the mask slid over him neutrally, and she moved on. Once he was a full member of the Vitale Society, he would know who these current members were, he would see them without their masks. He sipped from his goblet and grimaced: it tasted strange and bitter.

The soft rustlings of cloaked figures moving across the floor were silenced as the last of the goblets was handed out and the masked Vitales quietly retreated under the arch behind the altar to watch. Ethan stepped forward to the altar and pushed back his hood.

'Welcome,' he said, holding out his hands to the assembled pledges. 'Welcome to true power at last.' The candlelight flickered over his face, twisting it into something unfamiliar and almost sinister. Matt twitched nervously and took another swallow of the bitter herbal mixture.

'A toast!' Ethan called. He raised his own goblet, and before him, the pledges raised theirs. He hesitated for a moment, then said, 'To moving beyond the veil and discovering the truth.'

Matt raised his goblet and drained it with the other pledges. The mixture left a gritty feeling on his tongue, and he scraped it absently against his teeth.

Ethan looked around at the pledges and smiled, locking gazes with one after another. 'You've all worked so hard,' he said affectionately. 'Each of you has reached his or her personal peak of intelligence, strength and leadership ability now. Together, you are a force to be reckoned with. You have been perfected.'

Matt managed to politely restrain himself from rolling his eyes. It was nice to be praised, of course, but sometimes Ethan was a little too over the top: *perfected?* Matt doubted it was even possible. It seemed to him that you could always strive to be a little more, or a little less, something. You could always wish to be better. But even if he could, after all, be perfected, he suspected that it would take more than a few obstacle courses and group problem-solving exercises to do it.

'And now at last it is time to discover your purpose,' Ethan continued. 'Time to complete the final stage in your transformation from ordinary students into true avatars of power.' He took a clean and shining silver cup from the altar and dipped it into the deep stone bowl in front of him. 'With every step forward in evolution, there must be some sacrifice. I regret any pain this will cause you. Be comforted by the knowledge that all suffering is temporary. Anna, step forward.'

There was a slight uneasy stirring among the pledges. This talk of *suffering* and *sacrifice* was different from Ethan's usual emphasis on *honour* and *power*. Matt frowned. Something was wrong here.

But Anna, looking tiny in her long robe, walked without hesitation up to the altar and pushed back her hood.

'Drink of me,' Ethan said, handing her the silver cup. Anna blinked uncertainly and then, her eyes on Ethan, tipped back her head and drained the cup. As she handed it back to him she licked her lips automatically, and Matt tried to peer more closely at her. In the flickering candlelight her lips looked unnaturally red and slick.

Then Ethan led her around the side of the altar and

into his arms. He smiled and his face twisted, his eyes dilating and his lips pulling back in a snarl. His teeth looked so long, so *sharp.* Matt tried to shout a warning but realised with horror that he couldn't move his lips, couldn't draw the breath to call out.

He knew, suddenly, that he had been a fool.

Ethan sank his fangs deep into Anna's neck. Matt strained, trying to run towards them, to attack Ethan and throw him away from Anna. But he couldn't move at all. He must be under some kind of compulsion. Or perhaps something in the drink, some magic ingredient, had made them all docile and still. He watched helplessly as Anna struggled for a few moments, then went limp, her eyes rolling back in her head.

Unceremoniously, Ethan let her body drop to the ground. 'Don't be afraid,' he said kindly, gazing around at the horrified, frozen pledges. 'All of us –' he gestured towards the silent, masked Vitale behind him – 'went through this initiation recently. You must brace yourself to suffer what is only a small, temporary death, and then you will be one of us, a true Vitale. Never growing old, never dying. Powerful forever.'

Sharp white teeth and golden eyes shining in the candlelight, Ethan reached out towards the next pledge as Matt struggled again to shout, to fight. Ethan continued, 'Stuart, step forward.'

* * *

Elena smelled so good, rich and sweet like an exotic ripe fruit. Damon wanted to bury his head in the soft skin at the crook of her neck and just inhale her for a decade or two. Snaking his arm through hers, he pulled her closer.

'You can't come in with me,' she told him for the second time. 'I might be able to get James to talk to me because it's a question about my parents, but I don't think he'll tell me anything if someone else is there. Whatever the truth is about the Vitale Society and my parents, I think he's embarrassed about it. Or afraid, or . . . something.' Without paying attention to what she was doing, Elena shifted her grip and held on to Damon's arm more firmly.

'Fine,' he said stubbornly. 'I'll wait outside. I won't let him see me. But you're not to walk across campus at night by yourself. It's not safe.'

'Yes, Damon,' Elena said in a convincing imitation of meekness, and rested her head on his shoulder. The lemony scent of her shampoo mixed with the more essential *Elena* smell of her. Damon sighed with contentment.

She cared for him, he knew that, and Stefan had taken himself out of the picture. She was still young, his princess, and a human heart could heal. Maybe, with Stefan gone, she would finally see how much closer she was, mind and soul, to Damon, how perfectly they fitted together.

In any case, she was his for now. He lifted his free hand and stroked her head, her silky hair pliant beneath his fingers, and smiled.

The professor's house was barely off campus, just across the street from the gilded entrance gates. They'd almost reached the edge of campus when a familiar presence that had been lurking nearby at last came very close.

Damon wheeled round to scan the shadows, pulling Elena with him.

'What is it?' she said, alarmed.

Come out, Damon thought with exasperation, sending his silent message toward the thickest shadows at the base of a cluster of oak trees. *You know you can't hide from me.*

One dark shadow detached itself from the rest, stepping forward on the path. Stefan simply gazed at the ground, shoulders slumped, his hands loose and open by his sides. Elena gasped, a small hurt sound.

Stefan looked terrible, Damon thought, not without sympathy. His face seemed hollow and strained, his cheekbones more prominent than usual, and Damon would have bet that he wasn't feeding properly. He felt a twinge of disquiet. He didn't take pleasure in causing his brother pain. Not anymore.

'Well?' Damon said, raising his eyebrows.

Stefan glanced up at him. *I don't want to fight with you, Damon*, he said silently.

So don't, Damon shot back at him, and Stefan's mouth twitched in a half-smile of acknowledgment.

'Stefan,' Elena said suddenly, sounding as though the word had been jerked out of her. 'Please, Stefan.'

He stared down at the path under his feet, not meeting her eyes. 'I sensed you were nearby, Elena, and I felt your anxiety,' he said wearily. 'I thought you might have been in trouble. I'm sorry, I was mistaken. I shouldn't have come.'

She stiffened and her long dark lashes closed over her eyes, hiding, Damon was almost sure, the beginnings of tears.

A long silence stretched between them. Finally, irritated by the tension, Damon made an effort to ease it. 'So,' he said casually, 'we broke into the campus security office last night.'

Stefan looked up with a flicker of interest. 'Oh? Did you find anything useful?'

'Crime scene photos, but they weren't very helpful,' Damon said, shrugging. 'The folders were marked with black Vs, so we're trying to figure out what that means. Elena's going to talk to her professor about the Vitale Society, see if it could have anything to do with them.'

'The . . . Vitale Society?' Stefan said hesitantly.

Damon waved a hand dismissively. 'A secret society from back in the day when Elena's parents were here,' he said. 'Who knows? It may be nothing.'

Drawing a hand across his face, Stefan seemed to be

thinking hard. 'Oh, no,' he muttered. Then, looking at Elena for the first time, he asked, 'Where's Matt?'

'Matt?' Elena echoed, startled out of her wistful contemplation of Stefan. 'Um, I think he had some kind of meeting tonight. Football stuff, maybe?'

'I have to go,' Stefan said tightly, and was immediately gone. With his enhanced abilities, Damon could hear Stefan's light footsteps racing away. But to Elena, he knew, Stefan had been nothing but a silently vanishing blur.

She turned to Damon, her face crumpling in what he recognised as a prelude to more tears. 'Why would he follow me if he doesn't want to talk to me?' she said, her voice hoarse with sorrow.

Damon gritted his teeth. He was trying hard to be patient, to wait for Elena to give him her heart, but she kept thinking of Stefan. 'He told you,' he said, keeping his voice even. 'He wants to make sure you're safe, but he doesn't want to be with you. But *I* do.' Firmly recapturing her arm with his, he tugged her lightly forward. 'Shall we?'

CHAPTER

36

When he opened his door and saw Elena, James's face crumpled, just for a fraction of a second, and he stepped backwards, as if he was considering closing the door in her face. Then he seemed to think better of it and opened it wider, his face creasing into its familiar smile.

'Why, Elena,' he said, 'my dear, I hardly expected a visitor at this hour. I'm afraid this isn't the best time.' He cleared his throat. 'I'd be delighted to see you at college, during office hours. Mondays and Fridays, remember? Now, if you'll excuse me.' And, still smiling gently, he shuffled forward and *did* try to close the door in her face.

But Elena swung her hand up and stopped him. 'Wait,' she said. 'James, I know you didn't want to talk to me about the pins, but it's important. I need to find out more about the Vitale Society.'

His bright black eyes glanced towards her and away, as if embarrassed. 'Yes, well,' he said, 'the problem is of course that unchaperoned solo visits from a student – *any* student, you understand, my dear, no reflection on you personally – to a professor's home are, er, frowned upon. The wicked world we live in, you know,' and, with a soft chuckle, he pushed firmly against the door. 'There are times and places.'

Elena pushed back. 'I don't believe for a minute that you're trying to make me go away because my visit is inappropriate,' she said flatly. 'You can't get rid of me that easily. People are in danger, James.

'I know you and my parents were part of the Vitale Society,' she continued doggedly. 'I need you to tell me whatever it is that you've been hiding about those days. I think the Vitale is tied to the murders and disappearances on campus, and we have to stop it. You're my only lead at this point, James.' He hesitated, his eyes watering with emotion, and Elena fixed him with her gaze. 'More people are going to die,' she said harshly, 'but you might be able to save them. Will you?'

James visibly wavered and then seemed to give in all at once, his shoulders dropping. 'I don't know if anything I can tell you will help. I don't know anything about the murders. But you'd better come in,' he said, and led the way down the hall and through his house. The kitchen was shining clean, with spotless white surfaces. Copper pots and woven baskets were arranged on top of cupboards and cheery red dishcloths and towels hung from hooks. Framed prints of fruits and vegetables hung on the walls at intervals. James sat her down at the table, then busied himself with making her a cup of tea.

Elena waited patiently until he finally settled across from her, with cups of tea in front of them both. 'Milk?' he asked fussily, handing her the jug but without meeting her eyes. 'Sugar?'

'Thank you,' she said. Then she leaned across the table and placed her hand on his, keeping it there until he raised his eyes to look at her. 'Tell me,' she said simply.

'I don't know anything about the murders,' James said again. 'Believe me, I wouldn't have kept this secret if I thought anyone was in danger from it.'

Elena nodded. 'I know you wouldn't,' she said. 'Even if there isn't a connection, if the secret is about my parents, I *deserve* to know,' she told him.

He sighed, a long breathy sound. 'This was all a long time ago, you understand,' he said. 'We were young and a bit naive. The Vitale Society was a force for good, back then. We worshipped natural spirits and drew our energy from the sacred Earth. We were a positive force in the community, interested principally in love and peace and creativity. We served others. I hear that the Vitale Society has changed since those days, that darker elements have taken it over. But I don't know much about them now. I haven't been involved with the Vitale for years, not since the events I am about to recount to you.'

Elena sipped her tea and waited. James's eyes flew to her face, almost shyly, then fixed back on the table. 'One day,' he said slowly, 'a strange man came to one of our secret meetings. He was—' he closed his eyes and shivered. 'I had never seen a being of such pure power, or one who radiated such a feeling of peace and love. We, all of us, had no doubt that we were in the presence of an angel. He called himself a Guardian.' Involuntarily, Elena sucked a breath through her teeth, hissing. James's eyes snapped open and he gave her a long look. 'You know them?' At her nod, he shrugged a little. 'Well, you can imagine how he affected us.'

'What did the Guardian want?' she asked, her stomach dropping. She had met Guardians, and she hadn't liked them. It was Guardians who had, coldly and efficiently, refused to bring Damon back to life when he had died in the Dark Dimension. And it was Guardians who had caused the car accident that killed her parents in an attempt to kill Elena so that they could recruit her to their ranks. All the Guardians she'd met were female, though; she hadn't even known there were male Guardians as well.

Elena knew that, lovely as the Guardians appeared to be, they were not angels, were not on the side of Good or, for that matter, the side of Evil. They just believed in Order. They could be very dangerous.

James looked at her briefly, then fiddled with the tea cup and napkin in front of him. 'Would you like a scone?' he asked. She shook her head and stared at him, and he sighed again. 'You have to understand that your parents were very young. Idealistic.'

She had the sinking feeling that she was going to find out something deeply unpleasant. 'Go on,' she said.

Instead of continuing, though, James folded his napkin into tiny, precise squares, smaller and smaller, until Elena cleared her throat. Then he began again. 'The Guardian told us that there was a need for a new kind of Guardian. One who would be a mortal, on Earth, and who would possess special powers that she would need to maintain the balance between good and evil supernatural forces on Earth. Over the course of his visit, Elizabeth and Thomas, who were young and brilliant and good and deeply in love, and who had bright futures ahead of them, were chosen to be the parents of this mortal Guardian.'

He let the napkin unfold itself in his hands and looked at Elena meaningfully. It took her a moment to catch on.

'*Me?* Are you kidding? I'm not—' She shut her mouth. 'I have enough problems,' she said flatly. She paused as something he said sank in. 'Wait, why do you think my parents were being naive?' she asked sharply. 'What did they do?'

James drank a swallow of tea. 'Frankly, I think I need a little something in this before I continue,' he said. 'I've kept this secret for a long time, and I still have to tell you the worst part.' He got up and rummaged around in one of the cupboards, eventually pulling out a small bottle full of amber liquid. He held it out to Elena questioningly, but she shook her head. She was pretty certain she would need her head clear for the rest of this conversation. He poured a generous amount into his own cup.

'So,' he said, sitting down again. She could tell that he was still anxious, but also that he was beginning to enjoy telling the story. He was a natural gossip – the way he taught history was as gossip about the past – and this was even more familiar for him, because it was gossip about Elena's parents, people they had both known. 'Thomas and Elizabeth were both terrifically flattered, of course.'

'And . . .' Elena prompted.

James laced his fingers across his stomach and watched her, his eyes shadowed. 'They agreed that, when the child was twelve years old, they would give her up. The Guardians would take her away, and they would never see her again.'

Elena was suddenly very cold. Her parents had raised

her intending to *give her away*? She felt like all her childhood memories were shattering. In an instant, James was at her side. 'Breathe,' he said gently.

Gasping, she shut her eyes and concentrated on inhaling and exhaling deep breaths. That her parents, her beloved parents, had taken her on as some kind of temporary project, was devastating. She had never doubted their love until now.

She had to know the whole truth.

'Go on.'

'Honestly, that was the end of my friendship with your parents, and the end of my involvement with the Vitale Society,' he said, taking another long drink of his whisky-laced tea. 'I couldn't believe that no one else in the Society saw the problem with raising a child to the cusp of adolescence and then giving her up forever, and I couldn't believe that your parents – who I knew to be loving, intelligent people – would agree to such a plan. We graduated and went our separate ways, and I didn't hear from your parents again for more than twelve years.'

'You heard from them then?' Elena asked quietly.

'Your father called me. The Guardians had contacted them, ready to take you away. But Thomas and Elizabeth wouldn't let you go.' James smiled sadly. 'They loved you too much. They didn't think you were ready to leave home – you were only a child. They realised that they had agreed too quickly to the

Guardians' plan, that they didn't really know what was in store for you, and that they couldn't let their daughter go without knowing for certain that it was the best thing for her. So Thomas asked for my help protecting you. They knew I had dabbled in sorcery when I was in college –' he waved his hand modestly when Elena looked up at him – 'only small magics, and I had mostly given them up by then. But he and Elizabeth were desperate. So I gathered what knowledge I could, intending to help them.'

He paused, and a gloom settled over his face. 'Unfortunately, I was too late. A few days after our conversation, before I even set out for Fell's Church, your parents were both killed in a car accident. I checked up on you over the years, but it didn't seem like the Guardians had got their hands on you. And now, here you are. I don't think it's a coincidence.'

'The Guardians killed my parents,' Elena said dully. 'I knew it, but I didn't know . . . I thought it was an accident.' She was struggling to wrap her mind around the secrets of her childhood. At least in the end her parents hadn't been able to give her away. They had loved her, as she had thought.

'They tend to get what they want,' James said.

'Why didn't they take me then?' she asked.

He shook his head. 'I don't know. But I think there's a reason you're at Dalcrest now, where it began for you and for your parents. I think that some kind of task will arise here, and you'll come into your Powers.'

'A task?' Elena asked. 'But I *had* Powers once, and the Guardians took them away.' They had mercilessly stripped her of her Wings and all her abilities. Were they going to return them when the time was right?

James sighed and shrugged helplessly. 'Plans sometimes have curious ways of presenting themselves, even those that are fated from the start,' he said. 'Maybe these disappearances are the first sign of it. I don't know, though. As I told the class, Dalcrest is the hub of a lot of paranormal activity. I tend to think that, when your task presents itself, you'll know.'

'But I'm not . . .' Elena gulped. 'I don't understand what this all means. I just want to be a normal girl. I thought I could now. Here.'

He reached across the table and patted her hand, his eyes deep wells of sympathy. 'I'm so sorry, my dear,' he said. 'I didn't want to be the one to burden you with this. But I will give you any help I can. Thomas and Elizabeth would have wanted that.'

Elena felt as though she couldn't breathe. She had to get out of this cosy kitchen, away from James's avid, concerned eyes. 'Thank you,' she said, hurriedly pushing her chair away from the table and getting up. 'I have to go now, though. I do appreciate your telling me all this, but I need to think.'

He fussed around her all the way to the front door, clearly unsure of whether to let her go, and Elena was almost ready to scream by the time she reached the porch. 'Thank you,' she said again. 'Goodbye.' She walked quickly away without looking back, her shoes clacking against the pavement. When she was out of sight of James's house, Damon slipped from the shadows to join her. Elena held her head high, blinking away the tears that had pooled in her eyes. For now, this secret would be hers.

CHAPTER

37

Ethan had Chloe, holding her tightly in his arms like a parody of a lover's embrace. Matt moaned deep in his throat and strained towards her, but he couldn't move, couldn't even open his mouth to shout. Chloe's large brown eyes were fixed on his, and they were filled with terror. As Ethan bent his head to her neck, Matt held her gaze and tried to send her a comforting message with his eyes.

It's OK, Chloe, he thought. *Please, it won't hurt for long. Be strong.* She whimpered, frozen, her eyes on Matt's as if his steady gaze was the only thing keeping her from falling to pieces.

Keeping his eyes on hers and his breathing slow, Matt tried to emanate calmness, tried to soothe Chloe, as his mind worked frantically. Including Ethan, there were fifteen Vitales. All of them vampires. The other Vitales were watching quietly from behind the altar, letting Ethan take the lead and sire the pledges.

The bodies of four of the pledges lay at Ethan's feet now. They'd be out of the picture for several hours at least, their bodies going through the transition that would take them from corpses to vampires. Including Matt and Chloe, there were six pledges left. The longer Matt waited to fight back, the worse the odds would get.

But what could he do? If only he could break this involuntary stillness, if only he weren't a helpless prisoner. He tried again to move, this time focusing all his strength on lifting his right arm. His muscles tensed with effort, but after about thirty seconds of trying, he stopped in disgust. He was exhausting himself, and he wasn't moving a centimetre. Whatever held him was *strong*.

But if he could figure out a way to get free, then he'd be able to grab a torch from the wall, maybe. Beneath his robe, his pocket knife weighed heavily in his trouser pocket. Vampires burned. Cutting off their heads would kill them. If he could just hold the vampires off long enough to pull Chloe and whichever other pledges he could grab out of the room, then he could come back later with reinforcements and fight them with a chance at winning.

But if he couldn't break this spell or compulsion that

was holding him in place, any plan he came up with would be useless.

Ethan raised his head from Chloe's neck, his long sharp teeth pulling out of her throat, and licked gently at the red blood trickling from the wound in her neck. 'I know, sweetheart,' he murmured, 'but it's only for a moment. And then we'll live forever.' Her eyes glazed over and fluttered shut, but she was still breathing, still alive. There was still a chance for her.

At Ethan's feet, Anna stirred and moaned. As Matt watched in horror, her eyes snapped open, and she looked up at Ethan, her expression confused but adoring.

No! Matt thought. *It's too soon!*

As if he had caught the thought, Ethan turned to Matt and winked. 'The herbs in the mixture you all drank worked to thin your blood and speed up your metabolism,' he said, his voice as casual and friendly as if they were chatting in the cafeteria. 'I wasn't sure if it would work, but it looks like it does. Makes the transition go a lot faster.' His smile widened. 'I'm a biochem major, you know.' Ethan's mouth was smeared with blood, and Matt shuddered but couldn't look away from the golden eyes that held his.

It's possible, Matt thought for the first time, *that I might not survive this*. His stomach rolled with nausea. He really didn't want to become a vampire.

If the newly transformed pledges were waking up so

soon, the already slim odds would quickly become impossible. New vampires, he remembered from Elena's transformation back in the winter, awoke vicious, unreasoning, hungry and fanatically committed to the vampire who had changed them.

Ethan lowered his head to bite at Chloe's neck again, as Anna climbed to her feet with a fluid, inhuman grace. On the other side of the altar, Stuart was now beginning to stir, one long leg shifting restlessly against the dark wood of the floor.

His throat burning with unvoiced sobs of frustration, Matt felt his last flame of hope begin to flicker and die. There was no escape.

Suddenly, the door at the far end of the chamber burst inward, and Stefan swept in.

Ethan looked up in surprise, but before he or the other vampires could move, Stefan flew across the chamber and ripped Chloe from Ethan's arms. She fell flat in front of the altar, blood running down her neck. Matt couldn't tell if she was still breathing, still clinging to life as a human.

Stefan grabbed Ethan by his long robe and slammed him against the wall. He shook the curly-haired vampire as easily as a dog might shake a rat.

For a moment, the terrible fear that held Matt in its grip loosened. Stefan knew what was happening, Stefan had found him. Stefan would save them all.

The other Vitales were racing towards Stefan now as

he struggled with Ethan, their long robes flowing behind them as they smoothly came forward, moving as one.

Stefan was without a doubt much stronger than any of them. He flung a black-clad female vampire – the one who had handed him the goblet, Matt thought – away from him easily, and she sailed across the chamber as if she was no heavier than a rag doll, landing in a crumpled heap against the opposite wall. Smiling viciously, Stefan tore at the throat of another with his teeth and she fell to the ground and lay still.

But there were so many of them, and only one of Stefan. After just a few minutes of watching the fight, Matt could see that it was hopeless, and his heart sank. Stefan was much older, and much stronger, than any other vampire in the room, but together they outweighed him. The tide of the battle was turning, and they were overwhelming him through the sheer strength of their number. Ethan was free of him now, straightening his robes, and four of the Vitale vampires, working together, pinned Stefan's arms behind him. Anna, her eyes shining, snapped at him ferociously.

Ethan grabbed a torch from the wall behind him and eyed Stefan speculatively, absently licking at the blood on the back of his hand. 'You had your chance, Stefan,' he said, smiling.

Stefan stopped struggling and hung limp between

the vampires holding his arms. 'Wait,' he said, looking up at Ethan. 'You wanted me to join you. You *begged* me to join you. Do you still want me?'

Ethan tilted his head thoughtfully, his golden eyes bright. 'I do,' he said. 'But what can you tell me that will make me believe you want to join us?'

Stefan licked his lips. 'Let Matt go. If you let him leave safely, I'll stay in his place.' He paused. 'On my honour.'

'Done,' Ethan said immediately. He flicked his fingers in the air without taking his eyes from Stefan, and Matt staggered, suddenly released from the compulsion that had held him in place.

Matt sucked in one long breath and then ran straight for the altar and Chloe. Maybe it wasn't too late. He could still save her.

'Stop.' Ethan's voice cracked commandingly across the room. Matt froze in place, once again unable to move. Ethan glared at him. 'You do not *help*. You do not *fight*,' he said coldly. 'You *go*.'

Matt looked imploringly at Stefan. Surely he wasn't just supposed to leave, to abandon Chloe and Stefan and the others to the Vitale vampires. Stefan gazed back at him, his features rigid. 'Sorry, Matt,' he said flatly. 'The one thing I've learned over the years is that sometimes you have to surrender. The best thing you can do now is just leave. I'll be OK.'

And then, jarringly intrusive and sudden in Matt's

head was Stefan's voice. *Damon*, he said fiercely. *Get Damon*.

Matt gulped and, as Ethan's compulsion released him once more, nodded slowly, trying to look defeated while still signalling to Stefan with his eyes that his message had been received.

He couldn't look at the other pledges. No matter how much he hurried, some or all of them would die before he returned. Maybe Stefan would be able to save some of them. Maybe. Maybe he would be able to save Chloe.

His heart pounding with terror, his head spinning with fear, Matt ran for the exit and for help. He didn't look back.

CHAPTER

38

Bonnie didn't have her keys. She knew exactly where they were, but that didn't do her much good: they were lying on the bedside table next to Zander's neat plain single bed. She cursed and kicked at the door, tears running down her face. How was she going to get any of her stuff back?

Some guy opened the front door of the building for her. 'Jeez, relax,' he said, but Bonnie had already pushed past him and was running up the stairs to her room.

Please let them be here, she thought, clinging to the banister, *please*. She had no doubt that Elena and Meredith would comfort her, would help her, no matter what she had said to them during their fight. They would help Bonnie figure out what to do.

But they might be out. And she'd have no idea where to find them, no idea where they spent their free time these days.

How had she grown so far apart from her best friends? Bonnie wondered, wiping her hands across her cheeks, smearing away her tears. Why had she treated them so badly? They were just trying to protect her. And they were *right* about Zander; they were so right. She snuffled miserably.

When she reached the top of the stairs, she banged on their room door with her fist, hearing quick movement inside. They were home. Thank *God*.

'Bonnie?' Meredith said, startled, when she opened the door, and then, 'Oh, Bonnie,' as Bonnie threw herself, sobbing, into Meredith's arms. Meredith hugged her, tight and fierce, and, for the first time since she had jumped away from Zander and run for the fire escape, she felt safe.

'What's the matter, Bonnie? What happened?' Elena was behind Meredith, peering at her anxiously, and part of Bonnie noticed that Elena's white and startled face was marked with tears. She was interrupting something, but she couldn't focus on that now.

Past Elena, she caught sight of herself in the mirror. Her hair stood out around her face in a wild red cloud, her eyes were glassy and her pale face was smeared with dirt and tears. *I look*, Bonnie thought with a semi-hysterical silent laugh, *like I was chased by werewolves*.

'Werewolves,' she wailed as Meredith pulled her into the room. 'They're all *werewolves*.'

'What are you—' Meredith broke off. 'Bonnie, do you mean Zander and his friends? They're werewolves?'

Bonnie nodded furiously, burying her face against Meredith's shoulder. Meredith pushed her back and looked carefully into her eyes. 'Are you sure?' she asked gently. She looked to Elena, and they both turned and glanced out of the window at the sky. 'Did you see them change? It's not the full moon yet.'

'No,' Bonnie said. She tried to catch her breath, taking harsh sobbing gulps of air. 'Zander told me. And then – oh, Meredith, it was so scary – I ran, and they chased me.' She explained what happened, on the roof and on the lawn of the college.

Meredith and Elena looked at each other quizzically, then back at Bonnie. 'Why did he tell you?' Elena asked. 'He couldn't have thought you would have a good reaction to the news; it would have been easier to keep hiding it.' Bonnie shook her head helplessly.

Meredith arched an ironic eyebrow at her. 'Even monsters can fall in love,' she said. 'I thought you knew that, Elena.' She glanced at her hunting stave, leaning against the foot of her bed. 'When the full moon comes, now I'll know what to look for.'

Bonnie stared at her in horror. 'You're not going to *hunt* them, are you?' It was a stupid question, she knew. If Zander and his friends really were behind the murders and disappearances on campus, Meredith had to hunt them. It was her responsibility. All of their responsibilities, really, because if they were the only ones who knew the truth, they were the only ones who could keep everyone else safe.

But Zander, something inside her howled in pain. *Not* Zander . . .

'None of the attacks occurred during a full moon,' Elena said thoughtfully, and Meredith and Bonnie both blinked at her.

'That's true,' Meredith agreed, frowning as she thought back. 'I don't know how we didn't realise that before. Bonnie,' she said. 'Think carefully before you answer this question. You've been spending a lot of time with Zander and his friends. Did anything about them make you think they might hurt someone, really hurt them, when they're not in wolf form?'

'No!' Bonnie said automatically. Then she stopped and thought and said, more slowly, 'No, I don't think so. Zander's really *kind*, I don't think he could fake that. Not all the time. They play rough, but I've never seen them fight with anyone except one another. And even with one another, they're not really fighting, just sort of messing around.'

'We know what you mean,' Meredith said dryly. 'We've seen it.'

Elena tucked a lock of hair behind her ear. 'The

disappearances weren't during the full moon, either,' she said thoughtfully. 'Although I guess they could have been taking people and holding them prisoner, planning to kill them when they were in wolf form later, but that doesn't – I mean, I don't have much werewolf experience besides Tyler – but it doesn't sound very *wolfy* to me. Too sterile, sort of.'

'But . . .' Bonnie sank down on her bed. 'You think there's a chance Zander and his friends might not be the killers? Then who *are* the killers?' She felt bewildered.

Meredith and Elena exchanged a grim glance. 'You wouldn't believe some of the stuff that happens on this campus,' Elena said. 'We'll fill you in.'

Bonnie rubbed her face with her hands. 'Zander told me he was a good werewolf,' she said. 'That he didn't hurt people. Is that possible? Is there even such a thing as a *good* werewolf?'

Meredith and Elena sat down next to her, one on each side, and wrapped their arms around her. 'Maybe?' Elena said. 'I really hope so, Bonnie. For your sake.'

Bonnie sighed and cuddled closer to them, resting her head on Meredith's shoulder. 'I need to think about all this,' she said. 'At least I'm not alone. I'm so glad I have you guys. I'm sorry we fought.'

Elena and Meredith both hugged her more tightly. 'You've always got us,' Elena promised.

* * *

A wild hammering came at the door.

Elena glanced at Bonnie, who tensed visibly on her bed but kept her hands over her face, and then at Meredith, who nodded firmly to her and climbed to her feet, reaching for her stave. It had occurred to both of them that, if Zander wanted to talk to Bonnie, he knew exactly where she lived.

Elena flung open the door, and Matt tumbled in. He was wearing a long black hooded robe and his eyes were frantic as he gasped for breath.

'*Matt?*' she said in surprise, and looked to Meredith, who gave a tiny shrug and put her stave back down. 'What's the matter? And what are you *wearing*?'

He grabbed Elena by the shoulders, holding her too tightly. 'Stefan's in danger,' he said, and she froze. 'The Vitale Society – they're vampires. Stefan saved me, but he can't fight them all.' He quickly explained what happened in the secret chamber below the library, how Stefan came to his rescue, then sent him to get help. 'We don't have much time,' he finished. 'They're killing – they're changing all the pledges into vampires. I don't even know what Ethan's got planned for Stefan. We have to go back. And we need Damon.'

Meredith picked up her stave again and, grim faced, was taking her satchel of weapons from her closet. Bonnie was on her feet, too, fists clenched, jaw firm.

'I'll call Damon,' Elena said, picking up her phone.

Damon had dropped her off at the dorm after walking her back from James's house, but he was probably still nearby.

Stefan in danger. If he . . . if anything happened to him, if something happened while they were apart, while he was still hurt and it was her fault, Elena would never forgive herself. She wouldn't deserve to be forgiven.

Guilt was like a knife in her stomach. How could she have hurt Stefan like that? She was attracted to Damon, sure, even loved him, but she'd never had any question that Stefan was her true love. And she had broken his heart.

She'd do anything to save Stefan. She'd die for him if she had to. And, as she listened to the ringing on the other end of the line and waited for Damon to pick up, she realised that there was no question in her mind that Damon would do anything to save Stefan, too.

CHAPTER
39

Stefan hadn't had a plan when he agreed to stay in Matt's place. He just knew he had to save Matt, and now he hoped Damon would come for him. Stefan's wrists ached with a dull, throbbing insistent pain that was almost impossible for him to ignore. He tried once more to pull against the ropes that were holding him to the chair, turning his hands from left to right as far as he could to try and loosen his restraints, but it was hopeless. He couldn't shift them.

He looked around dazedly. The room seemed both serene and mysterious again now, as it had when he first kicked in the door. A good place for a secret society. Torches burned brightly, flowers were arranged around the makeshift altar. The Vitales had taken the time to clean up after binding him and killing the pledges.

The ropes were crossed over his chest and stomach and wound around his back; his ankles and knees were tied to the chair legs, his elbows and wrists to the arms of the chair. He was well trussed, but it was the ones around his wrists that hurt most, because they lay against his bare skin. And they burned.

'They're soaked in vervain so that you'll be too weak to break free, but I'm afraid it must sting a bit,' Ethan said pleasantly, as if he was explaining an interesting element of the secret chamber's architecture to his guest. 'See, I may be new at this, but I know all the tricks.'

Stefan rested his head against the back of the chair and looked at Ethan with fervent dislike. 'Not *all* the tricks, I suspect.'

Ethan was cocky, but Stefan was pretty sure he hadn't been a vampire for very long. If Ethan was still human, if he had never become a vampire, Stefan guessed he would look more or less the same as he did now.

Ethan crouched down in front of Stefan's chair to look up into his face, wearing the same warm, friendly smile as when he'd tried to convince him to join them. He looked like a pleasant fellow, someone you wanted to relax with and trust, and Stefan glared at him. The smile was a lie. Ethan was a killer whose mask was less obvious than those of the other Vitale vampires, that was all.

'You're probably right about that,' Ethan said thoughtfully. 'I imagine there are all kinds of tricks you've picked up in, what is it, more than five hundred years? Tricks that I don't know yet. You could be very useful to me in that way, if you decide to join us after all. There are lots of things you can teach us about all this vampire stuff.' He flashed that appealing smile again. 'I've always been a good student.'

Vampire stuff. 'What do you want from me, Ethan?' Stefan asked wearily. It had been a long night, a long few weeks, and the vervain-soaked ropes were hurting his arms, muddying his thoughts.

Ethan knew how old he was. Ethan knew what to offer him when they first talked about the Vitale Society. It wasn't a coincidence that he was the one in this room, then; Ethan wasn't looking for just any vampire. 'What's your plan here?' Stefan asked.

Ethan's smile grew wider. 'I'm building an invincible vampire army, of course,' he said cheerfully. 'I know it sounds a little ridiculous, but it's all about power. And power's never ridiculous.' He licked his lips nervously, showing a flash of thin pink tongue. 'See, I used to be one of the ordinary little people. I was just like everyone else on campus. My biggest achievements were good grades in exams or the fact that I had the leadership of some secret college club. You wouldn't *believe* how lame the Vitale Society used to be. Just white magic and nature worship.' He made a little self-deprecating grimace: *See how silly I was once. I'm telling you something embarrassing about myself, so trust me.* 'But then I figured out how to get some real power.'

One of the black-clad figures came up behind Ethan, and Ethan held up a finger to Stefan. 'Hang on a sec, OK?' He rose and turned to talk to his lieutenant.

After tying Stefan up, he had efficiently gone back to draining the pledges, one after another, dropping the bodies as soon as he finished with them. They had all gone through their transitions now and were back on their feet. They seemed irritable and disoriented, growling and snapping at one another and gazing at Ethan with undisguised adoration.

Typical new vampires. Stefan eyed them warily. Until they had fed thoroughly, they would hover on the brink of madness, and it would be easy for Ethan to lose control of them. Then they would be even more dangerous.

'The pledges need to eat,' Ethan said calmly to the robed woman behind him. 'Five of you should take them out and teach them how to hunt. You lead the hunting party and pick whoever you want to go with you. The rest will stay here and help guard our guest.'

Stefan watched as the Vitales sorted themselves out. Eight of Ethan's followers remained, stationing themselves by the sides of the room. Stefan had managed to kill one other during the fight, ripping her throat out, but the body had been tidied away somewhere.

Stefan gave a little involuntary moan. It was hard to think straight – he was so tired, and the vervain was starting to hurt him all over, not just on his aching wrists, but anywhere the ropes touched him through his clothes. *Damon, please come quickly. Please, Damon,* he thought.

'You're going to unleash nine newly made vampires on the campus?' he asked Ethan, his mind snapping back to the matter at hand. 'Ethan, they'll *kill* people. People who were your friends, maybe. You'll draw attention to yourselves. There are already police all over campus. Please, take them to the woods to hunt animals. They can live on animal blood.' He heard a pleading note enter his voice as Ethan smiled absently at him, as if Stefan was a child begging to go to Disneyland. 'Come on, Ethan, it hasn't been very long since you were a human, too. You can't want to stand by and have innocent students murdered.'

Ethan shrugged, patting Stefan lightly on the shoulder as he started to walk over to confer with another of his henchmen. 'They need to be strong, Stefan. I want them at their peak by the next equinox. And we've killed plenty of innocent students already,' he said over his shoulder.

'Equinox? *Ethan*,' Stefan shouted after him in

frustration. He looked frantically at the door through which the pledges and their escorts had left. It would take them a while to select victims. Not as many students were walking the campus alone at night these days. If he could get free, if Damon came *now* and freed him, they could still stop the slaughter. If all these brand-new vampires were allowed loose on campus, there would be a massacre.

Ethan couldn't have changed the rest of the Vitale Society all at once, he realised. The number of murders they would have committed newly made as a group would have been impossible to disguise as a few disappearances. This must have been the first mass initiation. *And who had made Ethan?* he wondered. Was there an older vampire somewhere on campus?

Damon, where are you? He had no doubt that Damon would come if he could.

Despite their rift over Elena, things had changed enough between him and Damon that he knew he could rely on his brother to rescue him. He had saved him before, after all, when they fought Katherine, when they fought Klaus. There was something rock solid between them now, something that wasn't there a year ago, or in the hundreds of years before that. He closed his eyes and heard himself give a dry, painful chuckle. It seemed like an inopportune moment to start having revelations about his own family issues.

'So,' Ethan said chattily, returning to his side and

pulling up a chair, 'we were talking about the equinox.'

'Yes,' Stefan said, an acid bite to his tone.

He wasn't going to let Ethan see how he was yearning towards the door, expectant. He needed to keep his cool, so that Damon could have the element of surprise on his side. He should keep Ethan talking, keep him distracted in case Damon came, so he fixed an expression of interest on his face and looked at Ethan attentively.

'At the time of the equinox, when day and night are perfectly balanced, the line between life and death is at its most weak and permeable. This is the time when spirits can cross between the worlds,' he began dramatically, moving one hand in a wide sweep.

Stefan sighed. 'I know that, Ethan,' he said impatiently. 'Just cut to the chase.' He might have to keep him distracted, but surely he didn't have to feed his ego.

Ethan dropped his hand. 'You remember Klaus, don't you?' he asked. 'The originator of your bloodline? We're resurrecting him. With him at the head of our ranks, we'll be invincible.'

Everything went still, as if Stefan's slow-beating heart had finally stopped. Then he sucked in a breath. He felt as if Ethan had punched him in the face. He couldn't speak for a moment. When he could, he gasped, '*Klaus?* Klaus the vampire who . . .' He couldn't even finish the sentence. His mind was full of Klaus:

the Old One, the Original vampire, the mad man. The vampire who had controlled lightning, who had bragged that he had not been *made*, that he just *was*. In Klaus's earliest memories, he had told Stefan, he carried a bronze axe; he was a barbarian at the gate, among those who destroyed the Roman Empire. He claimed that he began the race of vampires.

Klaus had held Elena's spirit hostage and tortured innocent Vickie Bennett to death for fun. He turned Katherine, first into a vampire, then into a cruel doll instead of a person, changed her until she was vicious and mindless, eager only to torment those she once loved. Stefan, Damon and Elena killed him at last, but it was nearly impossible, would have been impossible without the spirits of a battalion of unquiet ghosts from the Civil War tied to the blood-soaked battlegrounds of Fell's Church.

'Klaus who made the vampire who made you,' Ethan said cheerfully. 'It was another of his descendants who I found in Europe this summer on my trip abroad. I convinced her to turn *me* into a vampire. She taught me some tricks, too, like how to use vervain, and how lapis lazuli can protect us from the sun. I put lapis lazuli in the pins we wear now, so all the members have it on them at all times. She was very helpful, this vampire who changed me. And she told me all about Klaus.' He smiled warmly at Stefan again. 'See, you *should* like me, Stefan. We're practically cousins.'

Stefan shut his eyes for a moment. 'Klaus was insane,' he tried to explain. 'He won't work with you, he'll destroy you.'

Ethan sighed. 'I really think I can work it out with him, though,' he said. 'I'm very persuasive. And I'm offering him soldiers. I hear he likes war. There's no reason for him to turn us down; we *want* to give him everything he wants.' He paused and looked at Stefan, still smiling, but there was a note now in that wide smile that Stefan didn't like, a false innocence. Whatever Ethan was going to ask Stefan now, he already knew the answer. 'Does this mean you're not interested in joining our army, cousin?' he asked with mock surprise.

Gritting his teeth, Stefan strained against the ropes once more, but they didn't budge. He glared up at Ethan. 'I won't help you,' he said. 'Never.'

Ethan came closer, bent down until his face was level with Stefan's. 'But you will help,' he said lightly, a trace of self-satisfaction in his eyes. 'Whether you want to or not. See, what I need most of all to bring Klaus back is blood.' He ran his hands through his curls, shaking his head. 'It's always blood for this kind of thing, have you noticed?' he added.

'Blood?' Stefan asked uneasily. Young vampires were never sane, in his opinion – the initial rush of new senses and Powers were enough to bewilder anyone. He was starting to think, though, that Ethan's grasp on sanity might not have been that strong to begin with. He'd *convinced* someone to turn him into a vampire?

'The blood of his descendants, specifically.' Ethan nodded smugly. 'That's why I was so delighted to find that you were right here on campus. I made a hobby of tracking down the descendants of Klaus this summer, after I'd talked the first one I met into changing me into what she was. Some of them gave me blood willingly, when they heard what I wanted to do. Not all of Klaus's descendants are as ungrateful as you. I only need a little more, and then I'll have enough. Yours, of course,' and his eyes flicked up towards the door that Stefan had been surreptitiously watching all this time, waiting for Damon, 'and your brother's. I assume he'll be here any minute?'

Stefan's heart plummeted, and he stared openly at the door. *Damon, please stay away*, he thought desperately.

CHAPTER

40

Damon was moving fast, and Elena and the others had to race to keep up with him as they headed for the library. 'Typical Stefan, sacrificing himself,' he muttered angrily. 'He could have asked for help when he realised something was going on.' He stopped for a second to let the others catch up and glared at them all. 'If Stefan can't handle a few newly made vampires by himself, I'm ashamed of him,' he said. 'Maybe we should just leave him after all. Survival of the fittest.'

Elena touched his hand lightly, and, after a moment, Damon hurried on towards the library. She didn't for an instant believe he would leave Stefan a captive. None of them did. The taut, strained lines of his face showed that Damon was entirely focused on the danger his brother was in, their rivalry temporarily forgotten.

'It's not just a few vampires,' Matt said. 'There are about twenty-five of them. I'm sorry, you guys, I've been a moron.' He swung the stave Meredith had given him – Samantha's stave – determinedly in one hand.

'It's not your fault,' Bonnie said. 'You couldn't have known your frat – or whatever – was evil, could you?'

If anyone had spotted them as they crossed the campus, Elena was sure they would have been an alarming sight: she and Bonnie were clutching the large, sharp hunting knives Meredith had given them only half concealed under their jackets. Matt was holding the stave, and Meredith had her own stave in one hand. But it was past midnight, and the path they were following was deserted.

Only Damon wasn't carrying a weapon, and he clearly *was* a weapon.

His human façade seemed to have lifted, and his angry expression could have been carved out of stone, except for the glimpse of sharp white teeth between his lips and the seemingly bottomless darkness of his eyes.

When they reached the closed library, Damon didn't pause, forcing its metal doors open with the grinding sound of splitting metal. Elena glanced around nervously. The last thing they needed was campus security showing up. But the paths near the library were dark and empty.

They all followed Damon down to the basement and into the hallways of administrative offices. Finally, he stopped outside the door marked Research Office where he and Elena had once met Matt. 'This is the entrance?' he asked Matt and, at his nod, efficiently broke the lock on the door. 'You're all staying up here. Only Meredith and I are going down.' He looked at Meredith. 'Want to kill some vampires, hunter? Let's fulfil your destiny, shall we?'

Meredith slashed her stave in the air, and a slow smile tugged at the corners of her mouth. 'I'm ready,' she said at last.

'I'm coming, too,' Elena said, keeping her voice steady. 'I'm not waiting up here while Stefan's in danger.' Damon drew a breath, and she thought he was going to argue with her, but instead he sighed.

'All right, princess,' he said, his voice gentler than it had been since Matt told them what had happened to Stefan. 'But you do what I – or Meredith – tell you.'

'I'm not waiting up here,' Matt said stubbornly. 'This is my fault.'

Damon turned on him, his mouth twisting into a sneer. 'Yes, it *is* your fault. And you told us Ethan can control you. I don't want to get your knife in my back while we're fighting your enemies.'

Matt dropped his head, defeated. 'OK,' he said. 'Go down two flights of stairs, and you'll see the doors to the room they're in.' Damon nodded sharply and pulled up the trapdoor.

Meredith followed him down the stairs, but Matt

caught Elena's arm as she headed after them. 'Please,' he said quickly. 'If any of the pledges still seem rational, even if they're vampires, try to get them out. Maybe we can help them. My friend Chloe . . .' In the grim lines of his face, his pale blue eyes were frightened.

'I'll try,' Elena said, and squeezed his hand. She exchanged a glance with Bonnie, then followed Meredith through the trapdoor.

When they reached the entrance to the Vitale Society's chamber, Meredith and Damon pressed their backs against the elaborately carved wooden doors. Watching, Elena could see a similarity for the first time between them. Now that they were facing a battle, Meredith and Damon were both wearing eager smiles.

One . . . two . . . came Damon's silent count *. . . three.*

They pushed together. The double doors flew inwards, and the chains that had held them closed went flying. Damon stalked in, still smiling a vicious gleaming smile, Meredith erect and alert behind him, her stave poised.

Dark figures rushed at them, but Elena was looking past them, searching for Stefan.

Then her eyes found him, and all the breath rushed out of her. He was *hurt*. Tied firmly to a chair, he raised a pale face to greet her, his leaf-green eyes agonised. From his arm, dark red blood dripped steadily, pooling on the floor beneath his chair.

Elena went a little mad.

Charging across the room towards Stefan, she was only half aware of one of the hooded figures leaping at her, and of Damon catching it in mid-stride, casually snapping its neck and letting the body fall to the floor. Absently, she registered the smack of wood against flesh as Meredith caught another attacker with her stave so that it fell in convulsions as the concentrated essence of vervain from the stave's spikes hit its bloodstream.

And then she was crouching next to Stefan, and, for a moment at least, nothing else mattered. He was shaking slightly, just the faintest tremors, and she stroked his hand, careful of the wound on his forearm. Raised red ridges ran around his wrists below the rope, spots of blood on their surface. 'Vervain on the ropes,' he muttered. 'I'm OK, just hurry.' And then, 'Elena?' Below the pain in his voice, a dawning note of joy.

She hoped he could read all the love she felt in her eyes as she met his gaze. 'I'm here, Stefan. I'm so sorry.' She took out the knife Meredith had given her and began to saw at the ropes that held him, careful not to cut him, trying not to pull them any tighter. He winced in pain, and then the ropes around his wrists snapped. 'Your poor arm,' she said, and felt in her pockets for something to staunch the blood, finally just pulling off her jacket and holding it against the cut. Stefan took the jacket from her. 'You'll have to cut through the rest of the ropes, too,' he said, his voice strained. 'I can't touch them because of the vervain.'

She nodded and went to work on the ropes holding his legs. 'I love you,' she told him, concentrating on her work, not looking up. 'I love you so much. I hurt you, and I never wanted to. *Never*, Stefan. Please believe me.' She finished cutting through the ropes around his knees and ankles and chanced a glance up at his face. Tears, she realised, were running down her own face, and she wiped them away.

The thud of another body hitting the floor and a screech of rage came from behind them. But Stefan's eyes held hers unwaveringly. 'Elena, I . . .' he sighed. 'I love you more than anything in the world,' he said simply. 'You know that. No conditions.'

She took a long, shuddering breath and wiped the tears away again. She had to be able to see, had to keep her hands from shaking. The ropes around his torso were looped and twisted together. She pulled at them, finding where there was enough give to start cutting, and Stefan hissed in pain.

'Sorry, sorry,' she said hurriedly, and began to slice through the ropes as rapidly as she dared. 'Stefan,' she began again, 'the kiss with Damon – well, I can't lie and say I don't feel anything for him – but the kiss wasn't anything I'd planned on. I didn't even mean to be with him that night, it just happened. And when you saw us, that kiss, he'd just saved my life . . .' She was stumbling over her words now, and she let them trail off. 'I don't have any real excuses, Stefan,' she said flatly. 'I just want you to forgive me. I don't think I can live without you.'

The last of the ropes parted, and she eased them from around him before she looked up, frightened and hopeful.

He was gazing at her, his sculpted lips turning up in a half-smile. 'Elena,' he said and pulled her to him in a brief, tender kiss. Then he pushed her to the wall. 'Stay out of this, please,' he said, and limped towards the fight, still weak from the vervain but reaching to pull a vampire away from Meredith and sinking his fangs into its neck.

Not that she needed his help. Meredith was amazing. When had she become so good? Elena had seen her fight before, of course, and she'd been strong and quick, but now the tall girl was as graceful as a dancer and as deadly as an assassin.

She was fighting three vampires, who circled her angrily. Spinning and kicking, moving almost as fast as the monsters she was fighting, despite the fact that their speed was supernatural, she knocked one off his feet, sending him flying, and, in a smooth follow-up blow, bashed another in the face, leaving the vampire staggering backwards with his hands up, half blinded.

There were bodies littered across the floor, evidence of Meredith's skill and Damon's vicious rage. As Elena watched, Stefan tossed down the drained body of the vampire he had been fighting and looked around. Only Ethan and the three vampires surrounding Meredith remained on their feet.

Damon had Ethan on the run, backing nervously away as Damon stalked towards him, peppering him with sharp open-handed blows. '. . . my brother,' she heard Damon muttering. 'Insolent pup. You think you know anything, child, you think you want power?' With a sudden, violent movement, he grabbed Ethan's arm and jerked. Elena could hear the bone snap.

Stefan passed Elena, heading towards Meredith again, and paused for a moment. 'Ethan was laying a trap for Damon,' he told her dryly. 'I don't know why I was worried. Clearly, he didn't know what he was trying to catch.'

Elena nodded again, suppressing a grin. The idea of any brand-new vampire getting the better of Damon, with all his experience and cunning, seemed ridiculous.

Then the tide of the battle suddenly turned.

One of the vampires Meredith was fighting dodged her blow and, half bent over, flung itself at her, knocking the slender girl into the air. There was an endless moment where Meredith looked like she was flying, arms akimbo, and then she slammed headfirst into the heavy altar-like table at the front of the room.

The table wobbled and fell over with a thud. Meredith lay still, her eyes closed, unconscious. Elena ran to her and knelt down, cradling her head in her lap.

The three vampires Meredith had been fighting were worse for wear. One had blood steadily streaming down his face, another was limping and the last was doubled over as if something had been injured inside her, but they could still move fast. In an instant, they had surrounded Stefan.

As Damon growled and turned, shifting his stance to help his brother, Ethan saw his chance and launched himself at Damon. Faster than Elena's eye could follow, his teeth were gouging at Damon's throat, bright spurts of blood flying up. He had a knife in one hand and was trying to cut at Damon at the same time as he bit.

With a cry of pain and shock, Damon clawed at Ethan, trying to fling him away. Elena picked up her knife again and rushed towards them.

But two of the remaining vampires were on Damon in a split second, pulling his arms back. One caught Damon's midnight dark hair in his hand, yanking the older vampire's head back to expose his throat more fully to Ethan's teeth.

Off balance, Damon staggered backwards and for a moment caught Elena's eye, his face soft with dismay.

Terrified, Elena grabbed at the back of one of the vampires, and it threw her to the floor without even looking at her. Stefan, meanwhile, was caught in a struggle with another vampire, desperate to get to his brother. Damon was a better and a more experienced warrior than any of the vampires attacking him. But if they pushed their momentary advantage, used their superior numbers, they might bring him down before he could recover.

She clutched her knife tighter and jumped to her feet again, knowing in her heart that she'd be too late to save him but that she needed to try.

A snarling blur shot past her, and Stefan, free of his adversary, slammed into Ethan, throwing him across the room, sending his knife flying. Without pausing, he ripped one of the other vampires from Damon's arm and snapped its neck. By the time the body hit the floor, Damon had neatly dispatched the other one.

The brothers, both panting, exchanged a long look that seemed to carry a lot of unspoken communication. Damon wiped a smear of crimson blood from his mouth with the back of his hand.

Suddenly an arm was around Elena's throat, and the knife was wrenched out of her hand. She was being dragged upwards. Something sharp was poking her in the tender hollow at the bottom of her neck.

'I can kill her before you could even get over here,' Ethan's voice said, too loud by her ear. Elena flailed an arm backwards, trying to grab at his hair or face, and he kicked viciously at her legs, knocking her off-balance and pulling her closer. 'I could snap her neck with one arm. I could stab her with her own knife and let her bleed out. It would be fun.'

He was holding her knife, Elena realised, pressed against her throat. His other arm hung loose, and curiously bent. Damon had broken it, she remembered.

Stefan and Damon froze and then very slowly turned towards Elena and Ethan, both their faces shuttered and wary. Then Damon's broke into rage.

'Let her go,' he snarled. 'We'd kill you the second she hit the ground.'

Ethan laughed, a remarkably genuine laugh for someone in a life-or-death stand-off. 'She'll still be dead, though, so I think it might be worth it. You're not planning to let me leave here anyway, are you?' He turned to Stefan, his voice mocking. 'You know, I heard *all* about the Salvatore brothers from some of Klaus's other descendants. They said you were aristocratic and beautiful and terribly hot-tempered. That Stefan was moral, and that Damon was remorseless. But they also said that you were both fools for love, always for love. It's your fatal flaw. So, yeah, I think my chances are a lot better when I've got your girlfriend in my power. Whose girlfriend is she, actually? I can't tell.' Elena flinched.

'Wait a second, Ethan.' Stefan held out his hands placatingly. 'Hold on. If you agree not to bring back Klaus and let Elena go safely, we'll give you whatever you want. Get out of town, and we won't come after you. You'll be safe. If you know about us, you know we'll keep our word.'

Behind him, Damon nodded reluctantly, his eyes on Elena's face.

Ethan laughed again. 'I don't think you have anything I want anymore, Stefan,' he said. 'The rest of the Vitale Society, including our newest initiates, will be coming back soon, and I think they'll tip the scales back in my favour.' He tightened his arm around Elena's throat. 'We've killed so many students on this campus. Surely one more won't be missed.'

Damon hissed in rage and started forward, but Ethan called out, 'Stop right there, or—'

Suddenly, he jerked and Elena felt a sharp, stinging pain in her throat. She squeaked in horror and grabbed at her neck. But it was only a scratch from the knife.

As Stefan and Damon stood helpless and furious, Ethan's arm loosened around her throat. He made a hideous gurgling noise. Elena yanked away as soon as his grip weakened.

Blood was running in long thick rivulets from his torso, and his mouth opened in shock as he clutched at himself and slowly fell forward, a round hole in his chest filling with blood.

Behind him, Meredith stood, hair flying, her usually cool grey eyes burning like dark coals in her face. Her stave was coated in Ethan's blood.

'I got him in the heart,' she said, her voice fierce.

'Thank you,' Elena murmured politely. She was feeling . . . really . . . very peculiar, and it wasn't until she was actually starting to fall that she thought, *Oh no, I think I'm going to faint.*

Blurrily, she saw both Damon and Stefan rushing forward to catch her, and when she came to a moment later, she was held tightly in two pairs of arms.

'I'm OK,' she said. 'It was just . . . for a second, I was . . .' She felt one pair of arms pull her closer for a moment, and then they released her, shifting her weight over to the other set. When she looked up, Stefan was clutching her tightly to him. Damon stood a few feet away, his face unreadable.

'I knew you'd come to save me,' Stefan said, holding Elena but looking at Damon.

Damon's lips twitched into a tiny, reluctant smile. 'Of course I did, you idiot,' he said gruffly. 'I'm your brother.'

They looked at each other for a long moment, and then Damon's eyes flicked to Elena, still in Stefan's arms, and away again. 'Let's put out the torches and go,' he said briskly. 'We've still got about fourteen vampires to find.'

CHAPTER
41

It seemed as though he and Bonnie had been waiting forever in the tiny back office of the library, Matt thought. They had strained to catch a sound, to try and learn anything at all about what was happening down there. Bonnie paced, wringing her hands and biting her lips, and he leaned against the wall, head lowered, and kept a good grip on Samantha's stave. Just in case.

He knew about all the doors and passages and tunnels down there – though he had no idea where many of them led – but he didn't realise the soundproofing was so good. They hadn't heard a thing.

Then suddenly the trapdoor was pushing up, and Matt tensed, raising the stave, until he saw Elena's face.

Meredith, Elena, Stefan and Damon climbed out, covered in blood, but basically fine, if the eager way

Elena and Meredith were telling Bonnie what happened, their words tumbling over each other, was any indication.

'Ethan's dead,' Stefan told Matt. 'There were some other Vitales down there in the fight, but none of the pledges. He'd sent them out to hunt.'

Matt felt sick and weirdly happy at the same time. He'd pictured them dead at Damon and Stefan's hands, Chloe, all his friends from pledging. But they weren't. Not dead, not really. But transformed, vampires now.

'You're going to hunt them,' he said, aiming his words at Stefan and Damon, and at Meredith, too. She nodded, her face resolved, and Damon looked away.

'We have to,' Stefan told him. 'You know that.'

Matt stared hard at his shoes. 'Yeah,' he said, 'I know. But, if you get a chance, maybe talk to some of them? If you can, if they're reasonable and no one's in danger? Maybe they could learn to live without killing people. If you showed them how, Stefan.' He rubbed at the back of his neck. 'Chloe was . . . special. And the other pledges, they were good people. They didn't know what they were getting into. They deserve a chance.'

Everyone was silent, and, after a moment, Matt looked up to find Stefan regarding him, his eyes dark green with sympathy, his mouth pulled taut in lines of pain. 'I'll do my best,' he said kindly. 'I can promise you that. But new vampires – vampires in general, really – can be unpredictable. We might not be able to save any of them, and our priority has to be the innocent. We *will* try, though.'

Matt nodded. His mouth tasted sour and his eyes burned. He was beginning to realise just how tired he was. 'That's about the best I can expect,' he said roughly. 'Thank you.'

'So there's a whole room full of dead vampires down there?' Bonnie asked, wrinkling her nose in disgust.

'Pretty much,' said Elena. 'We chained the doors closed again, but I wish we could close the chamber off more permanently. Someone's going to go down there eventually, and the last thing this campus needs is another murder investigation, or another gruesome legend.'

'Ta-da!' Bonnie said, grinning brightly and pulling a little bag out of her pocket. 'Finally something I can do.' She held the bag up. 'Remember all the hours Mrs Flowers made me spend studying herbs? Well, I know spells for locking and warding, and I've got the herbs to use right here. I *thought* they might come in handy, as soon as Matt told us we were going to a secret underground chamber.'

She looked so pleased with herself that Matt had to smile a little despite the heaviness inside him at the thought of Chloe and the others somewhere out in the night. 'They might not work for more than a day or two,' she added modestly, 'but they'll definitely discourage people from investigating the trapdoor for that long.'

'You're a wonder, Bonnie,' Elena said, and spontaneously hugged her.

Stefan nodded. 'We can get rid of the bodies tomorrow,' he said. 'It's too close to dawn to do it now.'

Bonnie got right to work, sprinkling dried plants across the trapdoor. 'Hyssop, Solomon's seal and damiana leaves,' she said when she saw Matt watching her. 'They're for strengthening of locks, protection from evil and general protection. Mrs Flowers drilled me on this stuff *so* much I finally got them all down. It's too bad I didn't have her helping me with my homework in high school. Maybe I would have learned some of those French verbs.'

Damon was watching them, his eyes half hooded. 'We should look for the new vampires, too,' he said. 'You know vampires aren't pack animals. They won't hunt together for long. Once they split up, we can pick them off,' he told Stefan.

'I'm coming, too,' Meredith said. She looked at Damon challengingly. 'I'll just walk Matt home and then meet up with you both.'

Damon smiled, a peculiarly warm smile that Matt had never seen him direct at Meredith before. 'I was talking to you, too, hunter,' he said. 'You've got better.' After a second, she smiled back, a humorous twist of her lips, and Matt thought he saw something that might be the beginnings of friendship flickering between them.

'So the Vitales were definitely behind all the murders and disappearances?' Matt asked Stefan, feeling sick. How could he have spent so much time with Ethan and not suspected that he was a murderer?

Bonnie's face went so white that her few freckles showed like little dark dots on plain paper. And then her colour came flooding back, her cheeks and ears turning a bright pink. She climbed unsteadily to her feet. 'I should go and see Zander,' she said.

'Hey,' Matt said, alarmed, and moved to block the door. 'There's still a whole bunch of vampires outside, Bonnie. Wait for somebody to walk you over.'

'Not to mention that you have other commitments,' Damon said dryly, looking meaningfully at the herbs scattered across the trapdoor. '*After* you work your witchy mojo, *then* you can go and see your pet.'

'We're sorry, Bonnie,' Meredith said, shifting uncomfortably from one foot to another. 'We should have trusted you to know a good guy when you saw one.'

'Right! All is forgiven,' Bonnie said brightly, and plopped down in front of the trapdoor again. 'I just need to say the spell.' She ran her hands through the herbs. '*Existo signum*,' she muttered. '*Servo quis est intus*.'

As she scooped some of the herbs back into her bag,

she kept smiling and stopping and staring into space, and then bouncing a little. Matt smiled at her tiredly. Good for Bonnie. Someone ought to have a happy ending.

He felt a strong, thin hand take his and turned to see Meredith beside him. She smiled sympathetically at him. Nearby, Elena laid her hand tentatively on Stefan's arm, and they both had their eyes on Bonnie. Damon stood still, watching them all with an almost fond expression.

Matt leaned against Meredith, comforted. No matter what happened, at least they were together. His true friends were with him; he had come home to them at last.

The sun was low in the east when Bonnie climbed up the fire escape, her feet clanging on each step. As she came over the side of the building, she saw Zander sitting with his back against the rough concrete wall at the edge of the roof. He turned to stare at her as she came towards him.

'Hi,' she said. She'd been so excited to see him on her way over here, enough so that Elena and Meredith got over their guilt and started to laugh at her, but now she felt weird and uncomfortable, like her head was too big. It was, she realised, totally possible that *he* wouldn't want to talk to *her*. After all, she'd accused him of being a murderer, which was a pretty big mistake for a girlfriend to make.

'Hi,' he said slowly. There was a long pause, and then he patted the concrete next to him. 'Want to sit down?' he asked. 'I'm just watching the sky.' He hesitated. 'Full moon in a couple of days.'

Mentioning the full moon felt like a challenge, and Bonnie settled next to him, then squeezed her hands together and jumped right in. 'I'm sorry I called you a killer,' she said. 'I know now that I was wrong to accuse you of being responsible for the deaths on campus. I should have trusted you more. Please accept my apology,' she finished in a little rush. 'Because I miss you.'

'I miss you, too,' he said. 'And I understand it was a shock.'

'Seriously, though, Zander,' Bonnie said, and shoved him a little with her hip. 'You just tell me you're a *werewolf*? Did you get bitten when you were a kid or something? Because I know getting bitten is the only way to become a werewolf without killing someone. And, OK, I know you're not the killer now, but Meredith *saw* you with a girl who'd just been attacked. And . . . and you had *bruises*, really bad bruises everywhere. I think I had every right to think something was hinky with you.'

'Hinky?' Zander laughed a little, but there was an edge of sadness to it, Bonnie thought. 'I guess it's kind of hinky, if you want to put it that way.'

'Can you explain?' she asked.

'OK, I'll try,' he said thoughtfully. He reached down and took her hand, turning it over in his and playing with her fingers, pulling them lightly. 'As you apparently know, most werewolves are created either by being bitten, or by having the werewolf virus in their family and activating it by killing someone in a special ritual. So, either a terrible attack, which usually screws the victim up, or a deliberate act of evil to grab the power of the wolf.' He grimaced. 'It kind of explains why werewolves have such a bad reputation. But there's another kind of werewolf.'

He glanced at her with a sort of shy pride. 'I come from the Original pack of werewolves.'

Original. Bonnie's mind raced. *Immortal*, she thought, and remembered Klaus, who had never been a human. 'So . . . you're really old, then?' she asked hesitantly.

It was fine, she guessed, for Elena to date guys who had seen centuries go by. Romantic, even. Sort of.

Despite the crush she'd had on Damon, though, Bonnie always pictured dating someone close to her own age. Even Meredith's cute, smart Alaric seemed kind of old to her, and he was only in his twenties.

Zander snorted with sudden laughter and squeezed her hand tight. 'No!' he said. 'I just turned twenty last month! Werewolves aren't like that – we're alive. We live, we die. We're like everybody else, we just . . .'

'Turn into superstrong, superfast wolves,' Bonnie said tartly.

'Yeah, fine,' he said. 'Point taken. Anyway, the Original pack is like, the original family of werewolves. Most werewolves are infected by some kind of mystical virus. It can be passed down, but it's dormant. The Original pack is descended from the very first werewolves, the ones that were cavemen, except during the full moon. It's in our genes. We're different from regular werewolves. We can stop ourselves from changing if we need to. We can learn to change when the moon's not full, too, although it's difficult.'

'If you can stop yourself from changing, do some of you stop being werewolves?' Bonnie asked.

Zander pulled her closer. 'We would never stop being werewolves, even if we never changed at all. It's who we are. And it hurts to not change when the moon is full. It's like it sings to us, and the song gets louder and clearer the closer it gets to being full. We're *aching* to change by the time it happens.'

'Wow,' she said. Then her eyes widened. 'So, all your friends are members of the Original pack, too? Like, you're all *related*?'

'Um,' he said. 'I guess. But the relationship can go back pretty far – it's not like we're all first cousins or anything.'

'Weird,' Bonnie said. 'OK, Original pack, got it.' She snuggled her head comfortably against his shoulder. 'Tell me the rest.'

'OK,' he said again. He pushed his hair out of his eyes and wrapped one arm around her. It was getting a little cold sitting on the concrete, and she nestled gratefully against the warmth of his side. 'So, Dalcrest is on what's sort of a hot spot for paranormal activity. There's these things called ley lines, see . . .'

'Already know it,' Bonnie said briskly. 'Go on with your part.'

Zander stared at her. 'O . . . K,' he said slowly. 'Anyway, the High Wolf Council sends some of us to Dalcrest every year as students. So that we can monitor any dangers. We're kind of like watchdogs, I guess. The *original* watchdogs.'

Bonnie snorted. 'The High Wolf Council.' Zander poked her in the ribs.

'Shut up, it's not funny,' he said. 'They're very important.' She giggled again, and he elbowed her gently. 'So, with all the disappearances and attacks, things have been bad on campus this year,' he continued, sobering. 'Much worse than they usually are. We've been investigating. A pack of vampires in a secret society on campus is behind it, and we've been fighting them off and protecting people when we can. But we're not as strong as they are, except at the full moon, even if we change. And so the bruises. And your friend seeing me guarding a girl who'd just been attacked.'

'Don't worry. We took care of the Vitale Society tonight,' Bonnie said smugly. 'Well, the leader at least, and some of the others,' she amended. 'There's still a bunch of vampires on campus, but we'll get rid of them.'

Zander turned and stared at her for a long moment before he spoke. 'I think,' he said at last in a carefully neutral voice, 'that it's your turn to explain.'

Bonnie wasn't actually that great at properly organised, logical explanations, but she did her best, going back and forth in time, adding side notes and remembering things as she went along. She told him about Stefan and Damon, and how everything had changed when the vampire brothers came to Fell's Church last year and Elena fell in love with them. She told him about Meredith's sacred duty as a vampire hunter, and she told him about her own psychic visions and her training as a witch.

She left a lot of stuff out – everything about the Dark Dimension, and Elena's bargain with the Guardians, for instance, because that was really confusing, and maybe she should tell him about it later so he didn't just overload – but the telling still took a long time.

'Huh,' Zander said when she was finished, and then he laughed.

'What?' Bonnie asked.

'You're a weird girl,' he said. 'Pretty heroic, though.'

She pushed her face into his neck, happily breathing

in the essential Zander smell of him: fabric softener, worn cotton and clean guy.

'*You're* weird,' she said, and then, admiringly, 'and the real hero. You've been fighting off vampire attacks for weeks and weeks, to protect everybody.'

'We're quite a pair,' Zander said.

'Yeah,' Bonnie said. She sat up and faced him, then reached out and ran her hand through his soft pale hair, pulling his head closer to her. 'Still,' she said, just before their lips touched, 'normal is overrated.'

CHAPTER
42

Elena, Stefan, and Damon headed towards Elena's dorm together, and tension thrummed sharply between them.

Elena had taken Stefan's hand automatically as they walked, and he had stiffened and then gradually relaxed, so that now his hand felt natural in hers.

Things weren't back the way they had been between them, not yet. But Stefan's green eyes were full of a shy affection when they looked at her, and Elena *knew* she could make things right. Something had shifted in Stefan when Damon came to rescue him, when Elena untied him and told him how sorry she was. Maybe Stefan just needed to know that whatever was between her and Damon, he was first for her. No one was shutting him out.

Elena unlocked her door, and they all went inside. It had been only a few hours since she was last there, but so much had happened that it seemed like somewhere from a long time ago, the posters and clothes and Bonnie's teddy bear all relics of a lost civilisation.

'Oh, Stefan,' Elena said, 'I'm so glad you're safe.' She reached out and wrapped her arms around him and, just like when she took his hand, he tensed for a moment before hugging her back.

'I'm glad that both of you are safe,' she amended, and looked at Damon. His black eyes met hers coolly, and she knew that, without their having to discuss it, he understood that things weren't going to go on the way they had been. She loved Stefan. She had chosen.

When Stefan told them of Ethan's plan to take both of the brothers' blood and use it to resurrect Klaus, she was horrified. Not just because of the danger Stefan had been in, or because of the terrifying idea of Klaus alive again, and no doubt vengeful against them, but because of the trap Ethan had laid for Damon. He had planned to take the best of Damon – the reluctant, often marred, but still strong love he had for his brother – and use it to destroy him.

'I'm eternally glad you're both OK,' she said again, and reached out to hug Damon, too.

He came into her arms willingly, but, as she squeezed him tightly, he winced.

'What's wrong?' Elena asked, puzzled, and Damon frowned.

'Ethan cut me,' he said, the frown turning into a grimace of pain. 'I'm just a little sore.' He tugged at his shirt, fingering a torn edge, and pulled it up, exposing a swathe of pale taut skin. Against the white skin Elena saw the long cut was already healing.

'It's nothing,' Damon said. He shot Elena a wicked smile. 'A little drink from a willing donor and I'll be as good as new, I promise.'

She shook her head at him reprovingly, but didn't answer.

'Goodnight, Elena,' Stefan said, and brushed her cheek gently with the back of his hand. 'Good morning, really, I guess, but try to get some sleep.'

'Are you going after the vampires?' she asked anxiously. 'Be careful.'

Damon laughed. 'I'll make sure he takes care with the nasty *vampires*,' he said. 'Poor Elena. Normal life isn't going so well, is it?'

Elena sighed. That was the problem, wasn't it? Damon would never understand why she wanted to be an ordinary person. He thought of her as his dark princess, wanted her to be like him, to be *better* than ordinary people. Stefan didn't think she was a dark princess; he thought she was a human being.

But was she? She thought briefly of telling them

about the Guardians and the secrets of her birth, but she just couldn't. Not right now. Not yet. Damon wouldn't know why it upset her. And Stefan was so pale and tired after his ordeal with the vervain-soaked ropes that she couldn't bring herself to burden him with her fears about the Guardians.

As she thought this, Stefan staggered, just a fraction, and Damon reached out automatically to steady him. 'Thank you,' Stefan said, 'For coming to save me. Both of you.'

'I'll always save you, little brother,' Damon said, but he was looking at Elena, and she heard the echo of when he had said the same words to her. 'Even though I might be better off without you,' Damon added.

Stefan gave a tired smile. 'Time to go,' he said.

'I love you, Stefan.' Elena brushed her lips against his softly.

Damon gave her a brief nod, his face neutral. 'Sleep well,' he said.

Then the door was closed behind her, and she was alone. Her bed had never looked more comfortable or inviting, and she lay down with a sigh, looking up at the soft light that was beginning to break through the window.

The Vitale Society was gone. Ethan's plan had been stopped. The campus was safer, and a new day was dawning. Stefan had forgiven her, and Damon didn't leave, didn't turn against them.

It was, for now, the best she could hope for. Elena closed her eyes and fell willingly asleep at last. Tomorrow would be another day.

EPILOGUE

Ethan gasped, sucking in a long breath of air, and coughed his way awake, his whole body shaking. Everything hurt.

Gingerly, he patted himself down, finding that he was sticky with half-dried blood, covered with a score of small injuries. Reaching up, with delicate fingers he felt the already healing indentation in his back. The stave the girl had thrust into him had brushed his heart, but it hadn't pierced it. A half-centimetre to one side and he would have been dead. Really dead, this time, not undead.

Grabbing hold of a velvet-covered chair with one hand, he pulled himself to his feet and looked around. His lieutenants in the Vitale Society, his friends, lay dead on the floor. The Salvatore brothers, and the girls who were with them, had escaped.

Nervously, he felt in one pocket and sighed in relief as his hand closed on a small vial. Pulling it out, he looked at the thick red liquid within. Stefan Salvatore's blood. He fished in the same pocket and drew out a cloth bearing a long reddish-brown stain. Damon Salvatore's blood.

He had what he needed.

Klaus would rise again.

If you've got a thirst for
fiction, join up now

bookswithbite.co.uk

Packed with sneak peeks, book trailers, exclusive
competitions and downloads, **bookswithbite.co.uk**
is the new place on the web to get your fix of
great fiction.

Sign up to the newsletter at
www.bookswithbite.co.uk
for the latest news on your favourite authors,
to receive exclusive extra content and the
opportunity to enter special
members-only competitions.

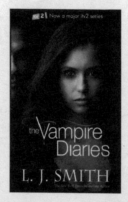

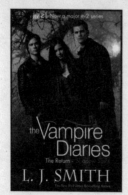
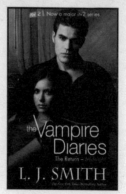

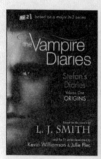

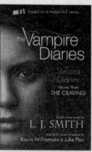
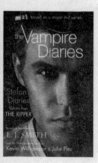
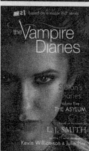
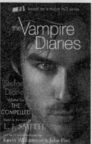

A WITCH in WINTER

When love is tangled up in magic, how can you be sure what's real?

Anna Winterson doesn't know she's a witch and would probably mock you for believing in magic, but after moving to the small town of Winter with her father, she learns more than she ever wanted to about power.

When Anna meets Seth, she is smitten, but when she enchants him to love her, she unwittingly amplifies a deadly conflict between two witch clans and splits her own heart in two …

www.ruthwarburton.com
www.hodderchildrens.co.uk

MIST

The last shred of the mist swirled and drew back, and she saw where she was. She was very, very far from home.

Midnight: a mist-haunted wood with a bad reputation. A sweet sixteen party, and thirteen-year-old Nell is trying to keep her sister, spoilt birthday-girl Gwen, out of trouble. No chance. Trouble finds Gwen and drags her through the mist.

Only Nell guesses who's behind the kidnap - the boy she hoped was her friend, the gorgeous but mysterious Evan River.

Final Friends

VOLUME ONE

They just wanted to finish high school,
but high school might finish them …

When Jessica Hart decides to throw
a party in order to get to know some
of the hot new guys at school, she could
never have predicted that by the end
of the night someone would be dead …

Most people figured it was suicide …
they figured wrong.